PHANTOM WARRIORS
BUNDLE 1

JORDAN SUMMERS

PHANTOM WARRIORS: BACCHUS

Bacchus is a desperate Phantom Warrior. Saddled with the quest to find a biologically compatible female species for his people, he stows away on a ship bound for planet Earth. There he discovers a world teeming with women, but how does he pick just one? Sex sounds easy enough or it would be, if Bacchus weren't from the Blood Clan. Where on Earth can he find a woman who doesn't freak out at the sight of blood and three-inch fangs?

Dog breeder Carrie Rittner has had a rough year. Between a broken engagement, threats to her safety, and an emotionally distant brother, she's ready to throw in the towel. The last thing she needs is a sexy 'bodyguard' trying to charm her pants off.

It'll take more than Bacchus' chemically charged pheromones, dominant nature, and forked tongue to convince Carrie that they're made for each other. He will have to release all his animal instincts, before giving her the ultimate love bite.

PHANTOM WARRIORS: ARCTOS

Photographer Caitlin Kelly thinks she's on a mission to save her friend, but when she gets to the wilds of Alaska, it turns out she'll be the one that needs rescuing. Caitlin doesn't hear the polar bear until it's too late. An attack leaves her bleeding in the snow. Her only regret as she faces impending death is that she's never been in love.

Arctos has come to Earth in search of a bride. The last thing he wants is to bond to a woman in order to save her life, but as a Phantom Warrior, he cannot let Caitlin die. Arctos believes the selfless act has destroyed the only chance he had of finding his true-mate.

When the snow begins to blow, the winds of fate take over.
Two strangers determined to ride out a storm are about to
discover that the worst day of their lives might just be the
best thing that's ever happened to them.

PHANTOM WARRIORS: LINX

Tabitha Shelley is determined to save her twin sister, Taylor
from her latest abusive boyfriend, even if that means taking
on the Russian mob.

Phantom Warrior Linx never met a woman he didn't like,
until he encountered Tabitha Shelley. His plans to sample
the female masses on Earth are disrupted, when Tabby draws
him into her personal war. Linx is ready to call it quits on his
search for a mate, when a spontaneous lap dance leads to an
unexpected night of passion.

Who knew a hissing Tabby could make a big cat like him
purr?

Before their new bond can be tested, the mob threatens
Tabby's life. But they will soon find out that it's never smart
to come between a Phantom Warrior and his mate.

PHANTOM
WARRIORS

Bacchus
JORDAN
SUMMERS

CHAPTER ONE

The Pleasurer straddled Bacchus, teasing him with her moist opening. He stared at her ripe breasts as she played with her nipples, popping first one, then another into her mouth and sucking greedily. It was a feat few Phantom women could accomplish. Bacchus watched, enraptured. It had been too long since he'd last partaken of such feminine delights.

He couldn't seem to catch his breath as his entire body tightened with arousal. She rimmed the head of his shaft. Bacchus felt his fangs unfurl. The urge to bite was strong, but he resisted the temptation. Acting before the woman achieved orgasm would show little restraint on his part.

It was hard enough to book a Pleasurer for the night. The workers' schedules remained full, with so many males to attend to and not enough pleasure workers or women to go around. Some men waited months for their turn. The last thing Bacchus needed was to get a reputation for being early off the mark.

He pushed aside the sudden guilt that surfaced at the way he'd obtained this particular Pleasurer. It would be a long time before Talon would forgive the extra duty he had assigned him tonight. But Bacchus had no choice. He'd been desperate.

Tomorrow he would stow away on a ship destined for Earth. It would take incredible skill and concentration to remain cloaked for the entire journey. He needed to relieve the tension burning through him before he left or risk discovery.

"Relax." The Pleasurer's silky voice meant to ensnare him as she finally lowered her body onto him.

Bacchus groaned as her ribbed channel swallowed him, sucking him deep, until he was nestled comfortably inside her. She began to move, gyrating her hips so that the fleshy protrusions caressed his length, stroking him like tiny fingers. Only members of the Claw Clan were blessed with sensual physical traits. That was why they made the best Pleasurers.

He gripped the furs beneath him and grit his teeth, lacerating the inside of his mouth with his fangs. Blood pooled, then poured down his throat. He swallowed the hot liquid to take the edge off his hunger, then bellowed, "More!"

The Pleasurer tossed her head back and her hands gripped his thighs, as she bounced up and down. A moan escaped from her throat as she ground her hips into him. Her claws tore his skin, leaving furrows of pleasure behind.

Bacchus' nostrils flared as the coppery mint scent of blood flooded his senses. He shot forward, latching onto one of her nipples and began to suck in time with her movements. She mewed, arching her spine to get closer. Bacchus sucked harder. The Pleasurer's breathing deepened as he laved and nibbled, teasing her with the tips of his fangs.

"Yes," she hissed. The woman grasped his head and buried his nose in her flesh. "Bite me," she demanded, increasing her speed.

Bacchus closed his eyes. The aroma of her blood beneath

her skin wafted like flowers on a breeze. He gripped her back, holding her in place so she couldn't change her mind and pull away. She wiggled closer. His forked tongue rasped her nipples twice more, then Bacchus impaled her with his fangs. He began to feed, while steadily pumping venom into her.

The Pleasurer screamed when the venom hit her bloodstream and sent her over the edge. Bacchus held her quivering body as it twitched from the explosive aftershocks. He wasn't sated. Not yet. His hips bucked in time with the draw of his mouth. She shuddered and her skin flushed anew.

Bacchus withdrew his fangs, licking away the stray drops of blood. The venom from his bite would continue to give her pleasure for the next few hours and would ease any discomfort she might feel later. He grasped the Pleasurer's hips and began to raise and drop her onto his hard shaft, while stroking the bundle of nerves hidden at the base of her skull.

The woman whimpered. "Please," she pleaded. Her eyes glowed from the mixture of pleasure and pain. "I don't know if I can—"

"More," he bellowed, cutting off her protest. Bacchus needed his senses filled and his body emptied in order to concentrate. Failure was not an option.

The Pleasurer's mouth descended to his shoulder. She blazed a trail of kisses to his neck, then sank her sharp, feline teeth into his skin.

Bacchus roared in surprise, then came hard with a jerk of his hips. Pleasurers never bit clients. It was against guild rules. She'd obviously made an exception for him. He stroked her erogenous spot, pinching and squeezing the nerves on her neck until the woman mewed and followed him into oblivion. She collapsed in a quivering heap on top of him, her breasts smashed against his chest, her lungs heaving.

"That was amazing." She sounded genuinely astonished.

Bacchus hid a pleased smile. "Do we have time for one more?" he asked, already knowing the answer.

The woman sat up and looked into his eyes, genuine regret in her gaze. "Sorry, Blood Warrior, but you know the rules. I have to attend to the next warrior on my list."

He kept his expression neutral to hide his disappointment. Just once, Bacchus would like to wake with a woman beside him, wrapped in his embrace. "I understand," he said. "Let me get your credits."

She slipped off his body, leaving him semi-hard. Unconcerned by his nudity, Bacchus rose and walked to the credit unit secured to the wall in his quarters. The unit had five colored stones on it that had to be pressed in the correct order for it to work.

Bacchus' hands flew over the stones. A moment later, a green credit crystal popped out. He handed the crystal to the Pleasurer.

She smiled and dropped it into a bag. "Would you like to book your next session?" The Pleasurer pulled out a device that held her schedule and looked at him expectantly.

Bacchus slowly shook his head. "That won't be necessary."

Something flashed in her eyes. With any other woman he would've thought it was disappointment, but not a Pleasurer. They saw nothing beyond the green of the credit crystals.

He showed the woman to the door. She stepped into the corridor, a faint smile ghosting her lips. Bacchus gave her a curt nod, then closed and sealed the entrance behind her. Black sweat-soaked strands of hair fell down his back and over his chest as he leaned his head against the door.

Tomorrow, everything would change. It had to.

His people were dying. *He was dying.*

Like the Atlanteans, a race of people who settled on Earth thousands of years ago before returning back to their home planet of Zaron, Phantom males outnumbered Phantom females thirty-to-one. Unless the Phantom people discovered a compatible female race capable of meeting all their unique needs and bearing their children, they as a people would cease to exist.

Since Atlantean women were also scarce, Phantom options were few. Many warriors chose to end their existence rather than live a life of never-ending loneliness. Others left Zaron never to return.

To outsiders, the Phantom people seemed like one large group, but they were actually made up of four distinct shifter species. Each group or clan had very different abilities and selective breeding habits, but all held the title of warrior.

The Blood Clan, which Bacchus called family, resembled Earth's mythical vampires and present day vipers. Their fangs transferred venom that could pleasure, numb or poison, depending on what venom sac the warrior accessed. They also fed on blood—though they could digest solids if necessary.

His reptilian group constituted the largest percentage of their population, followed closely by the Winged Clan, pterodactyl-sized bird shifters, the Claw Clan, which resembled saber-tooth tigers and other predatory cats, and the Tooth Clan, wolf-bear hybrids that could walk on two legs and would probably be considered mutant werewolves on Earth. Of course, the Tooth Clan could take a more pleasing form and resemble Earth's bears, but that was up to the individual shifter.

Phantoms grew up protecting their people's secrets. In the past, it had been a matter of life or total destruction. Today it was much the same, except their enemy was time. Which was why Bacchus found himself in his present predicament. He had never disregarded a direct order before.

Honor was as important as breathing to him. He took his duties as a royal guard for the Atlantean King seriously, but when he'd been ordered to remain on Planet Zaron, while Commander Orion went to retrieve a friend of the Queen's,

Bacchus knew he couldn't obey. Eros, the Atlantean King had left him no choice but to stow away.

Desperation permeated his people. Earth with its humanoid population remained their last great hope. Bacchus had volunteered to be the first warrior to attempt such an enormous undertaking. His future and the future of his people rested squarely upon his shoulders.

He may be the first to make the journey, but he wouldn't be the last if he succeeded. The Phantom people had given him very little time to secure a mate. If Bacchus failed, he feared self-destruction or rebellion.

Success and failure weighed heavily on his two hearts as he prepared for the long journey ahead.

* * * * *

Chapter Two

One week later...

Bacchus slipped off the craft shortly after it landed on Earth. They were in a place called Los Angeles, which was apparently filled with millions of humans. Bacchus hoped those millions included females.

Commander Orion had dropped off an Atlantean woman named Cassandra, then had taken off for someplace called New York. He'd probably notice a weight discrepancy, but would otherwise remain blissfully unaware of Bacchus' deception.

Bacchus had studied as much as he could about Earth before departure. Although he didn't feel comfortable on this new world, he knew he'd get by long enough to complete his mission. Bacchus tilted his face up to the sun, soaking in the heat.

The crisp ocean air tickled his nostrils and gently caressed his hair, leaving the taste of salt upon his forked tongue. This planet was similar to Zaron, but more exotic in flavor and color.

Earthlings began to arrive on the beach, shattering the

tranquility of the morning. Many ran in tight formation, wearing loose gray clothing that sagged on their bodies. Bacchus watched in fascination. There seemed to be no ritual behind their actions. They neither trained for combat nor executed stealth moves.

Strange, even for a primitive species.

Several people passed. He followed a woman down the wave-swept beach, taking care to blur his image in order to blend in with the environment. To the untrained eye, he would appear as a glimmer of light, a flash of sun on the sand, invisible to all until he deemed otherwise.

The woman's ass sashayed side-to-side with each step she took. Bacchus considered approaching, but decided against it when a nearby male called out her name. She waited for him to approach, then kissed the man. Together, they continued down the beach.

More people appeared on the sand. Their activities made no sense to him. Why were they running? As far as he could tell, nothing chased them.

Bacchus needed to learn more about this planet and its people. The vidlink had been helpful, but left out much information. The only way he could make up for the discrepancy was if he *absorbed* the knowledge. He frowned, not looking forward to what he had to do next.

He searched the sands for another Earth male. Bacchus couldn't take the chance with a female. The possibility of passing on his genetic coding and accidentally mating with her was slim, but still too great and far too important to squander indiscriminately. Bacchus was saving his code for his future mate. He refused to think that he might not find her on this planet.

Minutes passed without anyone coming by. The Atlantean female was close by, so he had to be careful. He couldn't afford for her to spot him and notify Orion. Bacchus stared down the beach, wondering if he should leave this place and go search another area. He was about to go, when

Cassandra began to peel off her clothing. He couldn't seem to move or breathe as she stripped, then stepped into the water.

Bacchus had lain with Atlantean women, so he knew about their enormous sexual appetites. They were tame compared to *his* true nature, but adventurous enough to whet his desire. His shaft hardened as she disappeared under a wave. Cassandra continued to frolic like a nymph, splashing and giggling as her blonde hair floated on the surface of the water behind her. He wondered if the female inhabitants of this planet would be as uninhibited.

Cassandra bobbed up, exposing her full breasts. Bacchus' body ached as her dusky nipples crinkled in the warm air. Atlantean women looked as if they shared that particular trait with the Earthlings, though he couldn't be sure until he saw one without their clothes on. Cassandra let out a squeal of delight.

He debated whether to materialize. It had been days since he'd had a woman writhing above him and longer still since one had come to his rest pad without receiving payment. Entranced by her nakedness and deafened by desire, Bacchus stepped forward. He didn't hear the man's approach on the sand until he was almost upon him.

Firm-framed with a shadowed jaw, the man slowed his pace as his gaze locked onto Cassandra. Bacchus could hear the man's heartbeat accelerate and sense his growing arousal. His arrival may have ruined his chance to lay with the Atlantean, but the man could make up for it by letting him absorb the information inside of him.

Bacchus lunged into the man's path, allowing himself to pass through the runner's body. He absorbed the man's essence, his knowledge, his experiences, and his *memories*. The man stumbled, but quickly righted himself. Bacchus felt a wave of nausea from taking in too much information. Emotions bombarded him.

So much pain. So much disappointment. And beneath it

all was something called love. Bacchus had read about that last emotion, but had never experienced anything like it. The feeling was…indescribable.

The details imprinted in the man's mind flowed into Bacchus at a dizzying speed, filling him with knowledge about the planet and the customs of its people. The male's name was Brady Rittner, but he preferred to be called Buzz. He fancied himself a space warrior underneath his unassuming façade. So why was he in so much pain?

Bacchus caught a glimpse of a woman crying in the man's mind. Who was she? And why did it hurt so much to see her like this? *Carrie*, the name whispered through his thoughts. It was followed by the word sister.

The information wasn't enough. Bacchus had to know more. He waded through pain that took his breath away, until he found what he was looking for. Carrie had been engaged to Buzz's best friend, Ryan. The man had discarded her, leaving her broken. Rage enveloped Bacchus. He wanted to hunt Ryan down and inflict the kind of pain he'd put Carrie through.

More memories swamped him. This time Bacchus saw a large box being lowered into the ground. Carrie and Buzz stood over the hole. Carrie was crying and holding her brother's hand. He'd pulled out of her grasp and walked away, leaving her alone at the side of the grave.

Buzz was mad at his sister. He blamed her for Ryan's death, though deep down he knew it wasn't her fault. His best friend wasn't perfect, but his passing had sent Buzz spiraling out of control. He'd lost his job and didn't feel like he had much to live for. The only thing that kept him from total destruction was his fear for Carrie's future. He didn't want her to be alone.

Bacchus couldn't believe the man's selfishness. Buzz's sister needed him and all he could think of was himself. His hearts ached for her. He needed to see for himself that she was all right. Checking on Carrie would delay his search, but what choice did he have? Bacchus couldn't call himself a Phantom Warrior if he turned his back on a female in need.

He had to locate her quickly. Once he observed that she was okay, Bacchus would be on his way and the hunt for a mate would begin in earnest. He turned back in time to see Buzz approach Cassandra. They spoke for several minutes. The man's gaze greedily drank in her nude form.

Lust rolled off him in waves, much like the Pacific caressed the shore. After a while, Buzz and Cassandra reached some kind of understanding. She climbed out of the water and got dressed. The couple hurried off the beach and headed toward a parking lot. Bacchus followed them to a nearby transport and slipped inside the car before they pulled out onto the street.

The ocean crashed onto the shore in white waves as they raced down the highway. Seagulls squawked above the water, dipping in for a quick meal amongst the shallows. A few came up with small fish flapping in their beaks, only to be swallowed a second later.

Invisible, Bacchus stared out the car window amazed at the shapes and colors of the various females wandering along the beach. He'd never seen so many females in one spot. Dressed in modest clothing and Pleasurer attire, there was something for any warrior on this planetary oasis.

Bacchus smiled. He couldn't wait to tell the others. He immediately pulled his thoughts back. He mustn't get too far ahead of himself. There was still a very good chance that the females here wouldn't be sexually compatible with his species. Their physiology was fragile compared to the Phantoms. Their primitive reproductive systems might not be able to handle the transformation process that occurred after mating.

Were their noses developed enough to respond to his pheromones?

Bacchus had faced many enemies over the years and fought more battles that he could recall, but none seemed as daunting as the task before him. How was he supposed to pick out a compatible female, when they all appealed to him in their own way?

As much as he was determined not to fail the Phantom people, Bacchus knew he couldn't select a random woman. He needed to find someone who would understand him, accept him for what he was.

The odor of fish and salt filtered through the transport window as they pulled up to a red light. More women rushed across the road, carrying towels and bags, their eyes hidden beneath black lenses and large hats.

Bacchus was tempted to jump out and taste the blood of one of the nearby females just to see if there would be a match, but he didn't. Honor dictated that he tend to Carrie first before he addressed his own needs. For her and her alone, he remained hidden and silent.

He replayed the memories he'd imprinted from Buzz's mind. The man seemed at a loss when it came to dealing with his sister. He loved Carrie, but thought she was making up stories about Ryan in an attempt to manipulate their sibling relationship. So, he'd stayed away, hoping the distance would make her face reality even though he couldn't.

Bacchus shook his head in disgust, then released the lingering guilt and sadness he'd sensed beneath the blame. Reluctantly, he searched Buzz's memories for more information about Ryan and Carrie. He saw them laughing and sneaking kisses, when they thought Buzz wasn't looking. Bacchus' gut clenched and he shoved the memory away. He didn't like seeing them together. Didn't like how happy they'd looked.

They continued driving down the coast. From what Bacchus could tell, they headed in the right direction to reach Carrie's home. That would make things much easier. Hopefully that's where they were going now.

He frowned when the car pulled in front of a building.

The building's windows were covered in crisp white shutters and a discreet sign displaying its name hung by the road.

Bacchus exited the car and followed the couple inside. After registering, they walked down a sand-colored hall to a room that faced the ocean. Buzz opened the door and ushered Cassandra inside, shutting the portal quickly behind him. The abrupt action left Bacchus standing in the hall, staring at the closed door. He grimaced at the momentary inconvenience, then concentrated and walked through the wall.

The pale gray room was bathed in light from the open shutters. Rich blue-green fabrics covered the bed, making it feel as if the hotel brought the ocean indoors. As Bacchus slowly looked around, sudden understanding dawned. Now he knew what kind of agreement the couple had reached. Cassandra moved fast with this Earth man. Perhaps she had a touch of Pleasurer in her after all.

Buzz strolled casually to the bathroom. Water came on a moment later. Cassandra tilted her head, listening. Her gaze strayed again and again to the closed bathroom door. Bacchus felt guilty for intruding upon their privacy, but he needed to ensure that Earthlings joined in much the same manner as Atlanteans and Phantoms. He didn't want his first joining with an Earth female to end in disaster or worst yet, death.

More splashing came from the shower. Bacchus laughed to himself, counting down the minutes it would take for Cassandra to give into her curiosity.

One...two...three.

Cassandra stripped out of her clothing. She'd shaved her mons, leaving a whisper of blonde peach fuzz behind. She padded down the same path Buzz took, her bare feet silent upon the carpeted floor. She didn't knock. Cassandra simply turned the handle and walked in. Steam bellowed out the door as Bacchus followed.

He reached the entrance in time to see Cassandra grab the

clear shower door and wrench it open. Buzz's hand snaked out and clasped hers. She gasped and her body flushed in response to his touch.

"Thought you weren't going to join me." Buzz's short hair lay slicked back on his head and his tanned body glistened beneath a thousand tiny droplets of water. Moisture clung to his lashes, hooding his eyes.

"You were expecting me." Cassandra didn't sound surprised.

Bacchus stared in fascination at the mating ritual taking place. Earth men were smaller *anatomically* than his species, but this one looked well enough endowed to please the Atlantean woman, if her widening gaze was any indication. She licked her full lips.

"See anything you like, baby?" Buzz choked, then cleared the thickness out of his throat.

Cassandra tore her gaze away from his rising shaft and glanced at his face. "Most definitely," she purred, doing a pretty good impression of a Claw Clan member.

"That makes two of us." Buzz's eyes lit with hunger as his gaze devoured her. "Come in, the water's perfect—like you."

Cassandra stepped into the shower and shut the door behind her

It was sheer torture to listen to their soft moans and watch as they caressed each other. The sounds alone were enough to drive any man insane. The ache in Bacchus' groin grew to dangerous levels. If he didn't find release soon, he wouldn't be able to maintain his invisibility.

Sweat beaded his brow and his shaft throbbed. His search for a mate couldn't start soon enough. Bacchus had taken one step out of the room, when Buzz's next words stopped him cold.

"This time is going to have to be hard and fast," he rasped.

Buzz opened the shower door and grabbed a foil wrapper

out of his pants. He tore it open with his teeth and quickly sheathed himself with the thin material inside. Bacchus was horrified, but couldn't tear his gaze away.

What had the man done to his shaft? Why would he do such a thing? Did it somehow enhance his size?

Buzz slipped back into the shower and immediately started kissing Cassandra. He lifted her off the ground. She automatically wrapped her legs around his lean hips. Buzz fumbled with his shaft as he searched for her moist entrance. He groaned when he finally found it, then thrust hard, burying himself to the hilt inside of her.

Cassandra's lips parted and she cried out as he pressed her against the wall tiles and drove into her hard and fast. Her breasts bounced with each thrust and her nails dug into his back.

"Buzz," she gasped.

The mention of his name seemed to spur Buzz on. He captured her mouth, devouring her as he rolled his hips to get even deeper. "So good," he snarled against Cassandra's lips. "What are you doing to me?"

Her eyes fluttered open. "Don't you like it?"

"Love it. That's the problem." He laughed mirthlessly. "Nothing this good ever lasts."

Bacchus held his breath, waiting to hear her response. This man was a fool to push a perfectly acceptable Atlantean woman away. Were Earthmen stupid enough to believe a good woman was easy to find? Did they mean so little to them that they were willing to discard them without thought?

The idea was unfathomable to Bacchus. He had seen enough. It was time for him to go, before he did something stupid like materialize and punch Buzz in the face. He made his way to the door.

Bacchus slipped Buzz's transport key off his key ring, then dropped the rest of the keys back onto the table. He shoved some of the replicator-created money that Cassandra brought with her into his pockets. He didn't bother to walk through the wall. 'Twas time to blend in and adhere to Earth customs. Bacchus opened the door and slipped outside, then headed to the parking lot.

He found a tote bag in the trunk of Buzz's car. It was filled with T-shirts, a pair of jeans, shorts, and rubber soled shoes. It was a tight fit, but somehow Bacchus squeezed into them.

Once he was dressed, Bacchus morphed his appearance to lessen the red of his eyes and pulled his long black hair into a queue at the nape of his neck. Buzz may not know it, but if Cassandra had her way, he'd be going back to Zaron with her. Atlantean women always got their way.

With Buzz's imminent departure looming on the horizon, Bacchus didn't have much time. He had to find Carrie and somehow let her know that her brother would soon be gone.

* * * * *

Chapter Three

Driving ended up being a bit more difficult than it first appeared, but Bacchus eventually got the hang of it. He quickly learned how to wave with one hand while honking and steering with the other, just like the drivers who passed him.

Bacchus still didn't quite understand why they'd put that red octagon-shaped sign on the side of the road, but it mattered not, since it now sat in his back seat, along with a couple of orange cones, the car's bumper and a small pine tree. It shouldn't have been planted so close to the sidewalk, anyway.

Finding things in Los Angeles was difficult with its one-way streets here, no entrance areas there. He'd barely missed the man holding the 'slow traffic ahead' sign. If he hadn't dove out of the way into a nearby pile of dirt, Bacchus would've flattened his feet. He could still hear the man's curses ringing in his ears and see his raised fist punching the air.

Bacchus arrived as darkness descended upon the palm-lined neighborhood he'd seen in Buzz's mind. He was grateful he'd made it. He wasn't sure he would with the car in two pieces. He pulled over to the side of the road and parked.

Take a quick look to make sure she's fine, then get back to searching.

Bacchus slipped out of Buzz's borrowed clothes, folding them neatly on the leather seat beside him before killing the engine. He sat in the car for a few minutes, listening to the sounds of the night. His forked tongue darted out of his mouth so he could scent the air for predators. The streets were relatively quiet, except for the constant hum of traffic on the freeways in the distance. Nearby dogs barked as underground sprinklers sprouted to life.

He could hear alien music thumping, couples making love, murmuring television sets, yet no ocean. Bacchus strained to listen for the gentle lapping of the distant waves. There it was, buried beneath the cacophony of existence. He stepped out of the vehicle, his feet falling silently on the pavement, and faded into the darkness.

Shrubs lined the sides of Carrie's small yard, creating a green wall of privacy around her little white home. Fragrant flowers surrounded the windowsills, their red and yellow blooms adding a burst of color to the otherwise plain palette.

Neat and obviously well tended, the space was cozy and seemed to fit the personality Buzz assigned to her. Curious, Bacchus allowed his image to solidify. He stood in the shadows, searching the windows for any sign of life.

Would she look like the image Buzz created in his mind? Would she have short brown hair and a pixie face? Or had she changed since then?

The questions filtering through his mind brought Bacchus up short. Her appearance shouldn't matter. That wasn't why he was here.

A light came on in the room at the front of the house. It was followed by the sound of up-tempo music. Bacchus held his breath and waited. A moment later, a fair-skinned woman stepped into view. Like taking an Atlantean energy blast to the gut, the air rushed from his lungs in a whoosh, leaving him winded.

Carrie had changed her hair since Buzz had last seen her. It was now shoulder length and blonde, without a trace of the brown that had been there before. Tiny boned but long of limb, she moved with the grace of a dancer as she walked from room to room, lights twinkling on in her wake. She came back into the main area with a rolled magazine grasped in her hand. Carrie brought the pages to her mouth and began to sing into it. She tossed her head back as she held a long note, while her hips swayed in time to the beat.

Bacchus stared, gaping, unable to look away. Blood rushed from his head straight to his shaft as she dropped the magazine and bent over to pick it up off the floor. She held it in her hand, carefully unfurling it, before placing it onto a side table. Bacchus knew without looking in a mirror that his eyes glowed red to match the heat churning inside of him. He could *feel* the color as it surged through his body, making demands.

Suddenly, observing Carrie wasn't enough. He needed to possess this woman, but he couldn't exactly march in and demand she mate with him. He didn't even know if it was possible for a Phantom to take a human as a mate, but the lack of knowledge didn't stop him from wanting her.

In his current condition, he'd scare her to death. And that was the last thing Bacchus wanted. He'd have to approach her when his beast was under control. But how? He hated the idea of deceiving Carrie. She'd been through so much this past year, but what choice did he have? She'd never believe the truth.

She pursed her lips. His dark gaze locked on her mouth. Bacchus longed to taste those lips to see if they were as sweet as they appeared to be.

His three-inch fangs unfurled without warning and hunger beat at his brow. Bacchus brought his hands to his temples and rubbed. His gaze traced the curve of her mouth down to her chin and over her throat. He could hear Carrie's blood pumping just below the surface of her milky skin. It called to him, demanding that he taste her. Bacchus had never felt anything like this urge. This went beyond simple lust into something deeper, darker, and far more primal.

What was happening to him? Did humans possess a hidden pheromone that affected Phantoms? It would explain a lot.

Bacchus swallowed hard and fought the instincts that told him to mark her. Helpless in the face of such overwhelming need, he continued to watch her.

* * * * *

Carrie turned off the stereo and tuned into her favorite show. Despite the noise, the quiet pressed in around her. She'd tried singing to fill the silence, but it hadn't helped for long. Ryan had brought the house to life with his raucous laughter. Always one to pull childish pranks, he kept her in stitches for the short time that they'd lived together. His goofy sense of humor was one of the reasons she'd said yes, when he'd asked her to marry him. As Brady's best friend, Carrie thought she knew him well. Thought she could count on him. Turned out, she didn't know him at all.

Despite the ugly breakup, she still missed him now that he was gone. The blame and guilt over his death lingered, but the pain wasn't quite as acute as it had been in the beginning.

She had always thought that she'd been in love with Ryan, but lately…Carrie wasn't so sure. She was beginning to think she'd wanted to be in love so badly that she'd simply convinced herself that she was.

Even her brother's desertion nine months ago didn't hurt as much as it once had. Carrie wasn't sure what that said about their sibling relationship. Oh, she loved her brother dearly and knew that Brady loved her, but there'd been a darkness growing inside of him for years. Ryan's death and the loss of his job had only hastened its spread. As much as she wanted to, Carrie couldn't save Brady from himself.

She stared at the empty spot beside her. Loneliness rose so quickly that Carrie barely had time to tamp it down. She loved this house, but she'd been thinking lately that a change might do her some good. She wasn't sure where she'd go yet, but it would certainly be easy enough to sell the place, since she was only a few miles from the beach.

With the money she'd make from the sale, she could settle Ryan's debt and maybe have enough to start over. Maybe she would even take the time to get back into her original field of study, not that there was a huge demand for herpetologists these days. She sighed.

There was nothing wrong with training and breeding dogs, but the job wasn't the same as working with amphibians and reptiles. Some girls loved warm and fuzzy, she loved cool and scaly. But then again, Carrie had always been a little out of step with her friends.

A particularly funny line from the TV show drew her back from her musings. Carrie laughed, temporarily forgetting about her plans. The screen switched to a commercial and suddenly the skin on the back of her neck prickled and heated.

Carrie looked at her alarm system to make sure it was set, then glanced out her living room window into her front yard. Darkness met her. The shadows clung to the bushes, making them seem particularly dense for this time of night. Her eyes strained to penetrate the inky mass.

No movement came beyond the hiss and spray of the sprinkler system. There was nothing to explain the sudden wave of hyper-awareness coursing through her body or the heaviness in her breasts.

Carrie looked down at the front of her shirt, noting her pebbled nipples and frowned. She crossed her arms over her chest. She might not be ready to start dating again, but it was obvious her body had other ideas. She gave the darkness one last glance, before dismissing the whole thing as an overactive imagination and settling back in her chair.

* * * * *

A car pulled into her driveway and cut the engine. Two men climbed out of the transport and headed for Carrie's front door. Bacchus sank deeper into the shadows. The taller of the two men raised his fist and banged on her front door.

He saw Carrie startle, then hurry to the door. The light on the porch came on and she opened the door. She immediately took a step back, when she saw who was there.

"Where's the money?" the taller man asked.

"Like I told you yesterday and the day before that and the day before that, I don't have it," she said. "Ryan never gave me anything."

"Mr. Bing is losing his patience," he said. The man took out a small object and flicked it with his thumb. Flame erupted from the end of it. "I'd hate for anything to happen to your house, while you're in it."

Carrie trembled and tears filled her eyes. "I'll get you your money. I told you I would."

"Chop! Chop! Next time we won't be leaving here without it." He motioned for the other man to head back to the car. He was about to follow, but stopped. "By the way, how's your brother doing?"

Blood drained from Carrie's face and her grip on the door tightened.

The man laughed. "See you tomorrow," he said, then hurried back to the car, climbed inside and drove away.

Bacchus didn't understand what had just occurred, but he recognized a threat when he heard one. What had Carrie gotten herself into? Did Buzz know that she was in danger? He searched the man's memories, but all he could come up with was a brief dismissal when Carrie had tried to tell him that Ryan had been in trouble before he died.

This changed everything…

Bacchus watched over Carrie's house until she went to bed. Once he was sure the men would not return, he drove around the neighborhood aimlessly, while he planned how to intercede.

The open window delivered cool air to the inside of the car, but did little to diminish his anger. He was so distracted by his strategizing that he almost missed a woman's muffled screams in the distance. He hit the breaks and the car skidded to a stop in the middle of the road. Bacchus listened, his hearts pounding in his chest. Silence ensued.

Had he imagined the cries?

Bacchus pulled over to the side of the road and turned off the engine. He glided out of the seat, his tongue testing the air for danger. It took two turns to the right, but he found what he sought. The trail of sweat and fear was faint, but he'd be able to follow it. Bacchus got back into the vehicle and made a U-turn.

It didn't take long to locate the darkened alley where the scream had come from. As he killed his lights, Bacchus saw a woman sprawled across the ground. Her knees were cut, along with her hands. Bruises marred her pretty face. Her eyes watered and her body trembled as shock took hold. The buttons on her shirt had been torn and her skirt was ripped, leaving her skin and underwear exposed. A group of men surrounded her, taunting her like a pack of hungry wolves. Each man had the word *fuego* burned into his skin.

Bacchus didn't know what the word meant, but from the smell, it wasn't anything good. Listening, he caught snippets of the conversation, something about pulling a train, which made no sense, since they were miles from the railroad tracks.

No one in the nearby houses responded to her pitiful cries. It was as if they didn't hear her. Or didn't want to. Televisions were turned up to their highest volumes and radios blasted distorted songs.

His forked tongue slithered out of his mouth once again. Bacchus tasted sexual need, along with depravity. So they planned to take this helpless woman once they finished beating her.

Rage boiled inside of him fueled by his unexpected hunger for Carrie. Bacchus stepped out of the car. His feet were silent upon the uneven ground as he moved closer to the men.

One of the men noticed his approach. "Nice ride," he said. "You lost, man?"

"No, I'm exactly where I want to be," he said.

The men exchanged confused glances.

"I think you'd better get out of here, *punta*," a dark-haired, pock-faced man said, stepping toward him in a manner Bacchus was sure was meant to be threatening. "This isn't a safe neighborhood." Aggression oozed from his pores.

The man had no way of knowing the creatures that he'd faced in battle in order to prove himself a warrior. His stern stance was little more than an annoyance that Bacchus could easily dispatch with no effort whatsoever. They thought they were the most dangerous predators out tonight. They were wrong.

Bacchus' gaze flicked to each man, before focusing on the woman who wept silently. Her brown eyes were both pleading and fearful. The beast inside Bacchus rejoiced. A good fight would alleviate some of the tension strumming through his body.

The young man pulled up his shirt to show Bacchus the gun hidden in his low-riding pants. "You'd better leave, *punta*. Not going to ask you again."

A bullet couldn't penetrate his flight suit, but it could leave a nasty hole in his head. Bacchus doubted any of these men were good enough shots to pull off that feat, especially with him moving in and out of their sights. Even so, he wouldn't give them the opportunity to try.

He felt his power flow until his eyes blazed red in the darkness like a demon from their religious texts.

The men gasped and stepped back.

In the next instant, Bacchus' fangs unfurled and venom shot out ten feet, spraying three of the men in the face. Screams rang out as the men wiped their eyes. The toxins would temporarily blind them while he took care of the others. Bacchus roared, blurring his image until he was a nightmare come to life.

He surged forward.

The young man who'd been speaking pulled his gun out and fired rapidly, but he wasn't fast enough. The bullets penetrated a wall nearby, sending plaster raining onto the ground. He kept firing until nothing came out.

Bacchus grasped the man's fingers and squeezed.

Crunch!

The man screamed in agony, as his bones snapped and crumbled to powder.

Bacchus kept his grip on the man and yanked him forward. He sank his fangs deep into his throat. Blood pooled in his mouth. He swallowed. The man's terrified wails increased, along with his struggles, but Bacchus refused to release his prize. Suddenly he went limp in surrender. The man may talk tough, but he behaved like prey.

He continued to feed. The man's blood tasted sour. Something tainted his body. Bacchus dropped him onto the ground and stepped over his prone form. He'd remain paralyzed for the next few hours due to the venom he'd expelled. Bacchus turned to face the final three, only to see two of them swivel and run. The third stood his ground, a knife clutched beneath white knuckles.

"Come on!" he shouted. "I'm not afraid of a vampire. I have a cross." He pulled his shirt open to show Bacchus the large silver chain around his neck, grasping it like a talisman.

The hypocrisy of the move did not escape him. Bacchus threw his head back and laughed, licking blood from his fangs as he did so. The young man's taste triggered his hunger. He fought the need for satiation.

"Do you expect me to fear the metal pressed against your chest, when *you* do not?" Bacchus asked.

"Vampires can't look upon crosses. It hurts them." The man glanced around as if help would suddenly appear. "Everybody knows that."

Bacchus brushed his clothing. "I did not," he said, then disappeared before the man's eyes.

The man frantically searched for him.

Bacchus reappeared behind him. The brush of breath on his neck was the only warning the man received before he plunged his fangs into his neck.

The man tried to stab him, but Bacchus caught the weapon before it could do any damage. He bent the knife blade with little effort and dropped it onto the ground.

He retracted his fangs to speak. "You shouldn't have done that," he said. "Your aggression just makes me hungrier." Bacchus gripped the man's chin and craned his neck for better access, then struck without mercy.

Bacchus drank until his hunger was sated. The rich fiery taste of blood filled every cell in his body. He was enjoying feeding so much that he almost missed the sound of the man's heart stuttering in his chest. Bacchus had no moral qualms when it came to killing, but there was no challenge in taking down human prey. He let the man fall to the ground. He landed with a thump. He'd think twice before he pounced upon a stranger again in a darkened alley. They all would.

The woman remained on the ground, her eyes wide with horror. She bled from so many places it was hard for Bacchus to concentrate. He took a couple of deep breaths, his body fading and solidifying repeatedly while he wrenched back control. The smell of blood permeated the air like coppery perfume. Finally, he stilled, his mind and beast firmly back under his command.

"It's okay." Bacchus held his hand out in a soothing gesture and lowered his voice. "I won't harm you."

The woman whimpered and hunkered down in an attempt to make herself smaller.

Bacchus heard her mumbling prayers under her breath and forced his fangs to retract. He hadn't intended to scare her, but he'd had no choice. The men would not have let her go without a fight.

"Where do you live?" he asked.

He needed to get her home, so her family could get her medical attention. Bacchus didn't think the men had sexually assaulted her, but the shock of the beating wouldn't wear off anytime soon.

The woman glanced up tentatively, eyeing his mouth as if she didn't trust what she'd seen. Bacchus relaxed. Soon she would doubt her recollection, which was for the best. She'd been through enough.

"A couple of blocks over to the east." She took a shuddering breath and clutched her tattered clothes to her chest, then struggled to her feet.

"I'm not familiar with this place," he said. "Can you guide me?"

She glanced warily at the men on the ground and nodded. "Are they going to die?" Tears welled in her eyes. "They were going to kill me after…"

Bacchus clenched his fists. He knew what they'd intended to do, even before he'd taken their blood and confirmed it. "They will not harm you again or I will return and finish what I started. Next time I will not be so merciful."

The men whimpered in response.

The instinct to kill was tempting. This wasn't the first woman to suffer at the hands of these men. Others had not been nearly as fortunate. Bacchus could have killed them easily, but he wasn't here to battle an enemy, however deserving of death.

"Come," Bacchus said before he changed his mind and put the men down for good. He reached out to support her, but she flinched and backed away. He let her, but kept a close eye on her in case she stumbled. Bacchus opened the car door and waited for her to step inside. "I'll be right back."

He strolled over to the incapacitated men. The three blinded ones wept in fear as they heard his purposeful footfalls, while the fourth and fifth lay supine, unable to move, their dark eyes filled with terror.

"If I ever see any of you around this woman again, I will kill you. I can do so at any time and you'd never see me coming." Bacchus allowed his fangs to unfurl as he bent over one of the paralyzed men. Venom clung to the sharp tip, dropping onto the man's white shirt. "Blink if you understand me," he snarled.

The man blinked rapidly and tears ran down his cheeks.

"Good." Bacchus smiled, flicking his forked tongue into the air. He could hear the rapid heartbeats of the two men who'd ran away before the fight. They were hiding not far from the alley. No doubt they'd retrieve their friends the second he left.

Bacchus didn't understand this planet. With all the resources here, including healthy women, why did they take so much for granted?

* * * * *

Chapter Four

Bacchus arrived on Carrie's awning-covered doorstep early the next morning, toting a briefcase containing notes on Ryan and her brother, Buzz that he'd scribbled after he'd dropped off the woman from the alley. The notes he'd made looked professional at first glance, but wouldn't hold up under scrutiny. He prayed to the Goddess that Carrie wouldn't ask to see them, since most were written in Phantom text.

Last night's encounter had changed things for him. Bacchus was still determined to save his people, but he also wanted to take Carrie away from this dangerous planet. She wasn't safe. No unattached females were safe here.

He tugged at the clothes he'd bought this morning, trying to get used to the fit. These clothes were not made for fighting. In fact, Bacchus couldn't tell what use they were at all, beyond covering his nudity. But between the clothes, the notes, and Buzz's memories, he should have enough to work his way inside Carrie's home.

Bacchus pulled his long, dark hair back into a queue, then pressed the button on the side of the door. He ignored the guilt churning in his gut. His deception was necessary, but that didn't make doing it any easier. The truth would come later once he was sure she was safe.

The bell chimed, echoing throughout the structure.

Silence pervaded.

Bacchus frowned and hit the button again.

He heard the pad of bare feet across the floor a second before a sleepy voice called out from the other side. "All right, all right, I'm coming. Keep your shirt on."

He looked at his green button down shirt and tweed jacket. He'd had no intention of taking off the garment, since it effectively concealed his flight suit.

Bacchus checked his reflection in the windowpane to see if the sunglasses he'd purchased at Venice Beach hid the red of his eyes. The lenses were dark enough to effectively conceal the unusual color, but not too dark. He shouldn't need to remove them during their conversation.

His body radiated heat thanks to the clothes and from being in such close proximity to Carrie. The heat sent his pheromones wafting into the air. Bacchus inhaled, catching their unique scent, then tugged at his collar. He didn't need this now. Not yet. He wrestled his beast for control as he waited for her to answer the door.

* * * * *

Carrie took one look out of the peephole at the handsome man standing on her front porch and cursed under her breath. Did he work for Mr. Bing, too? She looked again. The others who'd been sent had worn expensive suits, tailored to fit them perfectly. This man looked like he'd stepped out of a thrift shop. She glanced down at her wrinkled pajamas.

"One minute," she said and raced back to the bathroom.

Carrie quickly washed her face and brushed her hair, then threw on a comfy pair of sweats. She was about to walk out the door, when she spotted her pepper spray on her bedside table. Carrie hurried over and picked it up just in case she was wrong about him.

The police had told her there was nothing they could do until the men crossed the line. Of course by then she'd be dead. But the law was the law. It didn't always work like you needed it to. She tucked the can in the back of her sweats and pulled her T-shirt over it.

The man was still standing on her porch when she returned. Carrie slowly cracked the door open and blinked against the sunlight. She hoped he wasn't one of Mr. Bing's thugs or a door-to-door salesman hocking religion. She wasn't in the mood to face either one this morning.

Face-to-face, the man was even more handsome. At first glance, she'd thought his hair was short, but now Carrie could see it had been swept back into a tight ponytail. The black shade accentuated his pale skin. Skin that seemed to defy the Southern California sunshine.

"May I help you?" Carrie craned her neck to peer into his face, ignoring her accelerating heartbeat. Her hand moved casually to the pepper spray, so it would be within reach.

The man stared at her for several seconds, his gaze piercing despite his shades. Carrie had never had anyone look at her the way he was looking at her—not even her ex-fiancé, Ryan. It was unsettling.

"Do you speak English?" she asked.

A delicate, yet spicy fragrance emanated from his skin. The enticing aroma enveloped her, filling Carrie's lungs and permeating her pores. Her body swayed toward him and instantly relaxed.

He smelled so *good*…like fresh-baked cookies on Christmas morning or bread pulled from the oven of a French bakery. She had the sudden urge to start nibbling on his skin.

The thought made her take a step back. Carrie shook her head to clear it. Skin didn't smell *tasty*. And she wasn't the type of woman who liked to nibble on strangers. She inhaled again and her head swam. It had to be his cologne or maybe something floating in the smoggy air. People did not smell like this. She scrunched her nose.

* * * * *

Bacchus finally found his voice. Seeing Carrie up close had quite literally knocked him senseless. Her reaction to his pheromones had pulled him out of his stupor. "Are you Carrie Rittner?" he asked, knowing full who she was.

"Yes," she said. "Who are you?"

"I'm here on your brother's behalf," he said, which was the truth and a lie. If it weren't for Buzz, Bacchus wouldn't be here. He shifted so she could get a look at the car in the driveway. Since he hadn't passed any other transports that looked like it, he knew it was unique.

She gasped when she saw the 1968 vintage muscle car. "Where's Brady? What's happened to him? Is he all right? Tell me," she pleaded, then looked back at the car as if it held clues. "What happened to the bumper? How did it get that scratch down the door?"

Bacchus frowned. He hadn't meant to damage the vehicle. He'd done the best he could to keep it between the narrow lines.

"Is he…?" Carrie's voice trailed off and she grabbed the doorframe for support.

"No!" Bacchus said quickly. "Buzz is not dead. If you'll allow me to come in, I'll explain everything."

Her sigh of relief was audible, but she still eyed him with suspicion. "Do you work for Mr. Bing?"

"Who's Mr. Bing?" he asked.

* * * * *

Who was this man and why did he have her brother's car? That car was his baby. Brady and Ryan had restored it together. Her brother never let anyone drive it, aside from

Ryan. Carrie needed answers and didn't think she'd get them if she left him standing on the front porch.

"Okay," she said. "Come in and tell me what's happened." Carrie held the can of pepper spray behind her back, as she stepped aside for him to enter. The knot in her stomach grew from fist size to boulder in the span of a second as he crossed over the threshold. His mere presence seemed to engulf her home.

"May I have a seat?" he asked.

She'd been so startled by the car that she'd forgotten basic manners. "Of course. Would you like a cup of coffee Mr…Mr?"

"Please call me Bacchus," he said. "And yes, I'd love something to drink."

Her brow rose. "Unusual name, even for L.A."

He tilted his head. "I am an unusual *man*."

That he was, if first impressions were any indication. Carrie didn't comment. "Take a seat in the living room, I'll be right back." She kept her pepper spray out of view as she walked into the kitchen. "It'll take a minute for the coffee to brew."

Carrie kept Bacchus in her peripheral vision while she scooped heaping mounds of ground coffee beans into the filter. Her heart was pounding. What had happened to Brady? Had Bing's men gotten to him? Bacchus said he wasn't dead, but it had to be bad if he had her brother's car.

The aroma of French roast filled the air as she poured water into the carafe and flipped the switch to brew. She glanced at Bacchus. He sat on the loveseat, his gaze fixed at a point on the wall. What was he looking at? Suddenly his attention snapped to her.

Carrie froze, trapped in his gaze, powerless to escape. Her body tingled and her skin stretched taut. She knew she should be scared—and she was—but for some reason her body remained languid and strangely giddy like she didn't have a care in the world. What was wrong with her?

Working with animals gave her good instincts. Carrie's gut told her Bacchus wasn't there to harm her, but there was something odd about him that she couldn't quite put her finger on. She needed to watch him closely.

His alluring scent seemed to follow her into the kitchen. If Carrie didn't know better, she'd swear he was standing next to her…which was impossible since she could clearly see him in the other room.

It took forever for the coffee to finish brewing. Carrie walked into the living room, carrying a tray with a decanter and two mugs on it. The bittersweet aroma filled the air as she placed the tray onto the coffee table. She poured coffee into the cups, then took a seat in the wicker chair opposite Bacchus.

"Would you like sugar and cream?" she asked. "I have some in the kitchen."

"I prefer to drink it black." He lifted the cup to his lips and inhaled deeply. "This smells good."

"Be careful. It's hot," she warned.

He opened his mouth and a forked tongue appeared. Bacchus didn't look like the type to run with the piercing and mutilating crowd, but there was obviously more to him than met the eye.

Carrie watched in fascination as he dipped his tongue into the steaming brew a couple of times, then tipped the cup to his mouth like it was a shot of tequila. She glanced at her cup and watched the steam rise.

He should be screaming and holding his tongue, or at least turning red. Instead, Bacchus looked perfectly normal. Well, as normal as a guy with a forked tongue could look. Something about him was so…*reptilian,* she thought. The fact that Carrie found that kind of sexy said far more about her than it did him.

He's here because something has happened to Brady. Your brother might be lying in a hospital bed and you're fantasizing about a stranger.

Carrie put her cup down in disgust. "You said you were here on Brady's behalf. What's happened to my brother?" she asked. "Has he been arrested? Was he in an accident?" Neither of which would surprise her.

"None of those things." He poured himself another cup of coffee. "He sent me here to make sure you're okay. He's concerned about your safety."

She grimaced. "He could've come himself."

Bacchus shifted the cup in his hand. "He was otherwise occupied," he said, holding her gaze. "So I came in his stead."

Carrie couldn't stop staring at him. On the surface, he was like any other good-looking man in L.A., but it was what simmered beneath the surface that captured her.

Bacchus gave her a slow knowing smile.

Her face flushed. "Sorry." Carrie glanced at her feet to regain her composure. She'd never been forward when it came to men. As anti-feminist as it was, she liked it when a man made the first move. Carrie wanted them to take the lead, to be the dominant one.

"Don't be. I like it when you look at me." His voice rumbled in his chest, sending vibrations through her body.

Carrie's head shot up and her eyes widened. Was Bacchus flirting with her? *Would it be so bad if he was?* Her heart thumped loudly in her chest and she shifted.

Hello! Earth to Carrie. He's here about your brother. Remember?

She'd never thought of herself as an awful sister until now.

Bacchus placed his cup beside hers. "There's no easy way to tell you this. Buzz has decided to go away for a while."

"What do you mean go away?" she asked. "Where?"

"A place you have never heard of," he said.

"Where?" she asked again, determined to get a straight answer.

"Zaron," he said.

Carrie frowned. "Is that a country?"

He shrugged. "Of sorts."

"Why send you now? Brady never believed me when I told him Ryan was in trouble. He thought I was making it all up to get attention." Carrie stood and began to pace. "I know he blames me for Ryan's accident. If we hadn't been fighting on the phone when it happened, then maybe he would've seen the truck in time."

It didn't matter that the police had determined that the truck driver had been at fault. Guilt swamped her. Carrie couldn't help but think that he'd still be alive, if she hadn't distracted him. If he were, then she wouldn't be in this situation.

"Buzz told me what happened." Bacchus looked uncomfortable. "He's ashamed of his behavior."

"But not ashamed enough to come here and help me himself." Bitterness tinged her words. "When does he plan to leave?" Carrie plopped back down in her seat.

"His departure is imminent," Bacchus said.

"He must really trust you, if he shared all this with you." Carrie tried unsuccessfully to cover the hurt in her voice.

"Carrie," Bacchus said her name so softly, she almost didn't hear him. "I'm sorry. I know this must be painful to hear."

She scrubbed a hand over her face. "No, I was expecting something like this. I mean, it sucks, but I'm not really surprised." Her fingers fluttered nervously. "Actually, I was expecting much worse. I thought you'd come here to tell me that Brady was dead."

He reached across the coffee table and clasped her hand. Heat shot from his fingertips up her arm before blossoming throughout her body.

Carrie jerked her hand away in shock.

Bacchus' nostrils flared. Other than that tiny reaction, he seemed unfazed. "Your brother is very much alive. I'm sure

Buzz will eventually contact you after he's settled."

Her heart clenched. "He's not alone, is he?"

"No," Bacchus said without inflection. "He has found a woman who makes him happy."

Carrie had hoped that Brady had moved on with his life, but hearing that he'd met someone special from a total stranger made the fact that he hadn't phoned or come by to say farewell harder to take. She jumped up and started pacing again. "You're sure he's okay?"

"Positive. He's currently with his new…"

"Lover?" Her mouth twisted painfully as the word scalded her tongue. "Why didn't he take his car?"

"It was no longer needed," he said. "He's finally let go of the past."

Carrie's legs threatened to give out. Brady was leaving his past behind, which meant he was dumping the whole thing on her. What was she going to do? She glanced around. She'd have to sell the house. Heck, she might have to sell everything in it to cover Ryan's debt. Carrie took a deep breath. It didn't matter. If Brady could start over, then she could, too.

"Buzz needs to work through his issues, just like you need to work through yours," Bacchus said.

Her brow furrowed. "My issues aren't going to be solved by talking to someone or running away, but tell Brady thanks and that I wish him well."

"I think you've misunderstood why I'm here," Bacchus said. "I did not come here solely to convey this message for your brother. I am here to help."

* * * * *

Her skeptical expression said she didn't believe him. Her sharp blue gaze swept over his clothes and her frown deepened. "No offense, Mr. Bacchus," she said. "But I'm not sure you're up for the job."

Bacchus' brow arched. He couldn't tell her that she'd insulted him without admitting the truth. "Things aren't always as they appear," he said softly. "You of all people should know that."

Her lips thinned. "What do you intend to do?" she asked. "I've already called the police multiple times. Their hands are tied. They can't do anything until Mr. Bing's men cross the line and actually harm me."

"I will not let that happen," Bacchus' voice hardened. "When they return, I will talk with them." He could be very persuasive when he wanted to be.

"Talk?" Carrie snorted. "You're going to get yourself killed."

Bacchus stared at her. "Anything is possible, but that outcome is unlikely. Do you know about the credits?"

"Credits?" Confusion morphed her delicate features.

"I mean money," he corrected.

Carrie deflated before his eyes. "I knew nothing about Ryan's gambling or the missing money until those men showed up on my doorstep a few months ago. But I suppose I should've suspected something was going on. There were signs. Little things like missing checks and bank balance discrepancies that I ignored."

"It's not your fault," he said.

She grimaced. "It is, but I'm determined to fix it. Would you like more coffee?"

"Please." He held his cup out for her.

* * * * *

Their fingers brushed as Carrie poured, but this time she didn't pull away. "So how did you and Brady meet?"

"We ran into each other on the beach," he said, cryptically. "You could say, I've been inside his mind."

"Then you know what a dark, scary place that is." She finished pouring and sat the carafe down.

"Yes, I do." Bacchus peered over the top of the cup at her. The steam curled over his glasses like ghostly shadows. He didn't so much look at her as look right through her.

Carrie tried not to fidget under his close scrutiny.

"He may not express it well, but Buzz cares about you very much. I know this to be so. He worries about you in his own way. If he didn't, I wouldn't be here."

She sighed. "If he cared about me so much, he wouldn't have tossed away our relationship after Ryan and I broke up."

"He was a fool," Bacchus said. "They both were."

Carrie shook her head. "Everyone deals with loss differently. Brady chose to blame me, stick his head in the sand, and when that didn't work, run away," she said. "I couldn't do that. I had to stay and fight."

"Have you moved on with your life?" he asked.

"What do you mean?" she asked.

"Are you seeing anyone?"

Carrie laughed, but the sound held no humor. "I can't drag someone into this mess. It wouldn't be fair to them. In that respect, my brother and I are nothing alike."

"What if someone wanted to be part of your life?" It was an innocent question, but the look he leveled on her was anything but innocent. "Someone who wouldn't take no for an answer?"

Heat inflamed her, but Carrie made sure her expression remained intent. "Then I'd wonder what was wrong with them," she said. "Because only a crazy person would be that stupid."

"There's a difference between crazy and determined," he said softly.

"Not in this instance," she said. "I don't mean to be rude, Mr. Bacchus, but I'm going to have to ask you to leave. I have to get ready for work."

Carrie picked up as many extra hours as she possibly could, but they weren't enough. Nothing was enough.

Despite Bacchus' assurance that he was here to help, the only real chance she had of getting out of this mess was to sell everything and hope it was enough.

"What do you do for a living?" Bacchus asked.

The change of subject was so abrupt that Carrie answered without thinking. "I train and breed dogs."

"Did you study to do this?" he asked.

"Oh heavens no." She chuckled. "My degree is in herpetology."

His dark brow shot to his hairline. "You studied reptiles?" There was genuine interest in Bacchus' voice and something flared to life in his eyes.

For a second, they'd looked as if they had turned red, but that was impossible. *It had to be a play of sunlight against his lenses*, she thought, dismissively.

"Most people fear reptiles, particularly snakes. That includes my brother. Their first reaction is to want to kill the creatures. If only people understood how necessary reptiles are to the ecosystem, they'd think twice before they destroyed them." Passion filled her voice.

"I quite agree. So you don't fear them?" he asked. "Not even a little?"

"No," Carrie balked. "I find them fascinating. Always have. Their ability to survive and adapt to the planet, despite catastrophic changes to the environment, is miraculous really."

His lips quirked. "You sound like you wish you could be a reptile."

She shrugged. "Sometimes I think it would be cool. It would certainly be easier to live without all the emotional baggage."

"I'm not sure that life would be as enjoyable though," he said. "Without pain, life would feel incomplete."

She smiled. "Are you speaking from experience?"

"Perhaps." Bacchus gave her a secretive smile.

"You said you breed and train dogs, but I see no dogs

here." Bacchus glanced around the room. "Are they in your backyard?"

"No," she said. "There isn't enough space to breed dogs here at the house. The owners of the animals rent space at a kennel and give me access so that I can do my job."

"Sounds like an acceptable arrangement," he said.

"Believe me, it is. I'm only responsible for them during breeding periods and obedience training. Speaking of which..." She glanced at a clock on the wall. "I really have to go."

He tilted his head. "Would you mind if I came along?"

The idea of him watching her still sent tingles along Carrie's spine, leaving behind dark carnal thoughts and tempting erotic images. "Why?" she asked.

"I promised Buzz that I would protect you."

She examined him again. "You really don't look like a bodyguard."

"As I said before, looks can be deceiving."

True, she thought. Ryan had seemed liked the all-American guy, who had the perfect family and a nice education. And he was. But he was also addicted to gambling and didn't think twice about stealing from his friends and his business associates.

Carrie stared at Bacchus. His good looks were distracting. They made her think about things that she had no business considering right now. They also made her want to trust him. It had to be the stress. She was looking for relief—any kind of relief, to get her through the things she had to do over the next few months.

She worried her bottom lip with her teeth. Carrie didn't think there was any harm in having Bacchus go to work with her. She was pretty sure an obedience training class was scheduled for today. Besides, it would be nice to have someone watch her back for a while, even if it turned out that was all he could do.

"I suppose it would be okay," she said.

"Good." Bacchus grinned.

"I have to catch a shower before we go. Do you mind waiting outside on the porch?" she asked.

"Not at all," he said. "Take your time."

* * * * *

CHAPTER FIVE

A car slowly rolled by as Bacchus stepped out onto the porch. Two men glanced his way with narrowed gazes. He recognized them instantly. They were the same ones who'd dropped by Carrie's house the previous night.

Bacchus pulled his sunglasses down so they could get a good look at his glowing red eyes. Their tires squealed as they drove away, but he knew they'd be back. Their sudden appearance only added to the sense of urgency he already felt.

Carrie was in danger. Of that there was no doubt. Last night, Bacchus had shown mercy. Tonight, there'd be none.

Bacchus heard water come on in the house. Drawn to the sound and what it represented, he raced around to the backyard. Shrubs surrounded the small, green area, giving him complete privacy. Bacchus slipped out of his new clothes and dissolved in the sunlight. He passed through the back door, then headed down the hallway toward Carrie's bedroom.

She was removing her top, when he entered the room. A can labeled pepper spray was tucked in the waistband of her sweats. She placed it on the dresser. He frowned, doing a quick search of the memories he'd absorbed from Brady. Bacchus smiled as he realized what the canister contained. She'd armed herself before opening the door.

Smart woman. His respect for her grew.

Carrie turned toward the bathroom door, giving Bacchus an expansive view of creamy skin as her spine sloped its way down toward her ripe ass.

He swallowed hard, willing his fangs to remain retracted, and fought to keep from materializing. Spying on her like this was wrong, but Bacchus couldn't help himself. He followed her long, tapered fingers as they hooked her waistband and tugged. The material cleared her hips with a soft swish and pooled at her feet. She stepped out of her clothes, leaving them lying on the floor.

Goddess bless! His shaft rose like a phoenix, hardening instantly. Carrie turned to retrieve something in a nearby drawer.

Bacchus caught his first glimpse of her breasts. They were small, but firm. The pinks of her nipples flushed and puckered against her skin as if she sensed his eyes upon them. Her breathing deepened, and Carrie looked around before bringing her fingers to the pointed nubs and pinching the tips.

A low moan struggled out of her throat and her head dropped back as she played with her breasts. A flush started at her cheeks and spread over her body, giving her a rosy glow.

Bacchus knew she couldn't see him, but he held still all the same. His mind blanked as she teased her nipples. He wanted to rush across the room and push her hands out of the way so he could cover the ripe flesh with his mouth, feathering it with his forked tongue.

He followed the gentle swell of her breasts down her flat stomach and onto her mons. Light brown curls covered the delicate folds, hiding the feminine treasure from his gaze.

"You don't have time for this," she muttered.

Carrie released her breasts with a frustrated sigh, then went back to gathering the items she needed for her shower. Her gaze darted to the door time and again to ensure it remained secured.

He really couldn't blame her for being nervous. He didn't exactly come off as harmless. It pleased him that she was intelligent enough to lock the door for her own safety, even after she'd asked him to step outside. Bacchus noticed a cell phone amongst the items she'd gathered and grinned to himself.

Carrie stroked her arm.

Bacchus followed the movements, then flicked his tongue out to gather her scent. Now that he had it, he could find her anywhere in this city.

She walked the few steps into the bathroom and shut the door behind her. Bacchus told himself to leave, give her the privacy she sought. He'd already gone further than he'd intended. He wasn't the type of warrior to intrude on a female when he hadn't been invited.

Drawn by something primal, his feet traveled the short distance separating him from Carrie. Bacchus stood for several moments, staring at the closed door, listening to the steady ping of water. His body trembled and muscles ached as he fought to control his desire. It was a losing battle. He passed through the locked door. The second his eyes focused, his breath froze in his lungs.

Carrie stood inside a clear glass shower, her soapy hands gliding up and over her legs in luxurious strokes. She hummed as she reached for a sponge and brushed the soft material over her breasts. Her nipples stabbed skyward as if anticipating a warm lick.

So sensitive, he thought, enraptured by her body's response.

The spray covered her skin, leaving it glistening under the fake light. She rotated back to front, rinsing the suds from her body. She looked like a nymph under a waterfall, tempting, alluring. Bacchus curled his fingers into fists to keep from releasing his shaft.

His fangs unfurled and venom dripped along their length as he bit down, hard. Blood filled Bacchus' mouth, exploding his senses. He swallowed it and still he watched. He couldn't seem to tear his gaze away.

Carrie continued to bathe, moving onto her hair, which had turned light brown from the water. When she dropped the soap and bent to retrieve it, Bacchus knew he had to leave or risk pouncing on her. That would make him no better than the men who were threatening her.

He took one last look at her heart-shaped ass and caught a glimpse of her dewy quim. His shaft would feel at home there. He couldn't wait to sink into her flesh and fill her with his thick length. He'd pump her full of his crimson seed until she screamed in capitulation.

Bacchus closed his eyes, imagining the sound of her passionate cries. He had no doubt that the resonance would shatter his hearts. He departed quickly before he no longer had the will to do so. Bacchus dressed methodically, covering his flight suit with the clothes he'd purchased. His erection remained hard as Zaronian marble and would stay so until he sought his release inside this remarkable Earth woman.

By the time Carrie had dried and dressed in preparation for work, he'd regained a modicum of control.

"Ready?" She gave him a cheerful smile as she stepped outside onto the porch. She swept her purse up onto her shoulder and walked toward the garage door.

"More than you know," he muttered to himself, meeting her smile with a frown.

They drove in silence north on the 405 freeway to the 101, then made a left at the Topanga Canyon exit, heading into the hills. Bacchus watched as the houses thinned, leaving woods and hillsides behind. Several minutes later, they reached the kennel. Carrie pulled into the gravel lot and parked.

Dust swirled around them before clearing. Dogs barked in the background. Several other vehicles dotted the area. Part of Bacchus had hoped they'd be alone, but he knew that was a bad idea, since his control hung by a single strand of Zaronian thread.

He followed her along a dirt path leading to rows of buildings, which housed the kennels. The sound grew as they approached the pens. He saw people in a nearby field handling different breeds of dogs. The animals obeyed their hand-signaled orders…most of the time.

Bacchus smiled, enjoying the change of scenery and watching the light-hearted play between the animals. Leaves rustled in the trees surrounding the compound. Sun dappled the ground. The earth smelled richer, more pungent, fertile even. Or maybe it was his newly attuned mating senses kicking in. He turned to Carrie.

"Where are the dogs you handle?" he asked.

Carrie pulled up her schedule and cursed under her breath. "Today might not be the best day to hang out with me," she said.

"Why?" he asked in confusion.

"Um." Her face reddened. "Because with all the extra hours I've been putting in, I mixed up my schedule."

Bacchus' brow furrowed. "You aren't supposed to work today?"

"Um, no," Carrie said. "I am, but…"

He crossed his arms over his chest. "But what?"

"Obedience class isn't until tomorrow," she said.

"So what are you supposed to do today?" he asked.

"Breeding," she murmured and blushed again.

Bacchus schooled his expression so no emotion showed. Breeding dogs was part of her job description. She'd mentioned it earlier without any outward response, which meant her hesitation was due to his presence.

Interesting…

"Is there a problem?" he asked dispassionately.

Carrie swallowed hard. "No, I guess not."

"After you." Bacchus flipped his wrist, rotating his hand in a common Earth gesture.

Carrie stiffened, then started down the path in front of him.

Bacchus' gaze strayed repeatedly to her perfect bottom, which was cupped beautifully by a pair of denim jeans. He didn't know how long he'd be able to hold off touching her. Bacchus wanted Carrie to come to him or at least welcome him into her bed.

How did one get a human to do that?

So used to seizing what he wanted or paying for it, Bacchus didn't know. Perhaps once he dispatched her enemies, she'd feel grateful. Grateful enough to offer her blood. As plans went, it wasn't great, but Bacchus was desperate.

They reached the shed that housed a smaller chain-link kennel. The scent of feminine heat struck the second she threw open the door, overwhelming his senses. Several dogs paced within their individual pens, each releasing powerful pheromones. They may be a different species, but their need permeated the air, burning his nostrils, while stroking his inner beast.

His gaze darted from dog to dog, their whimpering sounds tore at his control. His skin began to itch as the urge to mate with Carrie stretched his muscles taut.

Carrie walked over to one of the pens and hooked a leash on a large tan female. She led the dog to a nearby pen located away from the prying eyes of the other animals in the room. She allowed the dog to slip into the small twelve by twelve wooden-fenced area, and then turned to Bacchus.

"I'll be right back. I have to go get the stud." She left before he could respond.

Bacchus stared at the bitch, her need rolling off her in waves. "I feel your pain," he whispered low and soothing to the dog. "At least your discomfort is about to ease, while mine continues to grow."

A deep bark sounded behind him, Bacchus turned as Carrie walked back into the building leading the largest dog he'd ever seen. He searched Ryan's memories for dog breeds, but found no point of reference. The male struggled as he passed each pen, trying to get at the females.

"Heel," Carrie said firmly and pulled him to her.

"Don't you think he's a little large for her?" Bacchus pointed to the much smaller female, who now whimpered at the change in the air. The other females followed suit. The male on the leash pulled harder and began to drool. If he had his way, he'd mount them all.

"They'll fit together just fine," Carrie said, focusing on her job.

"He's enormous. What kind of dog is that?" Bacchus watched the play of small muscles beneath her shirt as she tried to hold the animal steady.

"It's an Anatolian Shepherd."

"'Tis more like a horse," he balked. "The beast is mammoth."

Carrie laughed. "Yes, he is, and quite determined at the moment." She jerked him away from the other females, pointing him toward the pen where the bitch now danced anxiously.

The male finally caught the right female's scent and strained to break free, nearly dragging Carrie to the gated pen. The second she opened the gate and slipped the leash from his collar, the male bolted toward the female. Carrie barely had time too step out of the pen.

"He's anxious," she tittered, nervously running her hands along her pants.

Bacchus kept his gaze locked on the pen. "Can you blame him, when her heat calls to him?" He inhaled deeply and let his warm breath blow across her neck.

Carrie quivered, but didn't look at him. "I suppose not."

"Do we leave them now?" Bacchus asked his voice growing husky. He prayed she said yes.

"We can't," she said. "I have to make sure they breed. And help them if they have trouble."

"Why on earth would they need your help? Creatures have been mating for centuries," he said, trying to ignore his straining erection.

* * * * *

"Sometimes the females don't want to mate. They try to fight the males. When that happens, I have to step in and help hold her, so the male can do his business."

"Doesn't she understand that it's foolish to resist his dominance?" Bacchus asked. "A determined male is a formidable foe."

Carrie was afraid to respond as she stood against the chest-high wall and peered over the top. She watched the drooling male stick his nose in the female's sex and lick furiously.

Maybe it was her long dry spell or the present company, but Carrie seemed to feel every strong lap of the dog's long tongue as he moved, trying to position himself to mount her.

The bitch growled and whipped around. She snapped at him, but he remained undeterred. His tongue's strokes took on new urgency. The female snarled again, but turned her tail to the side to indicate her openness to breed. The male danced around to get into place, but she moved when he tried to mount her. Like any female worth her salt, she didn't want to make it too easy on him.

Carrie didn't hear or see Bacchus move, but she felt the heat roll off his body, when he stood behind her. His delicious scent seemed to grow stronger. She kept her gaze locked on the stud, afraid of what she'd see if she turned around.

The male became more and more aggressive, cornering

the female, so he could continue to consume her. Drool and her essence covered his muzzle until he looked like he was foaming at the mouth.

Embarrassment flooded her, when Carrie realized that watching the animals do their mating dance with Bacchus here actually turned her on. There was something about an aggressive male dominating a female that made Carrie's insides melt. He didn't ask permission once the offer was made, he simply took what was in front of him. She knew that kind of thinking belonged in the Dark Ages, but she couldn't help how she felt.

What are you doing? she asked herself.

The question was forgotten when Bacchus slid his hand along her arm, leaving gooseflesh in his wake. The stud took that moment to clamp down on the bitch's neck to hold her as he moved into place.

His enormous blood-red phallus rivaled that of some men Carrie knew. Totally unsheathed, its size was imposing. Carrie took a step back and encountered something far bigger. Bacchus groaned upon contact and his hand shot out to grab her before she could move away.

The dog's hips rocked, seeking the female's sopping entrance. Carrie's breathing deepened and her panties drenched as she watched, but it wasn't the dog that was turning her on, it was the man behind her.

He's here to protect you, not seduce you. Yet that was exactly what he was doing.

Her mind screamed at her to put a stop to it, but it had been so long since anyone had touched her with tenderness. Carrie's body was starved for human contact. Craved it to the point of desperation.

Ryan had stopped making love to her months before their breakup. Carrie had known something was wrong, but she'd still been blindsided when she'd found out that he'd cheated on her.

She'd been so stupid, so naïve, but she couldn't change

the past.

The stud's shaft missed the first couple of times, then finally slide home. The bitch whimpered and tried to pull away. The male growled and held her in place as his shaft stretched and filled her.

Carrie barely noticed Bacchus' lips graze her throat as the stud's hips began to piston with blurring speed. The female yelped, scrambling to escape, but it was too late. He'd already began to swell and knot, ensuring that they'd stay locked together until he'd pumped her full of his seed.

"Why are you doing this?" she whispered.

"Because I want to," he murmured.

Bacchus' free hand stroked down Carrie's side before finding the front of her jeans. His finger pressed in unerringly on her hidden bundle of nerves. She gasped as fire shot through her body.

"Do you like watching them?" He nibbled on her ear, his forked tongue teasing her lobe.

"I-I…it's my job," she practically moaned the words.

Carrie didn't see Bacchus smile, but she felt it as he licked along the column of her throat to her nape. When he reached the sensitive spot at the base of her neck, he nipped her. It wasn't a gentle rasp. The spot stung. The bite told her that this particular male was just as dominating as the one in the pen.

"You taste good," he purred.

Carrie's knees nearly buckled, when Bacchus opened his mouth and locked onto her neck. He held her in place with his unusually sharp teeth just like the male had done moments ago. He exhaled, then his forked tongue swirled over her skin. Carrie's body swelled and the ache between her thighs became relentless.

For a second, she thought she'd come on the spot.

Bacchus released her nape and kissed the spot he'd bitten, then continued to stroke her with his hand. "I think it's more than a job to you today," he murmured, increasing the pressure on the front of her jeans.

Carrie's eyes rolled back in her head.

"Getting turned on by watching creatures mate, is nothing to be ashamed of," he said.

"I'm not ashamed," she gasped. "I know the difference between fantasy and reality." He was the one blurring the lines.

"Tell me, what is your darkest fantasy? Do you burn for the forbidden like I do?" He kissed her throat, his lips lingering over her pounding pulse.

If he kept at this seduction, Carrie would go up in flames. "This is crazy," she murmured. "My brother hired you to help me. I doubt Brady had this in mind. We don't even know each other."

"Don't we?" Bacchus' voice was pure seduction. "I feel as if I've known you for a lifetime."

Carrie swallowed the pleas that hovered on her lips. She wasn't about to beg this man to take her. He was a stranger. A multitude of reasons to reject his advances floated through her lust-filled mind, yet none stayed long enough to break the spell.

She wanted Bacchus, even though logic told her it was wrong. Carrie ached for the pulsing shaft cradling her bottom. She wanted to feel him in her, on her—possessing her, if only for one torrid night.

"If you don't want this—don't want me—now is the time to say so," he growled. "I will still protect you with my life."

Carrie glanced over her shoulder in time to see Bacchus' stunned expression. Had he not meant to say that aloud? Or was he surprised that he had made the offer at all? Either way, it didn't matter. Carrie couldn't let him go. Not yet.

"Good," he snarled, taking her silence for the acceptance it was. Bacchus added another finger to the front of her jeans and pressed down.

Tremors shook Carrie as her orgasm slammed into her. She whimpered much like the bitch in the pen and bit her lip to keep from crying out.

It took several minutes for her to recover, but eventually the growling and whining coming from the pen brought her back to reality. The dogs were still locked together, their long pink tongues lolling out of their mouths as they panted for air.

It wasn't hard for Carrie to imagine Bacchus kneeling behind her, spearing her deep. He wouldn't be locked inside her like the stud, but Carrie knew there'd still be no escape.

* * * * *

CHAPTER SIX

Bacchus didn't want to drive all the way back to Carrie's home. He was worried that she'd change her mind before they arrived, but he had no choice. Too much was riding on their first joining.

Carrie quickly kenneled the dogs and phoned the owners to let them know they could pick up their prized pets in a few days. Her face remained flushed and her fingers trembled as she locked the gates and made notes on nearby paperwork.

Bacchus waited for her to finish. She dropped the pen into the holder and turned to him. He said nothing as he reached for her hand and led her toward the car.

Her dreamy expression was due in part to the orgasm, but also because of the intoxicating properties in his saliva and his pheromones. The biological properties couldn't force a woman to join. Nothing he'd done could. He'd only enhanced the pleasure she felt, which in turn made her more pliant. In the end, the choice was hers whether to act upon the sensations.

"Are you happy here in this place?" Bacchus asked.

Carrie blinked in surprise. "You mean Los Angeles?"

He nodded. "Yes."

"It holds a lot of memories for me—not all good," she said.

Bacchus tilted his head. "If you had a chance to leave, would you?"

"Funny you should ask. Lately, I've been giving that question a lot of thought." Her face scrunched. "I suppose it would depend on where I was going and who I was going with," she said, adding a small smile.

They drove to her home in silence. Each lost in their own thoughts. The sun was sinking fast as they pulled into her garage and climbed out of the car. Carrie plucked her keys out of her purse to open the front door, but stopped short of doing so. Instead, she placed her hand upon his chest, her fingers rubbing carelessly over the loose button on his green shirt.

"I'm not sure we should do this," she said. "You know the kind of trouble I'm in." Her blue eyes widened and her gaze darted around the yard. "I wouldn't want anything to happen to you. I couldn't handle anyone else getting hurt because of me."

Bacchus lifted her hand to his lips and kissed her knuckles one by one. "We will not do anything you do not wish to do." It was the truth and a lie. Bacchus knew he could make her *want* so badly that she'd beg him to take her, but that's not how he wanted their first time together to be. "You do not need to protect me. I'm here to protect you."

Carrie's lips parted as he continued to kiss her fingertips. "It's been a long time," she said, her voice breathless.

"We can take things as slow as you like," he said, praying to the Goddess for strength to follow through with his promise.

Carrie unlocked the door and stepped aside for him to enter. As soon as he did, she locked the door behind them and looked at him. "I want to see your eyes." She reached up tentatively and removed his sunglasses.

Bacchus stiffened. He wasn't sure how Carrie would react once she saw his eyes.

Carrie blinked in surprise. "Your irises are red," she said. "Really red. They're almost glowing. Are you having an allergic reaction of some kind? Was it the dogs?"

"No," he said, afraid to move. It wasn't the dogs causing the sudden change. The mating frenzy was upon him. Bacchus' jaw clenched as he battled for control over his thirst for blood. He searched Buzz's memories for a plausible explanation. "Contact lenses," he grunted.

"Red's an unusual choice." She stared in wonder, not fear. "The fit is so good that I can't even see the lenses. I couldn't pull off that color, but it looks good on you. Almost natural."

Bacchus released the breath he'd been holding. "I'm glad you like them. I like your eyes, too."

She smiled, her blue eyes crinkling at the corners. "Hungry?"

"Yes," he hissed. "But not for something to eat."

* * * * *

Carrie slid her hand down his chest until her fingers curled into the waistband of his pants and then tugged him down the hall to her bedroom. She still couldn't believe she was going to do this. Maybe Brady moving on without her was the push she needed to do the same.

Bacchus intrigued her more than anyone she'd met. It wasn't just his snake-like qualities, even though they appealed to the herpetologist in her. It was something more, something deeper that burned in his red eyes.

He looked at her as if she were truly precious to him, not just a warm, willing body that he could fuck and forget. That look and the emotions driving it was what propelled her to give in.

The scent emanating from his skin filled her small

bedroom. She couldn't take a breath without it expanding her lungs. Her body seemed to swell and moisten the longer she inhaled the aroma. Or maybe it was just being so close to Bacchus that was doing it.

Carrie released his waistband and grasped his belt. She worked the leather through the buckle, ignoring the trembling of her hands.

Bacchus eased her grip, then pulled her into his arms. His lips descended unerringly onto her mouth. Her heart stuttered on contact, then began to pound as he deepened the embrace. He curled his fingers into her shirt until he fisted the material.

Carrie heard a rip, but ignored it as her tongue reached out tentatively to caress the forked muscle in his mouth. She retreated away from the alien tickle. It was strange, but oddly pleasant.

It had been a long time, but Carrie had never forgotten the basic flavor of a man. Bacchus tasted different than anyone she'd ever kissed. His saliva seemed *flavored* like some kind of exotic Asian dish. Their tongues dipped and twisted, feeding their mutual need. He devoured her like a man who'd been starved, until her thoughts scattered.

Carrie pulled back and saw Bacchus' red eyes flash. His breathing was labored, much like her own. Her ripped shirt dangled precariously on her shoulders. She shrugged and the material fell to the ground. Her small breasts were still safely tucked inside the lace cups of her bra. His gaze drank her in.

"Remove it," he ordered impatiently. "I want to see all of you."

The command went from Carrie's ears straight to her sex. She pictured how the stud had stalked the bitch earlier. Now she knew what that dog felt like. The urge to flee was strong in her mind, but her feet refused to move.

His gaze swept her from head to toe. Carrie's nipples beaded and her womb clenched. She wanted the fantasy, not just a few seconds of domination, but would Bacchus play along?

"No," she said, her voice barely above a whisper.

Bacchus' burning gaze narrowed and he flicked the air with his tongue.

So serpent like, she thought, and moistened even more.

Bacchus closed his eyes and grinned. "If you want me to force you, that can be arranged. It's in my nature to take, to claim—to dominate." His face flushed as he took a step closer.

Carrie took a step back.

"You liked the way the Shepherd pursued the bitch, taking what she so readily offered," her purred and took another step forward. "That beast is nothing compared to the one lurking inside of me."

Carrie trembled, but not from fear. She'd never been so turned on her life.

Bacchus' feral grin widened. "I would like nothing more than to lap the juices pooling between your thighs, before I devour your essence. Though I must warn you that my shaft is much larger than the dog's puny appendage. I will fill you like no other. When I'm finished, you'll have no doubt who possesses you."

"Is that a warning?" her voice cracked.

"No, *eshe*, that's a promise," he murmured.

His words enflamed her. Carrie bit her lip to keep from moaning aloud, even as she backed away. Her legs hit the side of the bed, effectively trapping her unless she climbed over. Bacchus lunged before she got a knee on the bed and pinned her face down onto the mattress.

Carrie kicked out instinctively, though she didn't know why. Some dark fantasy hiding within her demanded that he force her compliance. If she weren't certain that she was safe in his arms, Carrie would've called a halt to the whole thing.

Bacchus' teeth clamped onto the back of her neck and a growl rumbled from deep within his chest.

She didn't remember his incisors being quite so sharp a

minute ago, when he'd nibbled on her lip, but Carrie wasn't about to complain. He bit down and her sex gushed, readying her for what would come next.

Bacchus released her throat, but kept her hands pinned above her head as he stripped away the rest of her clothes. Carrie wiggled to dislodge him, but the action only seemed to entice him further.

She turned her head to the side so she could see what he was doing. The black pupils in Bacchus' red eyes had narrowed until they were mere slits. He looked wild with passion, nearly insane with need. Carrie was too far gone to make sense of the changes she was witnessing.

"Do not move," Bacchus barked the command, before slowly releasing her.

Carrie wasn't about to go anywhere.

Within a minute, he'd managed to strip down to a thin bodysuit that covered his entire length.

Was he wearing long underwear? Carrie was about to ask, but then he parted the material and her mind ceased to function.

When Bacchus had said he was large, Carrie had assumed he was exaggerating. She was *wrong*. The man could give Priapus a complex.

Her eyes rounded as she drank in the sheer beauty of Bacchus' body. Along with the strange suit, he'd removed the queue holding his hair. The black tresses fell over his broad shoulders and down his back. The strands looked so soft that Carrie wanted to run her fingers through them. His muscles rippled, drawing her attention away. The snake tattoo she thought started and ended at his neck actually slithered down the right side of his body, encasing his chest and arms.

She wet her suddenly dry mouth. "You're magnificent, but…"

He gave her a pleased grin. "But what?"

Carrie nodded to the behemoth rising between his legs. "I

am not sure I can handle you."

Bacchus' lips quirked. "You will by the time I've finished preparing you."

He stepped forward, looking like something carved from marble. Carrie remained on her stomach, while her eyes drank in every inch of perfection. "What are you going to do first?"

His gaze heated. "Fulfill your every fantasy. When I'm done, maybe you can fulfill mine."

* * * * *

Embarrassed and more than a little intimidated that he could read her so well, Carrie sat up. "That's okay."

"I told you not to move! Now you'll need to be punished." He dropped to his knees behind her until his face was level with her ass. He smiled, his eyes smoldering with intent.

This time Carrie thought she caught a glimpse of some major canines in his mouth. She blinked and looked again, but they were gone.

Bacchus grabbed her legs and spread them, then leaned forward and took a long swipe with his forked tongue over the globes of her bottom.

Carrie's heart jumped and she craned her neck to watch. The move made it look like she was trying to get away.

Bacchus growled and clamped his hands down on her hips to hold her in place, then he pressed his nose into her cleft and inhaled.

Carrie mewed. "What are you doing?"

"Possessing you." He spread her nether lips with his thumbs and stuck his forked tongue into her wetness.

Carrie groaned and gripped the sheets to keep from pushing back.

"You taste like Zaronian moon cakes," he said, his lids lowering over his demonic eyes. He wedged his shoulders between her thighs, forcing her to open wider.

She had never felt this exposed.

Without warning, Bacchus speared her with his forked tongue and began to devour her in earnest. Carrie's hips moved of their own volition. She couldn't have sat still if she wanted to. His sharp teeth found her hidden pearl and worried it into a hard kernel. Carrie's body writhed in ecstasy. If he kept this up much longer, she was convinced she'd lose her mind. He ignored her pleas and continued to feast.

"Please." She rocked back, trying to get closer, reaching for that elusive peak that Bacchus refused to help her reach.

He released her and went back to thrusting his tongue inside of her. The forked end curled into her G-spot with unerring precision. Carrie cried out and clawed at the sheets.

Bacchus laughed. The tremors tortured her flesh as effectively as a flogging. He rose, settling his big body between her spread thighs. Carrie didn't care what he planned to do, as long as it brought her release. She felt his warm lips graze her nape and she whimpered as fantasy blended with reality. A second later, Bacchus sank his teeth into her flesh and thrust inside her.

Carrie opened her mouth to scream, but nothing came out. His lips drew on her skin, sucking hard. The dual invasion tumbled her over the edge. She shattered her like a clay pigeon hit by an Uzi. Her world tipped, then spun off its axis.

Bacchus rolled his hips, driving even deeper. Carrie whimpered beneath him, senses exploding, her attention narrowing to the spot between her legs where he filled her like no other. He released her neck and licked the spot.

Moisture, she assumed was sweat, trickled down the side of her throat, but she was too senseless to care. Bacchus chased the droplets with his forked tongue, catching them before they hit the sheets.

"I knew it," he murmured in her ear as he thrust inside

her. "I knew you were the one who could save me."

Carrie had no idea what Bacchus was talking about and couldn't focus with him moving inside of her. She'd never known sex could be like this. She was pretty sure he'd just ruined her for other men.

Her head swam as he licked her neck again. "I claim you, Carrie Rittner as my mate. From this day forth, you are mine."

* * * * *

CHAPTER SEVEN

The taste of Carrie's blood in his mouth, nearly sent Bacchus' body into spasms. She *was* the one. After all these years of searching, he'd finally found his mate. Carrie was the first to be claimed by a Phantom Warrior, but she would not be the last. As soon as word spread, they would come.

Bacchus' skin prickled as his built in genetic defense system alerted him that a ship was hovering nearby. He expanded his senses expecting to encounter Atlantean technology. Instead, a primitive force met him.

Phantoms…

His people had lost patience and sent a crew to check on his progress. Bacchus frowned. They would've had to leave within two days after he stowed away. They hadn't given him nearly enough time to accomplish his goal.

His gaze strayed to Carrie. Or perhaps they had…

He rolled his hips, feeling the tight squeeze of her channel. His body ached for release, but Bacchus couldn't allow it until he'd performed one final test. He nuzzled her neck tenderly and sank his fingers into her hips. "Are you still with me, my *eshe*?" *My life.*

"Yes," she croaked and closed her eyes as he plunged

into her, moving steadily. He loved the feel of her body clasping his shaft. Her channel may not be ribbed like Claw Clan members, but it was soft, moist, and pliant. Best of all, she'd come willingly to his bed without demanding an exchange of credits. Bacchus had no idea that joining could feel like this. The sheer beauty of it caused unexpected emotion to clog his throat.

He kissed Carrie again, then willed his form to shimmer and fade. Once he passed through her body, there'd be no turning back. If Carrie was his match like he suspected, she'd start to take on the characteristics of the Blood Clan people.

Bacchus sent up a single prayer to the Goddess, though in his hearts he knew he wouldn't let Carrie go, even if she didn't pass the final hurdle. He took a deep breath, then flowed through her body.

Carrie gasped and opened her eyes in surprise. "How did you do that? I didn't even feel you roll me over."

"It is a gift." Bacchus smiled, then inhaled deeply. Happiness radiated within his hearts when he detected his scent within her. She was his. Earth would be the Phantom people's salvation. He eased out of her, then slid home again. She panted as she sat up to straddle his thighs. Her small breasts bounced each time he thrust.

"This is more like it." Carrie rose onto her knees and took control of the rhythm.

Bacchus leaned forward until his mouth made contact with her rose-colored nipple. It pebbled against his tongue, stabbing the roof of his mouth as he began to suckle. Carrie's soft moans grew in volume and sweat coated her skin, leaving a salty residue behind.

Her movements became faster and more erratic, as she rode him into oblivion. Bacchus clenched his jaw and reached between her legs. One flick of his thumb nail sent her into orbit.

Carrie screamed and her body bowed above him.

Bacchus grasped her hips and thrust, once, twice, three times, then his seed burst forth like a shattered dam, showering her womb with life. The bellow that followed was a mixture of relief and triumph.

They lay entangled, chests heaving as they tried to catch their breath. Carrie draped his body in feminine warmth, as he stroked the length of her back, relishing the gift of their newfound connection.

When Bacchus could finally focus, his eyes met a matching pair of red orbs. His breath caught as joy and a far deeper emotion embraced his two hearts. She was the most beautiful Earthling he'd ever seen. Bacchus corrected himself. Carrie was the most beautiful Phantom woman he'd ever gazed upon.

He rolled her beneath him and slowly rocked his hips until his shaft hardened inside of her. Bacchus glided gently, while feathering Carrie's face with kisses. "You have made me so incredibly happy. I never dared dream the Goddess would bless me with one such as you," he said.

Carrie blushed, then reached for his head so that she could guide his lips to hers. The clinch was long and drugging as they savored each other's unique flavor. "Thank you for bringing me back to the land of the living."

"I intend to keep you here…if you'll have me." Insecurity suddenly filtered through his voice. Would she turn him down after all that they'd experienced together?

Carrie smiled and kissed him again. "How can I say no to a guy with a forked tongue?"

Pounding on the front door shattered the tender moment. Carrie scrambled off him and slipped her robe on. "Stay here. I'll be right back." Lights came on in her wake.

Bacchus' tongue slithered out of his mouth, scenting the air. Males! More than one. And his mate was heading right for them. He jumped out of bed and pulled his flight suit on. Bacchus had just sealed the material, when Carrie came running back into the room. Her pale and trembling body told him all he needed to know.

The pounding came again. This time louder.

"You have to get out of here," she said. "If they see you, they'll kill you."

Did she really think he'd leave her after what they'd just shared?

One look at her determined expression said she did.

Bacchus had so much to explain to her and so little time to do so. The men would come through the door any second now. He took her hands in his. "Listen, my *eshe*, remember how I told you that Buzz sent me here to protect you?"

She nodded slowly, her expression beginning to grow wary.

"It wasn't exactly the truth," he said. "I learned about you through Buzz, but it was my idea to come."

"You aren't a bodyguard, are you?" she asked softly.

He slowly shook his head. "No."

Carrie sighed. "Then you really need to go while you still can."

Bacchus straightened to his full height. "I am something far more formidable."

"Right." Carrie ran a quivering hand through her hair and glanced up at him with sad eyes.

Bacchus' hearts clenched over what he was about to do, but he had no choice. It was time for the truth. He smiled, exposing his fangs.

Her eyes locked onto his mouth. "Are those fangs?"

"Yes." He opened his mouth, allowing them to unfurl completely.

She frowned. "Are they real?"

"Yes."

"I can't believe a dentist would do that to you," she said, refusing to face what was right in front of her.

It was time to show his precious mate just *what* she'd slept with.

* * * * *

There was a loud crash in the other room as her front door crumbled under the assault.

Carrie didn't have time to think about what Bacchus had shown her. She'd make sense of it all later…if she survived.

"Run!" she shouted and headed for her bedroom door. She didn't get far before strong hands grabbed her and picked her up, then tossed her onto the bed. Carrie bounced and nearly fell off the other side.

"Stay here," Bacchus snarled. His eyes glowed red like they were lit from within as he rushed out the door.

Grunts and terrified screams followed.

Carrie leapt off the bed and scrambled after him. One second Bacchus stood in front of Bing's men, the next he was behind them, holding them by their necks. She hadn't seen him move. And from the men's startled expressions, they hadn't either.

Bacchus struck with blinding speed, sinking his fake fangs into the man who'd reached for a gun. Blood ran down the man's neck and onto his shirt, before soaking into his expensive suit.

His friend pounded on Bacchus' closed fist, trying to break his grip, but there was no getting away.

Bacchus swallowed a mouthful of blood, then released the man he'd been drinking from. The man landed on the hardwood floor with a loud thud.

Vampires aren't real, Carrie told herself, even as she watched Bacchus pull the man's accomplice close and sink his fangs into him.

This time he didn't appear to drink, but the man stiffened in his harms and fell all the same. Bacchus looked at them both dispassionately, then his gaze rose to find her.

Carrie trembled and took a step back. "You're not human," she said.

Pain swept over his handsome, bloodstained face. "I am

the same being who held you in his arms after we made love."

Tears welled in her eyes. "What are you?"

"We are the same you and I." He took a step forward.

Carrie flinched and he stopped. "I am nothing like you."

His beautiful lips thinned. "Correction," he said. "You *were* nothing like me."

"What does that mean?" she asked. "What are you saying?"

Bacchus sighed. "I'm saying that sleeping with me has changed you."

Her eyes widened in horror and Carrie felt the blood drain from her face. "Oh my god! We didn't use a condom. Did you somehow make me sick?"

Bacchus blanched. "I would never do anything to harm you." He sounded affronted that she'd even suggested such a thing.

"What…are…you?" If he said that he was a vampire, Carrie was going to lose it.

"On this undeveloped planet, I'd be considered an alien," he said.

Carrie's head swam and she grabbed the door to keep from collapsing. "Did you say alien?" she asked. "I don't suppose you mean the illegal kind?"

Hysterical laughter threatened to bubble up inside her. She tamped it down. Carrie had to keep it together for just a little while longer, then she'd allow herself to fall apart.

"You know I don't," he said.

Blood roared in her ears. Carrie clutched her head. This wasn't possible. Couldn't be real. Aliens didn't exist. Did they? She jerked her chin up. "Where's my brother?" Carrie glanced at the men at his feet. "Is he really alive?" Her voice cracked with emotion.

Sadness etched his features. "I never lied about your brother," he said softly. "He really has met someone. She just happens to not be from around here."

"Oh terrific! So she's an alien, too?" She threw her arms up. "This just keeps getting better and better."

"I know this is a lot to take in. I'd planned to break the news to you gently," he said.

"You've been lying to me from the start," she snapped, but a sob took some of the heat away. "Why am I always drawn to liars? First Ryan, now you."

Bacchus' expression hardened. "Do not compare me to him. We are nothing alike. What I did, I did for my people's survival."

"So lying and sleeping with me was some kind of sacrifice you made?" Anger quickly replaced her fear. Carrie stomped over to where he stood and poked him in the chest. "I'm no charity case. I don't need your pity."

"Careful, your eyes are beginning to glow." He grinned, but the warmth never reached his gaze.

"Yeah, right." Carrie headed back down the hall.

"Don't believe me?" Bacchus called out after her. "Look in the mirror and see for yourself."

He was lying. He had to be. He'd lied about everything else. Why not this? Carrie marched into her bathroom determined to prove him wrong. She turned the light on and gasped, when she caught sight of her reflection.

"What happened to my eyes-ss?" she lisped. Gone was the familiar blue that she'd had all her life. It had been replaced with a startling ruby shade. "What's-ss happening? Why do I have a lisssp?" Carrie felt like she had a mouthful of marbles.

She opened wide to see what was causing it and fangs unfurled before her eyes. Carrie screamed and took a step back. They couldn't be real. It wasn't possible. She touched one with the tip of her tongue and winced as blood welled. Panic took hold. She turned to run, but Bacchus stood in the doorway, blocking her escape.

"What did you do to me?" she shouted.

There was a mixture of love and pain, shining in his red

eyes. "All your life, you've wanted a man to dominate and claim you. I fulfilled your fantasy, even the one you were afraid to say aloud." His gaze held hers, refusing to release her until she faced the truth.

Carrie opened her mouth and closed it several times before speaking. "I admit I fantasized about someone like you, but not this-ss…I don't know what to think of this-ss."

"This." He turned her to face the mirror once more. "Is my fantasy. *You* are my fantasy." Bacchus brushed her hair away from her face. "When I passed through you, I absorbed your hopes, dreams, and emotions. I know what lies in your heart, Carrie. And now, thanks to that exchange, you know what lies in mine. Look deep and you'll find my love," he said, daring her to try.

Carrie was afraid to at first, but she'd never been a coward. She closed her eyes and let her mind explore her thoughts. It didn't take long before she encountered Bacchus' presence. It was followed by such a strong wave of love that it brought tears to her eyes.

She pushed through the onslaught until she sensed his emotions and witnessed the life he'd lived before they'd met. Carrie had felt his bone-deep loneliness and his pain, along with the joy of discovery that came the moment he'd laid eyes on her.

It would take a while to get over his deception, but could she really turn her back on a man who'd lived with a level of honor that rivaled that of medieval knights?

No.

Carrie opened her eyes and looked at him. Wasn't she the one who'd said it was time to start living again? Hadn't she thought a change might do her good? She chuckled to herself to stop the rising panic. Traveling to another planet was about as far of a move as she could envision.

She couldn't believe she was about to ask this question, but couldn't seem to stop herself. "If I go with you, what will I do on your planet?"

Bacchus' eyes lit with hope and her heart clenched. "The Blood Clan, our clan, is reptilian in nature. You'd fit right in with our healers."

"What about—us-s-s?" she asked, not sure what answer she was hoping for.

"If you'll have me, I will spend my lifetime attempting to make this moment up to you. It is not in my nature to deceive, but I knew you wouldn't accept the truth. Not without proof anyway."

"I'm scared," Carrie said honestly.

"I know." He clasped her face and pressed his lips to hers. "As your mate, I can sense your fear and it pains me greatly. I would give anything to take it away and have you look upon me like you did a few hours ago."

In her heart, Carrie knew he was telling the truth. "What happens now?" she asked, strangely exhilarated at the prospect of starting a new life. This would probably all turn out to be a fantasy. She was probably lying in a hospital bed, suffering from a severe head injury. But what if?

Bacchus glanced at the ceiling. "A ship is near. It will come and pick us up after it drops off its cargo, then we'll return to Zaron."

"Cargo?" she asked.

He gave her a child-like grin. "More warriors have come. They wish to find what I've found in you."

"This is so much to take in," she whispered.

Bacchus touched her chin, tilting it until their gazes met. "Our joining would not have worked, if your heart had not chosen me first."

Carrie turned back to the mirror, tears floating in her red eyes. "My appearance is going to take some getting used to." She sniffled. Not that she was a big mirror queen to begin with, but a girl didn't walk around everyday with three-inch fangs sticking out of her mouth. She'd scare the hell out of Brady the next time he saw her. Would she ever see her brother again?

"You will see him," Bacchus said.

"How did you?" she asked.

"We have all the time in the galaxies to explore each others thoughts," Bacchus said, nuzzling her neck.

Carrie knew that she needed to move on with her life. Ryan would've wanted that for her. "Can I visit Ryan's grave before we leave?" she asked, her lip trembling.

"Anytime you wish, *eshe*. We can return to Earth for regular visits. You can even keep your house, if that is your wish."

She snuffled again. "Sss-wear?"

Bacchus smiled and crossed his heart. "I swear."

Carrie frowned at her rumpled reflection. She looked so different with red eyes and fangs. Yet inside, she still felt the same. She held the same thoughts she had before the—what had Bacchus called it? Transfer?

Thanks to the exchange, which was slowly sinking in, Carrie knew he was telling the truth about Brady. She'd seen her brother's new girlfriend in Bacchus' memories as clearly as if she'd been watching a movie. Tears filled her eyes as she realized Brady had finally found the happiness he'd been searching for after Ryan's death. Perhaps, it was time for her to do the same.

She looked into her bedroom. She didn't need this place anymore. It was part of her past and had no room in her future. Carrie turned the faucet on and splashed her face with cool water, then met Bacchus' gaze in the mirror. "Are you a reptile or a vampire?"

"Some would say both, but I would say neither." He grinned.

"Will my fangs-ss go down?" She glowered at her reflection. "Or do I have to live the rest of my life like this?"

He reached out hesitantly. "I will teach you how to control them and many, many more things as your powers grow."

"Powers-ss? As in plural?" Carrie's eyes widened as she

tapped on her new teeth with the tip of her nail. "This isn't the end?"

Bacchus smiled. "For us, *eshe*, this is only the beginning."

* * * * *

EPILOGUE

Bacchus awoke slowly as skin caressed his chest. The dream of having a woman of his own was so vivid that he almost believed he could smell her feminine musk. Hair tickled his nose and he brushed it aside. The feel of it brought him instantly awake. He opened his eyes.

Carrie lay next to his body, her soft length curled against his chest, seeking warmth. He grinned and pulled her close, tucking her under his shoulder.

How many years had he dreamed of waking with a woman by his side? One hundred? Two? Bacchus couldn't remember. All he knew for certain was that the happiness he felt was not an illusion born out of loneliness. Carrie was here and had been by his side for several months now.

She'd settled into work quickly and had fast become one of their best healers—a feat that did not surprise him given her passion for the subject matter. Bacchus kissed the side of her head.

She snuffled, then muttered, "Is it time to get up already? I don't smell any coffee."

Bacchus laughed, hugging her close. He hadn't been able to convince her to leave Earth without the ground beans she craved so dearly. He'd even had to bring her coffeemaker along, though he had warned her that it wouldn't work on Zaron. It had taken him a while to create a machine that would replicate the bitter brew, but now that he had, she expected him to make it for her every morning.

His lips brushed her forehead. 'Twas a small price to pay for the joy that she brought to his two hearts.

#

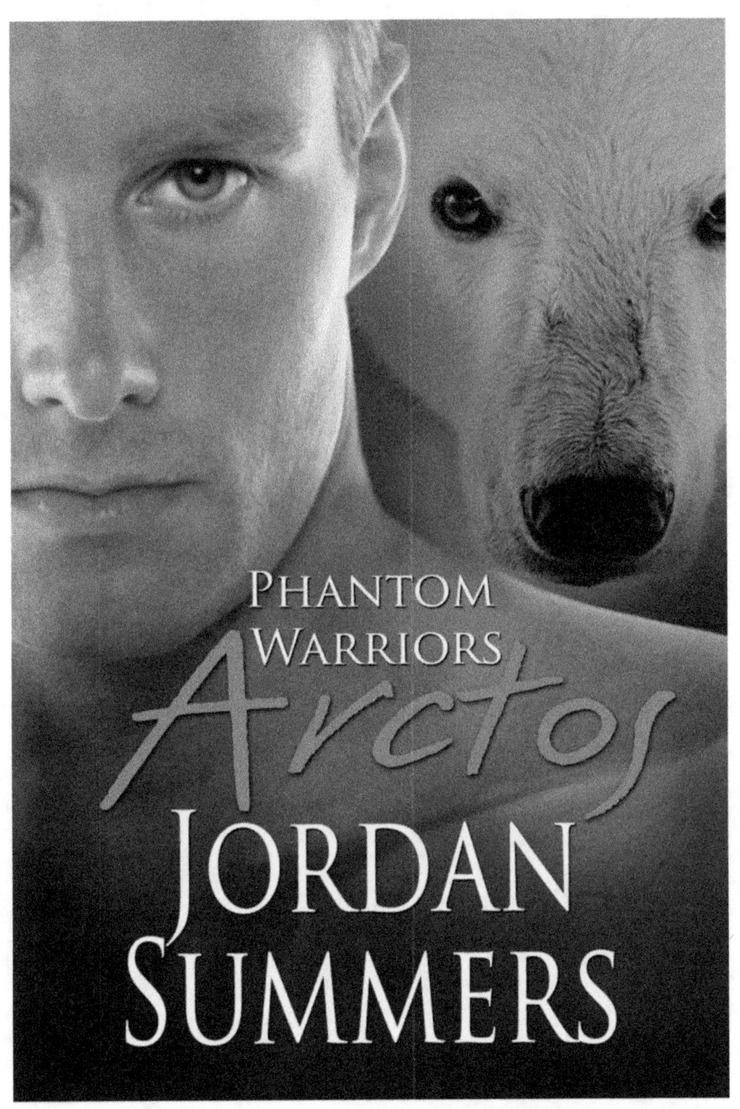

PHANTOM
WARRIORS
Arctos
JORDAN
SUMMERS

CHAPTER ONE

Arctos smelled her before he saw her. He'd been watching the polar bears play when the soft flowery, feminine scent reached his sensitive nose. The aroma had been so fleeting that he'd almost ignored it like the bears had, but something inside him had urged him to investigate.

He found the girl hiding in the snow a quarter mile away. She had small hands and equally small feet. Standing, she'd barely reach his chest. She was a tiny speck of a thing barely noticeable against the sea of white. He glanced at the bears in the distance.

What was a *child* doing so far from the nearest town and so close to danger?

Protective instincts spurred by bone-deep honor prompted him to act. Arctos took a step in her direction to find out, when the child shifted to the side. The small, seemingly insignificant movement revealed lush round curves. The kind of curves that could only be found on a woman in her prime. He stumbled in surprise. Her scent came again, this time stronger. The delicious aroma filled his lungs, leaving Arctos breathless and achingly hard. How could he have made such a mistake?

Arctos watched as the woman wiggled her butt and burrowed into the high snowdrift. He'd yet to see her face, but she now had his undivided attention. He couldn't seem to pull his gaze away from the round little globes as they twitched from side to side. His hands itched to touch them, taste them, stroke them, and squeeze them. He clenched his fists, fighting the sudden urge. The beast snarled inside of him, demanding to be let out. It wanted to see this woman for itself. Scent her. Mark her. But Arctos forced the beast down to keep his presence cloaked and continued to observe.

What was she doing out here all alone? Didn't the woman understand the danger she'd put herself in? Arctos did and he didn't like it. Anything could sneak up on her like he had. Wolves, bears…other men. His muscles tightened and his jaw clenched as anger washed through him. She should take better care.

The woman reached into the bag tucked at her side and pulled out what looked to be a weapon. Arctos stared in disbelief as she pointed the device at the white bears in the distance. Surely she wouldn't…

She pressed the trigger and a rapid-fire sound filled the air. Arctos' hearts clenched and his ardor quickly cooled. This was *not* the type of female he wanted as a mate, no matter how intoxicating she smelled. If he wanted a bloodthirsty mate, he would've found a nice Phantom female from the Blood Clan to settle down with. It mattered not that the women on his planet were few in number.

Arctos glanced at the bears and waited for their large bodies to drop into the snow, but nothing happened. He looked back at the woman and frowned in confusion. Had she missed the shot? It seemed unlikely given the range and the lack of obstructions, but it was always possible. She raised the weapon again.

He growled, a deep rumbling sound that seemed to come from the depths of his bowels. No way would he give her a second chance to make a kill.

* * * * *

Caitlin Kelly hunkered down lower in the snow-bank to ward off Northern Alaska's biting wind. She raised her equipment and gazed through the scope, focusing before taking careful aim. Two polar bears wrestled in the fresh powder, flashing deadly claws and powerful teeth as they vied for dominance and the mating privileges of a nearby female. Funny, she could've sworn there'd been four of them earlier.

She set the scope down and replaced it with an even longer lens, then fired. The click, click, click rattled out in quick succession as she captured the bears' every move. "Big payday, here I come," she murmured.

Caitlin had made sure to stay down wind, since polar bears weren't exactly known for their sunny dispositions.

Unlike most bears, polar bears loved sneak attacks. It wasn't uncommon for them to come up behind their prey and be on them before the prey even knew they were there. It helped that they blended seamlessly in with their environment. There'd only been one fatal polar bear attack in decades, but Caitlin had no plans to become number two.

She focused on her prey and continued to shoot. "That's right, smile pretty."

Caitlin kept her attention glued to her subjects, watching for any sudden changes in behavior that would indicate that they'd detected her presence. Risk wasn't a job requirement for a nature photographer, but it was certainly an occupational hazard.

She switched out lenses on her camera and fired off a few more shots. "Come on, baby, show me some claws." With any luck, she'd make enough on these photos to pay for this unexpected trip to Alaska. Caitlin had only planned to stay for a few days, but four weeks had passed in a blink. She'd somehow missed her last rent payment and what little savings she'd had, had now dwindled to dust.

Caitlin had her old college roommate, Allie to thank for her current financial crisis. At least partly. Allie had called last month in a panic, leaving a cryptic message. She'd dropped words like 'severe pain' and 'not getting better' into the voicemail. When Caitlin tried to phone back, she couldn't reach her.

After replaying the message a dozen times, Caitlin decided there must have been some kind of an accident. That could be the only explanation for the brief message and the lack of further contact. Even though she'd recently lost her job, Caitlin had thrown her things into a bag and rushed to the airport. It had been the longest nine-hour flight of her life—and the most expensive.

Caitlin had arrived in Alaska haggard and beyond worried. She'd been so out of it that she'd walked right by Allie at security. There were no slings, scars, or broken bones visible when her friend stopped her. In fact, Allie appeared to be in perfect health. Caitlin's anger over the deception had lasted all of five minutes, before quickly being replaced by relief.

It turned out that Allie had phoned because she was *heartbroken…*

Heartbroken over the fact that despite there being a ton of single men in Alaska, she hadn't been able to snag a husband yet. She was convinced that if Caitlin came to help that she would somehow succeed.

As if that was ever a goal worth achieving, Caitlin thought, then rolled her eyes.

As the child of multi-divorced parents, who put the capital 'B' in bitter, she had learned early on that marriages weren't worth the paper they were notarized on. Prince Charming didn't exist. And if he did, she'd tell him to get back on that white steed and move along. This *princess* didn't want any part of him and she was way past believing in fairytales.

Caitlin had tried to tell Allie this, but her friend wouldn't listen to reason. She was convinced the man of her dreams was out there somewhere waiting to be found or worse yet, searching for her. Pathetic! Caitlin shook her head and sighed.

It was more likely that he was somewhere sitting on a couch, scratching his ass, tossing back a few cold ones, while the delightful aroma of beer farts filled the air.

Ah, romance…

She glanced once more through the camera lens. The bears were still frolicking; two balls of white against a blanket of soft powder, but it no longer mattered since sometime during her musings she'd lost the light. Go figure. If Caitlin didn't get some cash soon, she'd have to resort to waiting tables.

She shuddered at the thought. Allie had given her a 'worst waitress ever' ribbon when they were in college. Caitlin had no plans to repeat the experience if she could help it. Nope, she'd just have to come back tomorrow and try again. She wasn't looking forward to the long hike back to her snowmobile or the freezing twenty-mile ride into town.

It's either that or camp here. Your choice.

She stared at the endless sea of white. *So not happening.* Caitlin lifted the camera and put it in the bag. She'd just zipped it up, when a deep rumbling growl sounded behind her. Her breath locked in her lungs. *It couldn't be. She'd kept them in sight the whole time.*

The sound came again. This time louder and closer.

The blonde hair on Caitlin's neck stood on end and she froze, too frightened to move, too scared to blink. Maybe the bear hadn't seen her yet. Even as the thought crossed her mind, Caitlin knew she'd never be that lucky.

Bears had an exceptional sense of smell. She put her camera bag down and slowly turned to find a thousand pound male polar bear standing twenty-five feet away, panting and watching her.

With her white coat and matching pants and gloves, Caitlin had no doubt he thought she was a chubby oversized baby seal, a delicacy for a polar bear. She knew enough about bears to know there was no way she could outrun him. And the rifle she'd brought wasn't going to do much at this close range, even if she could reach it in time. She'd never been a good shot on the best of days. Panic wouldn't help her aim.

He took a step forward, his massive paws making soft crunching noises in the snow. He snorted and lowered his head. Crap! This was not how she'd planned to die.

I'm never going to make the cover of a national magazine. Never going to get my own Discovery show. Never going to get the chance to...fall in love.

Caitlin whimpered and scooted deeper into the snow bank, praying it would somehow protect her, but knowing in the end that it wouldn't. She pulled her camera bag close to her chest and hugged it. The bear lunged. Caitlin screamed and threw up her hands in front of her face in a pathetic attempt to ward off the attack.

There was a loud thud followed by a roar of anger. Caitlin's eyes flew open in time to see a silvery white monstrosity flying through the air toward them. Another bear. Oh God, now there were two.

* * * * *

Arctos could still sense the woman, but he could no longer see her. Had the bear managed to reach her? Was she lying in the snow bleeding to death? She moaned. He felt his two hearts jump into his throat. He didn't dare take his eyes off the hungry bear that was doing its best to rip his guts out for a chance to eat such a tender morsel.

Too bad. He'd seen her first.

The male bear—though large—was no match for a Phantom Warrior in his prime. Twice as thick and a good half-foot taller, Arctos was part of the Tooth Clan on Zaron. His people could shift between bear and wolf-like creatures and disappear at will. They were the largest of the Phantom Warriors and the fiercest when it came to battle. He didn't want to hurt the bear, but he would if it didn't give up and leave its intended prey.

His long claws swiped at the polar bear's snout, leaving a streak of red behind. The bear grumbled and rose to his hind legs. Arctos did the same in a show of dominance and aggression. The bear bellowed and waited. When Arctos didn't back down, he dropped to the ground and rushed him in a flurry of teeth and deadly claws.

Arctos braced for impact.

A thousand pounds of bear slammed into him, sending him skidding across the icy snow. Sharp claws connected as the bear turned and attacked with surprising speed. Warmth trickled down Arctos' side. He ignored it and kept fighting. There was far more than a meal at stake for him.

Swipe for swipe, they scratched, bit and wrestled with each other. The polar bear stumbled, but came at him repeatedly determined to run him off. Arctos could tell the bear was tiring. It wasn't moving as fast as it had earlier. With any luck, it would give up soon and leave. Very few fights ended in death, but Arctos would kill him if necessary.

The male gave up several minutes later, but not before he'd managed to spill more of Arctos' blood. The bear ambled off, glancing over his shoulder from time to time to see if his perceived rival was still guarding the food.

Poised for another battle, Arctos watched him go. Once the thick musk of bear cleared the air, a more familiar coppery odor reached his nose. He glanced down at the crimson snow beneath his feet. It was only then that he saw the claw marks marring his silvery white fur and recalled the trickle of warmth. Arctos took a step and swayed from blood loss. The wound wouldn't kill him, but it would definitely slow him down.

He ignored the pain and concentrated on breathing, waiting for his head to clear. The injury wouldn't completely heal when he shifted back, but at least the transformation would seal the wound enough to stem the bleeding, giving him time to get the woman to safety.

Arctos sucked in a deep breath and prepared to change form. Pain seared his flesh as he temporarily shimmered out of existence. His wound stretched, ripping wider, then quickly knitted together. Naked, Arctos stumbled as he adjusted to his human form once more.

He brought his hand to his tender side. Only the faintest streaks of blood remained. Gone were the deep furrows from where the bear had struck. It would be fine as long as he didn't put too much strain on the injury.

He closed his eyes and concentrated until his uniform appeared, then turned to check on the woman. She was slumped over like she'd fallen asleep in the snow. Arctos' hearts pummeled his ribs, when he saw the ugly scarlet stain spreading across her white coat. He'd failed.

The thought was almost incomprehensible. Arctos had never failed at anything in his life. Ever. He'd always been a fiercely fast hunter, one of the best fighters, and a strategic planner. Nothing went unchecked. His safeguards had their own safeguards. He prided himself on his preparedness. He was always ready for anything. *Almost anything.*

He'd been so focused on the woman and her movements that Arctos hadn't seen the creature until it was nearly on top of her. He thought he'd reached her in time, but the metallic aroma swirling in the air told a very different story. He stared at the ever-growing pool of blood in bewildering disbelief. He'd failed her. The woman moaned, snapping him out of inaction.

Arctos pushed his shame aside and rushed forward. With trembling hands, he brushed a wisp of golden hair out of her face. His breath caught as he released the silken strands.

The woman's cheeks were pale pink from the cold and so

were her lips. The fading color accentuated the tip of her upturned nose and her pointy little chin. Taken separately, her features were nothing to contact the ship about. He'd seen Phantom and Atlantean women who were stunning by galactic standards. Their beauty commanded armies and ruled over kings.

This woman wasn't like that. She'd *never* be like that. She was…

Arctos brushed more hair away and looked again. Taken together, her 'ordinary' features formed a rather interesting, some might say intriguing, combination. Strong, yet soft. Foreboding, yet alluring. She drew him in, while somehow remaining aloof.

His fingers hovered over her cheek. Even without touching her, he could feel the heat draining from her supple skin. It wouldn't be long before her life-force followed. He had to get the bleeding to stop. Arctos curled his hands into fists, then forced them to open. He had to examine the wound.

Arctos found the opening to her clothing and slid the metal down. It hissed in the silence. He peeled the material back and swallowed hard before lifting the shirt beneath. Claw marks gouged her pale flesh, slicing deep. Humans couldn't shift and he had no way of closing the wound. Even if he somehow managed, the injury would likely become infected—that's if she didn't bleed to death first.

He'd wanted to give her a choice. Heck, he'd wanted to have a choice, when it came to deciding his future, but an Earth beast had taken everything away. The irony was not lost on him. The stain continued to spread. He had to act now or lose her forever. There was only one way that he knew of to save her.

The proposition was risky. If he succeeded, it would change both their lives forever. If he didn't pass through her, sharing his essence and genetic material, then she'd die for sure. Arctos knew that even if he did there was a chance that she wouldn't make it. He hadn't been able to test her to see if she was compatible to mate with a Phantom Warrior. *What if she wasn't?* He shoved the thought away, refusing to accept it as even a possibility. She had to live.

Arctos concentrated on the woman. "Please forgive me," he whispered, pressing a chaste kiss upon her lips. His form shimmered, then faded to nothingness so he could pass through her body and back out again.

The woman's eyes flew open, storm gray and piercing. She stared at the sky, her gaze unfocused, then slowly closed her eyes once more. The blood trickled, then stopped. That was a good sign, right?

Arctos nudged her shoulder. The woman didn't move. Not a flinch, not a whimper. He frowned. From the rise and fall of her chest, he could see that she was breathing. So why wasn't she moving? The transference meant that they were partially bound. Had it somehow failed, too?

Humans were fragile by nature. Women even more so. The smallest injury could result in a fatality. Fear and panic gripped Arctos for the second time in his long life. Something inside of him that he never knew existed, threatened to burst. He couldn't lose her. Refused to lose her.

"You will not die. Do you hear me?" Arctos ran his hands over her body. Nothing appeared to be wrong other than the now healing bear scratch. Had he missed something? He decided to check again to be sure. At least that's what Arctos told himself that he was doing as he slowly re-inspected every inch of her.

Definitely not a child. The inappropriate thought crossed his mind before he could stop it.

He cleaned the blood off using his intense body heat to melt the snow. He didn't want the stain to frighten her when she awoke—if she ever awoke. Helplessness swamped him. Arctos didn't know what else to do.

"Live!" The choked command sounded more like a plea.

The woman's lashes fluttered open. She looked at him

and at his hands, which were resting near her breasts, then said, "What do you think you're doing?"

Arctos jerked his fingers back. "I—" was all he got out before her soft gray eyes crossed and she passed out again. "That went well." He shook his head in disgust. He didn't even catch her name. This was not how he'd envisioned their first introduction to go.

What did you expect? You are a stranger to her and unworthy of her regard.

He grit his teeth and reached for her. Grateful at least that she was no longer bleeding. Arctos' muscles clenched as he lifted her and held her against his chest. She was light for a female, barely a wisp of air in his arms. Under normal circumstances, he wouldn't even notice her. But this situation was turning out to be anything but normal. He closed his eyes.

"Goddess give me strength." He inhaled.

The sweet musky scent of her skin teased his sensitive nostrils. Arctos forced himself to loosen his hold for fear that he'd bruise her, then readjusted the woman so she sat higher against his body, making it easier for travel. Her warm breath brushed his neck, tickling his ear.

Ignore it. Ignore her. At least until you know she's truly okay.

She exhaled again and gooseflesh raced along his spine, settling heavily in his groin. Arctos cursed under his breath. This wasn't going to work. There was no way he'd be able to travel quickly with her caressing his ear and taunting his body.

He juggled the woman again until she was hanging partially over his shoulder, then reached down to gather the bag she'd been clutching to her chest. He glanced at her rifle and quickly dismissed bringing it. As long as she was with him, she wouldn't need the gun. Guilt settled heavily upon his chest once more. His best efforts hadn't been enough to keep her safe.

"I will protect you with my life," he vowed. "I'll die before I'll allow anyone or anything else to harm you." He may have failed her once, but he'd never fail her again.

Arctos turned in a slow circle and extended his senses. Like a beacon of energy crashing upon him, he felt the pulse of the nearby population. Many life-forms resided there. She'd likely come from that town. He locked the location into his mind. "West it is," he said, and began to walk.

* * * * *

Caitlin awoke cocooned in warmth and gently rocking from side to side. She snuggled deeper and her nose came in contact with hard warm flesh. She sniffed, then sniffed again. A slightly musky, not entirely unpleasant aroma greeted her. Why did her whole body ache? She cracked one lid open just enough to peek at her surroundings and saw nothing but a wall of black material. She frowned as she tried to recall where she was.

Steady breathing and the squeaky crunch of boots hitting packed snow reached her ears. Her eyes flew open, but all Caitlin could see was the wide back her face was smooshed against. She pushed away and the world tilted. Her stomach lurched and she nearly threw up. Fortunately panic set in and saved her from embarrassment. She thrashed wildly, kicking with her feet and flailing her arms in an attempt to get away.

"Easy, you've been injured," a deep male voice said, without breaking stride. "If you don't stop struggling, you're going to hurt yourself." His grip on her firmed.

"Let go of me," she demanded, straining to remember the details of the last few hours. Had it been hours or minutes? She couldn't recall. Where was she? How did she get upside down? Her thoughts scrambled then reassembled themselves into working order.

There was a bear. A really *big* bear. And another bear. Then pain. Lots of pain. Followed by a tingling sensation like all her limbs had gone to sleep at once, then nothingness. Her heart began to thump wildly in her chest. What had happened to the bears?

She craned her neck to look around, catching a sideways glimpse of the man carrying her. There was something *familiar* about him. Had they met? She couldn't recall. Where had he come from? Better yet, how had she gotten away? It was all a blur of white fur, teeth, claws and blood. Caitlin began to shake uncontrollably.

"Listen, Caveman, I really must insist that you put me down immediately," she said through chattering teeth.

The man stopped, then shifted her until he could look into her face, but otherwise made no move to oblige her request.

A snowflake landed on her nose. Caitlin looked around, then glanced up at the sky. It was snowing. Hard. The man didn't seem fazed by the steadily falling powder. In fact, he wasn't even breathing hard.

Caitlin stopped struggling and took a good look at her...*rescuer*. His face was harshly beautiful with tantalizing sharp cheekbones, a sensual mouth, and dark unfathomable eyes. Trapped by his gaze, she continued to stare. She'd never seen anyone quite like him.

Her attention shifted to his hair. At first she'd thought it was covered in snow, but now Caitlin realized it wasn't snow at all. His hair was white, so white that it would probably glint like silver tinsel in sunlight. They definitely hadn't met. He wasn't the kind of guy that a girl forgot.

She licked her suddenly dry lips and asked, "Who are you?"

He continued to stare at her, until she felt unnerved by the rapt attention.

Caitlin cleared her throat. "I asked you a question."

His lips quirked and a dimple winked out from his cheek, softening his features. Such a simple movement, not even one of conscious thought, but it still managed to do strange things to Caitlin's insides. How could she have found him harsh-looking only moments ago? A woman would have to be blind not to realize the man was gorgeous.

It had to be the shock from the bear attack, she thought. What else could it possibly be? Caitlin prided herself for having a level head. She wasn't prone to bouts of lust. She'd never fallen for a pretty face. It just didn't happen.

"My name is Arctos," he said, staring at her like he'd never seen a woman before.

"Arctos." She rolled his name over her tongue, testing the sound of it. Caitlin looked at him again. Despite the oddity of it, the name did somehow fit him. He didn't look like a John or a Steve with that strangely colored hair and those sharp assessing features. "How did I get here? Actually, strike that last question. Where are we?"

"I found you. You were hurt." He broke eye contact. "As to where we are, we are heading toward a denser population. Though the snow is making the journey… difficult."

Difficult? Try impossible. Caitlin looked up at the sky. It was still daylight, but wouldn't be for much longer. Soon the temperatures would start to drop, reaching dangerous levels. Already a chill rode the air, promising a quick death.

She stared at Arctos. The outfit he had on wasn't thick enough to ward off the oncoming cold. Hers might, but not without shelter. She shivered as a breeze swept the falling snow into her face. "We need to get inside before nightfall."

"Do not worry. I have excellent night vision," he said, puffing out his impressive chest. The man winced as he did, but his expression remained stoic.

Caitlin looked at the snow near his feet. Red spots dotted the ground. She reached out and touched his side. Her white glove came away covered in blood. "You're hurt," she said, gently touching him again. "How bad is it?"

He sucked in a breath as her padded fingers probed. "It is nothing," he said through gritted teeth.

She held her glove up to his face. "This doesn't look like *nothing* to me," she said, watching him closely. "You need a doctor. How far are we from town?"

"I believe the term is a mile. Perhaps five," he said.

She glanced around at the falling snow. With the wind, the steady snowfall was drifting and morphing into a blizzard. "We might be able to make it," she said, even as doubt set it. Without markers, it was so easy to get lost in a storm. Heck, even with markers an experienced hunter could get turned around. If that happened, a mile or two could be the difference between life and death. "Mind putting me down? We can make better time if you don't carry me. It'll also take the strain off your injury."

Arctos looked like he was about to refuse her request, but at the last second, he acquiesced. "As you desire, but at the first sign of distress, you're going back."

Distress? Was he serious? She wasn't the one bleeding into the snow. Caitlin kept her thoughts to herself as he carefully put her down. The loss of warmth was instantaneous. She bounced from foot to foot to get the blood circulating and so he wouldn't see her shiver. "You're sure it's a few miles to town."

"Yes." He paused and glanced up as if in thought. "Definitely more than three, but less than six."

Snow quickly filled his footprints. How had he covered fifteen miles? "You carried me the whole way?"

He looked at her as if she'd suddenly sprouted snakes for hair. "Of course, you were injured."

She glanced down at the front of her coat and saw a huge blood stain. The world tilted for a moment before righting itself. Caitlin unzipped her coat and yanked her shirt up. Four pink ribbed lines scored her abdomen.

"It must have missed," she said, but the amount of blood told her otherwise. She forced her brain to focus on something else, anything else.

When she'd found the polar bears, Caitlin had been over twenty miles from town as the crow flies. She'd needed a snowmobile to reach the spot. She'd left it parked a half a mile away, afraid it would spook the bears. How had Arctos moved so quickly without a vehicle or at least sled dogs? It just didn't make sense. He was injured for Pete's sake. Caitlin was about to ask, when a howl rose on the wind. The hair on her neck bristled.

"We'd better hurry," she said. "Don't want to get caught out in the open by the wolves. They probably smell our blood."

Arctos' eyes appeared to flash from brown to red and back again. "I won't let anything harm you," he said with such conviction that Caitlin actually believed him.

The howl came again. This time it was the wind warning of the approaching storm. "We might be able to outrun the wolves, but we won't outrun the storm. Not with injuries," she said.

He arched a brow. "Your concern for my well-being is…unnecessary."

"Unnecessary?" She balked. "You saved me from being eaten by polar bears. I'd say that I owe you. And I always repay my debts." Caitlin glanced around, scanning the horizon through the blowing snow for any manmade objects. "Look over there and tell me what you see." She pointed at something a couple hundred yards away, hoping it wasn't just a clump of trees.

Arctos looked. Blinked a few times, then said, "It's a dwelling of some sort."

There weren't any lights on, but that didn't mean anything in Alaska. A few miles outside of a small town meant no electricity. If someone was home, she didn't think that they'd be turned away, but it paid to be cautious, since everyone in Alaska tended to be armed.

She shielded her eyes and looked again. "I can't tell if the structure is sound from here, but at this point it'll have to do. We need to get out of this storm."

* * * * *

Arctos stared at the small shelter in the distance. He sent his senses out, searching the area for threats. The wolves were closing in from two sides, but they were still a great distance away and would pose no threat. They smelled the blood on the wind, but what they hunted was bigger game like the caribou herd making their way across the tundra a half a mile from their location. Arctos sent out a warning, alerting the pack that there was a larger predator in the area. It would be enough to deter them from pursuing them.

That done, he turned his attention back to the cabin. It was empty and might serve as the perfect place to rest for the night. He chastised himself for not making better time. He should've had her safely tucked back with her people by now.

He glanced at the woman. He'd been right. She barely reached the center of his chest. Nowhere near big enough to defend herself. He was amazed she'd managed to survive this long without protection. Was she who the Goddess had chosen for him? Bitterness rose. He'd never know for certain now that the first bond was in place.

"What is your name?" he asked, pushing aside the useless emotion. In his haste to get her to safety he'd allowed his manners to slip.

She blushed, her cheeks turning even pinker. "Caitlin. Caitlin Kelly," she said. "We'd better get moving."

Caitlin. Her name tasted sweet on his lips and suited her small stature. Arctos watched her march out into the snow toward the structure. Not only did she not look like the women he'd known on Zaron, she didn't behave like them. Her diminutive size belied her hidden strength. She was not a woman used to being coddled. That much was abundantly clear when she'd demanded to be put down.

Other than her initial panic from finding herself in a stranger's arms, which was understandable, Caitlin didn't appear fussed by their present situation. Her bravery was admirable. If anything, she'd responded practically. First seek shelter, then tend to his wound. Arctos wasn't quite sure what to make of her.

The women he'd known would've been screaming about the cold and demanding that he find them food and shelter immediately. Instead, Caitlin had been the one to spot a dwelling and make the decision to spend the night.

How utterly…*fascinating*.

Arctos followed at a short distance—which was a mistake, because it gave him a clear view of her small bottom as it swished from side to side with each step. Caitlin didn't seem to notice as she picked her way over the snow. Arctos could do nothing but pay attention. It was as if she'd strapped a hunk of raw meat on her luscious ass.

Mesmerized by the gentle swaying motion, his hungry gaze devoured every inch of her. Despite the pain in his side, his shaft hardened, demanding release. He shouldn't want this woman…but he did, and Arctos was beginning to think that it had nothing to do with the bond he'd forced upon her. He growled in frustration.

The deep rumbling sound traveled on the wind. Caitlin jumped and let out a little squeak, then picked up her pace. Her focus became single-minded as she rushed toward shelter. Had Arctos not been watching, he wouldn't have believed she could move so fast.

Don't run! The plea echoed in his mind.

Arctos wanted to scream the command as his body instinctively reacted. He took a step and froze, balanced on a blaster's edge, as centuries of training and breeding spurred him to give chase. He shuddered as the bear roared inside his skull. Sweat broke out across his forehead a second before sharp incisors burst through his gums. His beast struggled for its freedom, no longer content to wait for its mate, determined to run her to ground.

Claws sprung from his fingertips as he fought the urge to hunt, to catch, to claim. The warrior in him knew Caitlin wasn't running from him. She was scared and hurrying toward the structure. Arctos latched onto that thought and clung to it, even as his raw instincts demanded action.

He raised his head and inhaled. Her warm scent wafted past him before being carried away by the wind. "Patience," he growled, forcing his claws and teeth to recede. Far easier said, than done.

*****

CHAPTER TWO

The snow was coming down hard by the time they reached the rickety shack. The structure looked even worse up close than it did from a distance, which didn't seem possible. Caitlin stared at the wooden hut wondering if they'd fall through the floor upon entry.

Wind whistled through the trees, whipping her hair around her face. If nothing else, the place would block out some of the cold. She climbed the two steps up to the door and knocked, then waited.

"There is no one inside," Arctos said. His warm breath teased her ear, making it tingle.

Caitlin shrugged in a lame attempt to brush the sensation away. "How do you know?" she asked.

"I know," he countered, then pushed the door open.

The hinges creaked as the door swung wide. Caitlin stepped forward, her eyes squinting to adjust to the darkness. Arctos put her pack down near her feet, then walked inside, his big body brushing hers as he did so. She sucked in a breath as a shiver skittered along her spine, turning her nipples into hard points. Caitlin chalked it up to the cold, refusing to acknowledge that it could be anything else.

Arctos moved silently in the shadows. Given his impressive size, Caitlin was surprised by his agility and stealth. She couldn't see exactly what he was doing until a flame flared to life, nearly blinding her. She blinked away the spots, then scanned the shack as he continued to feed the growing fire.

The cabin turned out to be in better shape than it appeared from the outside. Despite the Spartan furnishings, the dwelling somehow managed to be cozy with its small table for two and over-sized chairs situated near the hearth. An elk pelt covered much of the floor, keeping the cold from seeping into bare feet.

A neatly stacked pile of wood, enough to heat the place for the night, stood next to the now crackling blaze. A thin, crude mantel had been erected over the hearth. It housed a row of well-worn paperbacks that clung precariously to its narrow ledge.

Caitlin recognized several of the titles. At least they'd have something to do, while they waited out the storm, she thought. Her traitorous gaze slid of its own volition to Arctos' wide shoulders.

She cleared her throat and tore her eyes away, focusing instead on a small door on the left toward the back of the cabin. "I'm going to see what else is here. Check if they have any…uh…blankets," she said, not waiting for a response.

Caitlin poked her head inside the room and saw a decent sized bed and what looked to be a primitive bathroom. She'd kill for a hot bath. Excited, she rushed toward the room and threw open the door, only to find a porcelain washbasin, a freestanding claw-tub, and a portable self-contained flush toilet. There was a cast iron pot next to the bathtub with a set of potholders wrapped around its metal handle.

Her heart sank. So much for having a hot bath. Unless she wanted to melt snow in the fireplace and fill that tub, it wasn't going to happen. Caitlin supposed she should be grateful that whoever had built the shack had at least sprung for the toilet or she'd find herself making several trips outside. She shuddered at the thought of squatting in the snow.

Despite her chosen profession, Caitlin wasn't much for roughing it. Sure, she'd camp if she had to, but *only* if she had to. She much preferred taking day trips. That way she could work all day and sleep in a real bed at night. At least there was a bed, she thought. Caitlin spotted a rusted first aid kit under the washbasin. It looked old, like it hadn't been replenished in a while. Didn't matter. It would have to do.

The tinkling sound of her cellphone reached her. Tearing out of the bathroom, Caitlin rushed into the main room, only to find Arctos standing over her bag with some kind of weapon drawn. His eyes were narrowed and his muscles tense.

She skidded to a halt. "What are you doing?" she asked, not daring to get any closer for fear he'd fire and kill her bag.

Her gaze shifted to the weapon once more. The size of a small stun-gun, it didn't have a discernible barrel. Caitlin did not recognize the gun model, but that didn't mean anything. She was in no way a weapons specialist. She'd only learned to shoot a pistol and a rifle because of her job. A camera was her weapon of choice.

"There is something inside your belongings," Arctos said, his gaze never wavering from the pack.

Caitlin would've laughed, if he hadn't looked so serious. "It's just my phone. What you're hearing is the ringtone for my friend, Allie. A little odd maybe, but hardly suspect."

The cell rang again.

"I really need to get that." She pointed to her bag. "Allie's probably worried sick that I haven't returned."

His brow furrowed. "It's a communication device?"

"Yeah, like I said, it's my cellphone." Caitlin put the first aid kit on the table, then took a step closer. "I promise it won't bite."

His gaze met hers. Arctos studied her as if gauging the truth of her words then lowered his weapon.

Caitlin reached into her bag and rummaged around for her phone, praying she got to it before it went to voicemail. "Hello?"

"Where are you?" Allie shouted over thumping music. "You were supposed to meet me at Rob's party. Mike's here already."

Caitlin scrambled to remember. Party? Party? Party? She recalled Allie mentioning something about a fireman fundraiser. Was that tonight? She searched her brain. Oh crap, it was and she'd agreed to go with Mike. Ugh! Caitlin knew she should've never let Allie talk her into going on a double date. "I—"

Allie cut her off before she could say another word. "No more excuses. I let you out of the last two parties. You promised. I told Mike that you would be here. *You* told him that you'd be here. He's stoked to get to know you better. Told me to pass along that he thinks you're cute."

"Yeah, I bet." Caitlin didn't mean to sound cynical, but in her experience 'cute' was code for small. Most guys used her size as an excuse to not take her seriously. Some went out of their way to convince her that she needed someone to take care of her. They didn't realize that she'd been taking care of herself since she was nine years old.

Something sloshed and Allie broke into giggles. "Cat, you won't believe how many smoking hot men are here tonight. The room is full of hard bodies."

"A firemen pun, seriously?"

"Gosh, I just realized what I just said." Allie laughed harder. "Sorry, it was an accident. Now are you coming or what?"

Caitlin grimaced at the phone. Her friend had started the party early by the sounds of it. She'd never been big on parties. The idea of making small talk for hours was about as welcome as butt hives. She much preferred quiet dinners and casual lunches to loud music and shouting. "I can't," she said, not feeling an ounce of remorse.

"What do you mean you can't?" Allie shrieked.

"Hon, try to use your indoor voice. You don't want those hot guys thinking you're a screeching harpy"

Allie scoffed. "Can't or won't? Do I need to remind you that you promised?" She lowered her voice to less ear-shattering levels.

Caitlin sighed. "I know I did, but some things are beyond my control. Have you looked outside lately?"

"No, why? Hang on."

She could hear shuffling as Allie made her way through what sounded like quite a crowd. Everyone in the small town must be there. The noise slowly died to a dull roar.

"I'm back," she said, then gasped loudly. "It's blowing like stink out there. Where did you say you were?"

Caitlin paused. All she knew for sure was that she was a few miles from town, but that could be in any direction. "Um, I'm in a cabin."

"Whose cabin?" Allie asked.

She turned her back on Arctos. "No idea. We just needed to find shelter from the storm."

"What do you mean 'we'? You had better not have stood Mike up for another guy. Even I wouldn't do something like that," she said, indignantly.

Caitlin glanced over her shoulder, but Arctos didn't appear to be paying any attention to her. "It's not like that," she said. "You know I'd never do anything so rude. Not on purpose anyway." She scrubbed a hand over her face. "Listen, it's been a long day and I'm beat."

"I get it. You don't feel like going through the whole story. That's cool. Give me the condensed version," Allie said, sounding more sober than she had moments ago.

Caitlin took a deep breath. "I was attacked by a polar bear. Arctos saved me. We almost made it back to town, but we got caught in the storm."

"Who's Arctos? Is that an Inuit name?" Allie asked.

Caitlin glanced at Arctos' silvery white hair. "No, definitely not Inuit. Maybe Norwegian. I don't know for sure. Not really important."

"Does this Arctos have a last name?" Allie asked, sounding more than a little perturbed, which was her normal tone when she began to worry.

Caitlin frowned. She hadn't asked. Weird, that would normally be something that came up right away. Instead, she'd felt at ease in his presence. Enough so that she'd looked past her usual dating protocols. *Where had that thought come from?* She and Arctos were *not* on a date. "I think you missed the most important part of the story. The guy saved me from being a polar bear snack," Caitlin said a little too defensively.

Allie sighed. "I'm grateful that he did. Beyond grateful. But where is he from? Does he live around here? I'd feel a whole lot better if someone here knew him and could vouch for him."

Caitlin felt her face heat. She hadn't even asked. "I don't know," she whispered.

"What am I going to tell Michael, when he asks where you are and why you aren't here? I can't exactly tell him you're in a cabin with another guy. That's not going to go over well. He really likes you, Cat."

"He doesn't know me well enough to say that," she said.

"Just because you don't believe in love at first sight doesn't mean that it doesn't exist," Allie said.

It wasn't like she'd planned to get trapped in a cabin with a stranger. It just happened. Caitlin didn't know why she was arguing. Arctos wasn't even her type. He was far too good-looking and outdoorsy. Not to mention *huge*. Because of her size, Caitlin had always avoided big men. She didn't like feeling helpless—ever.

"I have a question for you and I want you to really think

about it before you answer," Allie said. "If you haven't asked for coordinates, then how do you know you're close to town? You could be miles away. Shoot, for all you know, it's his cabin you're standing in."

Fear clamped onto Caitlin's shoulders, sinking its steely fingers into her bones. Was that why Arctos knew no one was home? Her knuckles turned white as she gripped her phone. Had she been wrong about him? Caitlin inhaled and did a quick soul search, then slowly let the breath out. The fear disappeared with it. She wasn't wrong about Arctos.

"Cat, are you still there?" Allie asked.

"I'm here," she said.

"Do you want me to contact the State Troopers? I think there's a few of them here tonight at the party. It might take a while before they can find you, but at least they could start searching now. I'd hate to have you trapped in a cabin with a crazy toothless wild man."

"He's not toothless," she said absently. Caitlin glanced over her shoulder again. Arctos stood by the fire, his gaze focused on the storm raging outside. Even in repose, he exuded power and savage grace.

He carried you for miles, she reminded herself. Would a crazy mountain man do something like that? Her gut said no way. If he wanted her dead, she'd already be dead.

"I'm fine," she heard herself say, knowing it was the truth. "Don't call out the troops just yet. I'll be back tomorrow as soon as the storm dies down." Caitlin snapped a picture of Arctos with her phone and emailed it to her friend. "Please apologize to Mike for me. I'll make it up to him when I get back to town."

"Cat, I don't mean to alarm you, but I just heard someone say that the storm is expected to last for days. Do you have enough supplies?"

"Yep," Caitlin said automatically, knowing it wasn't the truth. She hadn't checked the kitchen yet, but she couldn't imagine there'd be much in the cabinets. Food tended to attract bears. And she was pretty sure all she had in her pack were a couple of protein bars.

"Hang on, my phone just beeped," Allie said. A second later she returned. "Whoa! Is that the crazy mountain man? Mike is so not going to be happy, when he sees this."

Caitlin sighed. "He's not crazy. Geez, give me a little credit. Please don't show the picture to Mike." Even as she said the words, Caitlin knew it was only a matter of time before her friend spilled the beans. Allie had never been able to keep a secret. Not that Arctos was a secret, but still…

"Who cares if he's crazy if he looks like that!" Allie said. "I swear you have all the luck."

Caitlin flushed. "I wouldn't exactly call this situation lucky. I was almost eaten by a polar bear and now I'm trapped in a cabin with a stranger."

"If I were you, I'd make the best of it, even if it is *his* place. He's yummy. I bet his got a big—"

"I'm not…It's *not* like that," Caitlin said, cutting Allie off before she could finish that statement. Who knew how many people were standing around her, listening in. "Pull your brain out of the gutter. He's not interested in me and I'm not interested in him. We're just riding out the storm together."

"You could always get him interested. With a body like that, I bet it wouldn't take much," Allie said.

"I can't," she said.

Allie snorted. "That's a shame. Truly a waste a perfectly good man. Sometimes, Cat, if I didn't know any better, I'd swear you were a nun in a past life. You need to try to loosen up and live a little. You can start by doing him."

"Thanks for the advice, Mom. I'll keep it in mind—for when I get back to town."

A deep male voice interrupted before Allie could respond. "Hey darlin', want to dance?"

"Hey yourself," Allie purred.

"Sounds like Rob has found you," Caitlin said, rolling her

eyes.

Despite her friend's assertions, Caitlin wasn't uptight. She was choosy. There was a difference, even if it didn't exist in Allie's world. Just because she didn't jump every man who made a play for her didn't mean that there was something *wrong* with her. She went out with plenty of men. Just the other day she'd gone out for coffee with Michael. Okay, so maybe Allie had been there, too, but it had been pleasant.

So maybe it *had* been a while since Caitlin had dated someone steadily. And so what if she couldn't remember the last time she'd had a man spend the night. She had been busy working, trying to build her career. Dating didn't pay the bills. And neither did photography apparently.

Allie should be grateful that she'd agreed to meet Mike for another date. It hadn't exactly been on her list of priorities. He was a nice enough guy. Said all the right things and made all the right moves. Definitely more her type than Arctos, but there'd been something missing. There wasn't that indefinable spark that promised passion. Since Caitlin wasn't looking for any other promises from a man that spark was absolutely mandatory.

"Hon, I have to go," Allie said. Caitlin could hear Rob pouring on the charm in the background. "Sure you're going to be okay?"

She glanced at Arctos. "Yeah, I'll be fine. Just remember to tell Mike that I'm sorry."

"Here, I'll let you tell him yourself," Allie said, then giggled.

"No!" she shouted.

"Hello?" Mike said.

Caitlin stared at the phone as if it had suddenly grown purple tentacles. How could Allie do this to her? "Uh-hi Mike," she said, plotting how to kill her friend.

"Where are you?" he asked. "I thought you'd be here by now. You didn't forget, did you?" Hurt colored his tone.

She tapped her forehead with the cellphone, then crossed her fingers. "No, I didn't forget." The lie slipped from her lips. Caitlin didn't want to hurt his feelings anymore than she had to. "I'm stuck in the snow," she said, glancing at Arctos.

No longer fascinated by the storm raging outside, he'd turned his attention to her, his expression unreadable.

"I was really looking forward to seeing you again," Mike said.

Caitlin walked across the small space toward the kitchen. "Yeah, me, too. Sorry."

"Where are you?" he asked.

Why did everyone want to know where she was? "I'm in a cabin. Had to get out of the storm."

"Are you close? I could come pick you up. I have a snowmobile at the house," he said, sounding hopeful.

"Um, that's okay. It's really blowing out there. I don't want you getting caught out in the storm, too" she said. "Let's just plan to get together when I get back to town."

Undeterred, he said, "I don't mind. Just tell me where you are and give me an hour. I'll come get you."

A large hand closed over hers, disconnecting the call before she could answer. "Hey! Why did you do that?" Caitlin turned to find a very unhappy looking Arctos glowering at her.

* * * * *

Arctos watched her beneath heavy lids, rage simmering below his calm surface. He'd listened carefully to the conversation. Partly to gain insight into the woman that he'd saved, but mainly to see if the partial bond had begun to take effect.

He hadn't been prepared for Allie's hurtful allegations, but he understood why she'd made them. Caitlin was her friend. She wanted to protect her. Not surprising. He would've dismissed the whole conversation had it not been for Allie next words.

Caitlin had been promised to another male tonight. And not just any male. One named Michael.

The anger over the news struck like a blow to the head, leaving him dizzy and more than a little confused. It had taken every fiber of Arctos' being to control his shift, when his instincts demanded that he hunt this 'Mike' down and destroy him.

The urge was made worse by the fact that Caitlin had dismissed him outright, and then made plans to see the male upon her return. He could've handled all that, but then the male in question spoke. He planned to come and take Caitlin away. Arctos couldn't allow that to happen. Not now. Not ever.

Arctos hadn't realized that he'd moved until his hand closed over hers, effectively ending the call. It shouldn't matter that Caitlin wasn't interested in him in that way, but it did. He wasn't used to being dismissed by females. Quite the opposite in fact. Women found his appearance appealing and were quite eager to share his bed. Well, all but one woman. The most important one. His mate. Arctos stared at Caitlin, hoping to read her thoughts.

Maybe she's not yours, the thought gave voice to his fear.

She shifted under his regard and crossed her arms over her chest. Her defensive posture only stoked his anger and sudden insecurity.

Arctos opened his mouth to tell her the truth about what had happened today. Guilt stilled his tongue. How could he explain that he'd not only taken away her future by saving her life, but soon he'd be taking her away from this planet? He couldn't. Not yet.

He wandered over to the lone window at the front of the cabin. Snow fell in sheets, blotting out the growing darkness. Somewhere out there Michael was waiting for her. Did she love him? The thought lanced his hearts. How could he live with a mate that longed for another? Would fate be so cruel?

Arctos sighed and glanced back at Caitlin. In the end, it would not matter for she was his now. The bond could not be broken.

Arctos allowed himself to take one last long look at her. Huddled by the kitchen, she appeared so tiny and defenseless. Anger had brought color back to her face, giving her cheeks a rosy glow. Perhaps not so defenseless, he mused.

At some point, she'd pulled her hat off. Her tangle of golden hair glistened in the firelight like the myriad of stars that surrounded Zaron. He longed to run his fingers through it. To feel its softness once more.

"If you wanted me off the phone, all you had to do was say so," she said, avoiding his gaze. "Thanks to that little stunt, Michael is going to be worried sick. I wouldn't be surprised if he puts together a search party to come find me."

He could try, but there was no way Arctos would let the man anywhere near her. The Goddess might not have spoken, but his actions had sealed their fate. Something primal rose inside of him, snarling and growling, determined to fight to keep its claim. Arctos watched her closely, then quietly said, "He would be a fool to start a search in these conditions." Though he knew that had their positions been reversed that he'd stop at nothing to find her.

"Mike's not a fool. He's a very smart man. In fact, he's a teacher," she said. "It was rude of you to hang up on him."

"I didn't," he said. "You did."

Her mouth dropped open. "I did no such thing."

"He did not know of my existence. He will believe that you acted of your own freewill."

She snorted. "By now, he knows all about you, including what you look like. Allie's probably shown your picture to everyone at the party," she said, her gray eyes melting into worry.

Good! Arctos was glad that Mike knew, but he made sure not to show it.

Caitlin glanced his way. "Maybe I should phone him back and try to explain."

"And tell him what?" Arctos asked. "That you intend to spend the night with me? Perhaps the males here react differently than where I'm from, but I would not like to hear that my mate was staying with another man," he said. "Even if it was a man that she has *no interest* in." His voice dropped to dangerous levels, all but daring her to deny the truth.

So much for being stealth on the phone. *Yay me.*

Her jaw opened and closed a few times as one excuse after another flitted through her mind. In the end, Caitlin groaned in frustration. "I liked you better when I was asleep," she snapped.

* * * * *

Chapter Three

Caitlin slipped off her mittens and unzipped her coat, revealing a pink, form-fitting long-sleeved shirt. She dropped the coat and gloves into a nearby chair, then unlaced her boots and toed them off, before shimming out of the bottom of her snowsuit. The movement so similar to the movement she'd made when he'd first come upon her. Those softly rounded globes once again had his full attention.

Arctos' mouth went dry as he feasted upon the lush curves hidden beneath her protective clothing. He'd known they were there, but he'd greatly underestimated their scale and impact on his senses. His nostrils flared as he inhaled. Her sweet musky scent had returned, banishing the sourness that had arose during her phone conversation. The delicious aroma now permeated the small space, leaving him hard and aching. Self-preservation made him retreat.

"I'll get us some food," he said in a low rumble. He hoped the hint of anger disguised his true condition.

Caitlin flinched. "Do you want me to check the kitchen first?" she asked, pointing to the cabinets behind her. "Could save you a trip."

"I already have. There's no meat," he said. "It contains

something called beans, but there's not enough to sustain us if the snow continues to fall." Arctos rushed past her. "I'll be back as soon as I can."

"Wait!" Caitlin grabbed his arm before he made it to the door.

His whole body tensed at her gentle touch and didn't relax until she released him. Arctos forced his gaze to meet hers. Big gray eyes locked with his and something inside of him melted. "You have nothing to fear from me. I am not crazy," he said, before he could stop himself.

"I know." Caitlin's cheeks bloomed with color. "Sorry that you heard that. Allie can be pretty dramatic, but you didn't have to hang up on Mike. It wasn't his fault. He was only trying to help."

He nodded and started to leave, but she stopped him again. Arctos swallowed hard and desperately tried to ignore the warmth from her fingers seeping into his arm.

"Be careful. Okay? You don't want to have to tangle with another polar bear," she said, glancing into the darkness. The sharp tang from her fear burned his nostrils.

Arctos grinned. He couldn't help it. She may not want him, but she *was* worried about him. It was a start. He'd never had anyone worry about him. Not since he'd come of age.

Her concern was unwarranted, yet it still warmed his two hearts. He brushed her face with the back of his knuckles. Arctos didn't know why he'd done it, only that he couldn't resist. He'd needed to touch her like he needed his next breath.

Caitlin quivered on contact, but made no move to get away.

Interesting...

Arctos slowly pulled his hand back, his fingers tingling from where they'd touched. "Do not fear for my safety, Little Cat," he said. "Any bear should know better than to tangle with me."

* * * * *

Caitlin's face glowed with the fire of a thousand suns as she watched him melt into the darkness. Even though the cabin was tiny, she had hoped that Arctos hadn't heard her mainly whispered conversation with Allie.

Sure her friend had brought up a lot of good points. Caitlin didn't know anything about Arctos, including his last name, but he wasn't crazy. Rude maybe, but not crazy. Why had he hung up the phone on Michael? It didn't make sense. Maybe he was just tired of listening to her talk about him. Okay, so maybe she *had* been the rude one.

The fact that he'd told her that she had nothing to fear only made her embarrassment worse. He'd looked so hurt when he said it. God, she sucked. Talk about ungrateful.

Caitlin covered her face with her hands and shook her head. Somehow she'd managed to hurt two men's feelings in one day. First Mike and now Arctos. It had to be some kind of record. She stared at the cellphone and thought once more about phoning Michael back.

Arctos was right. What would she say to him if she did call? *Hey, I'm spending the night with a hot mountain man. I'll catch you later.* So not going to happen. She'd just have make it up to Mike once she got back to town. Her heart sank. Suddenly the idea of seeing him again didn't seem as appealing as it had before. What was wrong with her? She'd never been fickle in her life. It had to be the stress of the day. She'd worry about it, worry about him later.

She had more important matters to consider…like how she was going to apologize to Arctos. There had to be something she could do to make it up to him. He'd saved her life after all.

Caitlin glanced around the small cabin. Her gaze locked on the two cupboards at the back of the room. He'd mentioned something about beans. She crossed the few steps it took to reach the kitchen and threw open the cupboard doors. One held plates, a few cups, a thermos, and silverware. The other had some coffee, a few cans of chili, beans and dried noodles. More than enough for a meal.

"Chili-mac it is," she said, racing into the other room to retrieve the cast-iron pot.

Pot in hand, Caitlin stared at the door to the cabin as she slipped her boots back on. As much as she wanted to avoid going outside, there was no way around it. She needed snow. She forced herself to cross the room and open the door. Wind whipped her hair around, temporarily blinding her.

Caitlin pushed it aside and scanned the darkness for predators, but it was impossible to see in whiteout conditions. How would Arctos find his way back? Her heart leapt into her throat, choking off her air. What if he was lost in the blizzard? What if he was lying out there now, freezing to death? *Don't think about it. He said he'd be fine.*

She clung to that assurance as panic wrapped its vicious fingers around her neck. He'll be back. He has to come back. Caitlin forced her feet to move. She quickly filled the pot, packing it tight with snow, then slipped back inside, slamming the door behind her. Tears welled in her eyes. She scrubbed them away.

Get a hold of yourself.

She waddled under the weight of the big pot as she made her way to the fire. A small hook inside the fireplace poked out of the brick. Caitlin hadn't noticed it before, but there was no doubt what it was used for. She hooked the pot handle over the hook, added a couple of logs, and waited for the snow to melt.

Within an hour, she'd downed five cups of coffee and bitten all her nails to stumps. More time passed. Caitlin had never been good at waiting. She much preferred action to sitting around. The wait would've been bad enough, but coupled with worry, it became interminable. Caitlin couldn't remember the last time she'd been *this* worried. Not even when Allie had called her and she'd thought there'd been an accident had she been this concerned.

Why? Something was definitely wrong with her. She barely knew Arctos. In truth, she didn't know him at all. Yes, he'd saved her life. And yes, she was grateful, but he was a stranger. So why all the fear and panic? Was this some kind of weird Stockholm syndrome? It just didn't make sense.

The door handle jiggled and her heart jumped. A second later the wooden door swung open. Arctos looked like a ghost coming in from out of the snow. Without his snowsuit, he would be impossible to spot...just like the polar bears. A shudder ran through her.

Arctos walked into the room and dropped two large rabbits onto the floor. Their eyes met briefly, then he looked at the table she'd set and frowned. Not exactly the reaction she'd been hoping for. It didn't bode well for the apology she had planned.

Caitlin looked down at the plate in front of her. The setting wasn't fancy, but she'd taken care to make it as nice as possible. She had found a clean sheet in a trunk in the bedroom and some candles in the bathroom. Caitlin used the sheet as a tablecloth and lit one of the candles, placing it in a glass to create a pseudo-centerpiece. It was in no way fancy, but she'd thought it looked nice.

Arctos shut the door behind him, but otherwise hadn't moved from the entryway. "What is this?" he asked, in obvious confusion.

"Dinner," Caitlin said, her voice losing some of the confidence she'd felt earlier. "I wanted to apologize for earlier."

"Apologize for what?" he asked.

He wasn't making it easy. "The phone call, Allie, Michael, everything," her voice trailed off.

His brow furrowed even more. "What is that smell?"

"Chili-mac." Maybe he wasn't a fan of chili-mac. "If you don't like it, I can try to cook one of the rabbits." Caitlin had never cooked a rabbit in her life. Her culinary skills were better suited to canned goods and microwaves, than fresh foods. The mold growing in her refrigerator at home could attest to that, but she'd give it a try if that's what he wanted.

Why was she working so hard to please this man? He was a stranger. After tonight, she'd probably never see him again. For some reason, that made her feel even worse. She had to be exhausted. There was no other logical explanation for why she was behaving this way.

Arctos looked at the pot over the fire, then back at her. "I'll wash up and be right in," he said, then walked back outside to scrub his hands in the snow.

Caitlin shivered as she watched. Arctos didn't seem to notice the cold or if he did, he certainly didn't seem to be in any hurry to get out of it. Which meant that the only reason he'd stopped earlier was because of her. Caitlin's heart sank. She'd botched this day up and good. Before he walked back in, she planted a smile on her face and dished up the food.

* * * * *

She'd prepared food for him like a mate would do. Arctos had tried to cover his shock, but he'd failed miserably. While he'd been hunting, he'd convinced himself that the Goddess was mistaken in her choice of mate for him and that the bond had not formed. It made sense given that this woman was already spoken for. He'd heard the man with his own ears. He'd seen her reaction to him.

Arctos had been determined to come back and keep his distance, then he'd smelled the food. Its aroma had wafted on the wind, drawing him to its source. It didn't take long before he realized the scent was coming from the cabin. Stubbornness alone kept him from acknowledging the truth. He'd purposely stayed out an extra hour to prove that she meant nothing to him. And it had worked…until he laid eyes on her again.

Caitlin had looked so happy, almost relieved when he'd stepped through the door. Her gray eyes had sparkled in the firelight and she'd scooted to the edge of her chair as he walked into the room.

And how had he responded? He'd froze like a deer trapped by a wolf pack. Even his breath had stuttered in his lungs, as his brain fought to catch up with what he was seeing. Arctos knew that cooking him a meal didn't mean anything to her. At least not the same as it meant to him. But he was having a hard time convincing his beast that was the case. Caitlin now had its full attention and that was never a good thing.

Arctos used the time needed to wash his hands to recover from the surprise and get his beast under control. Breathing deeply, he let the cold embrace him. Even in his human form, he could barely feel it. His body was made for harsher temperatures than the Earth could produce. He scrubbed his hands and arms with snow until they turned bright pink. Knowing he couldn't put it off any longer, Arctos turned and walked back into the cabin.

Caitlin was smiling when he entered, but her scent didn't match her expression. She had dished up the food while he was out. It smelled different than anything he'd ever eaten, but he was willing to give it a try for her sake.

"What did you say this is called?" He took a seat across from her.

"Chili-mac," she said, then picked up her fork and speared a bite.

Arctos watched her chew. She made little humming noises in the back of her throat while she did so. It made him wonder what kind of noises she'd make if they made love. He shifted as his flight suit tightened against his groin, then sniffed the food once more. Caitlin continued to watch him, her gaze reserved, but hopeful.

"Have you ever had chili-mac?" she asked, taking another bite.

"No." He met her shimmering eyes.

"It's pretty good, if you like chili."

Arctos didn't know if he liked chili, but it didn't matter. Caitlin had prepared this meal for him and he intended to eat every bite. He lifted his fork tentatively. "Smells good," he said, not wanting to hurt her feelings. In truth, it smelled odd. The predator in him wanted meat. Though he detected some kind of meat, it wasn't anything he was familiar with. "What are the red things?" he asked, pushing them around his plate.

"Beans," she said and frowned a little.

He poked at something else. "And the long pale skinny things?"

"Noodles," she said slowly. "You've really never had noodles and beans before?"

He shook his head. "No, this is the first time. My diet is made up of mainly protein."

"Ah." She laughed and her shoulders relaxed a little. "You're one of those kind of guys."

Arctos took a bite and chewed it quickly. It actually tasted far better than it looked. Sweet, yet spicy and full of flavor. "I don't know what you mean," he said, watching her closely. Did she suspect his true nature? Without the final bond, he didn't know for sure.

"True carnivores," Caitlin said as if that was obvious.

Arctos nodded in agreement. She had no idea how accurate that statement was.

"I've met a few guys like you, but not many," she said around another bite.

His lips twitched. He could almost guarantee that she'd *never* met anyone like him, but he wasn't about to correct her. Instead, Arctos plunged his fork into the food and looked at her. "I admit I do love succulent meat. The sweeter, the better," he said, allowing his gaze to slowly scroll over her from head to foot, before reversing direction. By the time he finished, Caitlin's ears were glowing.

She cleared her throat. "Yes, well, I'm glad you like the chili-mac."

"Thank you for making it," he said. "Had I known you were planning to prepare a meal for me, I wouldn't have hunted the rabbits."

"How did you catch them by the way?" Caitlin asked. "I didn't see any holes, so you couldn't have used your gun. Did you use a trap?"

Arctos shifted again. He'd caught them with his teeth and claws. He didn't want to lie to her, but he could hardly tell the truth. "Neither was necessary," he said, noncommittally. "What are you drinking?"

"Coffee, want some?"

"Sure." He watched her pour the dark liquid into his cup. It was hot and bitter to the taste, but strangely good. Arctos finished his cup in record time and asked for another.

* * * * *

Caitlin was only too happy to oblige. Arctos seemed to be genuinely grateful that she'd cooked for him. For a minute, she'd thought she had made a huge mistake. Fortunately, when he'd returned from cleaning his hands, he'd been in a better mood. It had bolstered her confidence enough to actually enjoy the meal.

She still couldn't believe that he'd never tasted beans or noodles. Where had he been living, under a rock? Caitlin would never be able to survive on meat alone. She loved noodles too much.

"So." She pushed her empty plate back. "Do you live around here?"

Arctos put his fork down. "No, I'm just visiting."

"Me, too." She grinned.

"You do not live here?" From his perplexed expression, she could tell he was surprised by her answer.

"Why would you think that?" she asked.

"Because of the bears and Michael. You said--"

She held up her hand, cutting him off. "I don't want to talk about Mike. Okay? I feel bad enough about the situation. I've never stood anyone up before."

Arctos looked like he had no idea what she was talking about, but nodded in acceptance anyway. "What would you like to discuss?" he asked.

"You," she said. "I mean you saved my life, but I don't know anything about you." Caitlin played with the edge of the material covering the table to give her hands something to do.

"Does it matter?" he asked, his expression serious.

Surprised by his question, she paused. His gaze didn't waver. If anything it grew even more intense.

"Yes," she said. "It does to me."

He sat back and crossed his leg until his foot rested on his knee. "Very well, ask away. I will do my best to answer your questions if that is what you truly desire."

She dished up more chili-mac onto his plate, then scooted back, mirroring his actions. "How did you get me away from the polar bear?"

"I challenged it," he said matter-of-factly. "The bear wasn't about to give you up without a fight...and neither was I."

Caitlin's stomach fluttered at his unexpected confession. She pushed the odd sensation aside, not wanting to get sidetracked from the most important point. "What do you mean you challenged it?"

He picked up his fork and took a bite. The tension stretched between them. Caitlin thought for a moment that Arctos wasn't going to answer, but he surprised her again.

"I fought it in order to protect you," he said quietly.

Caitlin's heart sped in her chest. He couldn't be serious. She'd never had anyone fight for her. Not even on the playground. She wasn't the type of woman that men fought over, much less took on a bear for.

Sure, she cleaned up well, but Caitlin knew deep down that she'd never be anything but blissfully average. She'd learned that long ago and made peace with it. "Thanks," she said, knowing it sounded lame and rather unsubstantial under the circumstances.

"Don't thank me," he snapped. "I failed."

Startled by the veracity of his claim, Caitlin slowly looked down at her body and said, "Doesn't look like you failed to me."

"You were injured. Horribly," he croaked, as if it hurt to say the words.

Caitlin didn't understand where his pain was coming from. They'd survived the ordeal. He should be happy or at the very least grateful. "Without your help, I'd be dead," she said. "So I'm going to call it a win."

They fell silent once more. Caitlin took the opportunity to mull over what she'd learned thus far. Not much, she decided, since it was obvious that there was more going on here than she realized.

Arctos cleared his plate. "The meal was delicious."

"No, it wasn't, but thanks for saying so." Caitlin picked up their plates and deposited them in the sink. She just couldn't let it go. She had to know. "I don't understand how you managed to fight off a polar bear and only get a scratch."

"Is it important?" His dark eyes held so many secrets, so many promises. Secrets she was dying to know, but didn't think she was ready to hear.

"No." Caitlin shook her head, then added, "It's just that I've never had anyone do something like that for me."

"I'm sure Michael would've done the same in those circumstances," Arctos said. There was an edge to his voice that hadn't been there before.

"Doubtful," Caitlin replied without thinking, then glanced at his side. She hadn't managed to get him patched up yet. She should've done that before he went out hunting. The last thing they needed was for the predators to follow the blood trail back to the cabin.

She might have gotten a scratch, but he'd been injured during the encounter with the bear. Injured defending her. Fighting for her. It was probably why she had so much blood on her jacket. Even though it went against everything that she believed in, Caitlin felt a small thrill from Arctos' heroics. "Take your shirt off," she said, reaching for the first aid kit.

*****

Arctos stilled at her uttered command. In his current condition, he didn't think undressing was a good idea. "Why?" he asked, wondering what she was up to.

"I need to bandage your wound and put some salve on it. We don't want it to get infected." She rummaged around in the small metal box.

"It won't," he said.

Caitlin stopped what she was doing and looked at him. Her brow rose as she stared. "Don't tell me that you're afraid of a little ointment and a bandage. You can take on a bear, but not some medicine that might sting." She laughed, then went back to gathering materials.

Arctos' body tensed. He wasn't afraid of anything—or at least he hadn't been until he'd met her. He rose slowly out of his seat, then grasped the corners of his flight suit and pulled it apart, baring himself to the waist.

"That's bett..." The word died on her lips as her gaze locked onto his chest. Her throat worked convulsively as she struggled to speak.

Had he known this would be the effect, Arctos would've removed his clothing long ago. It took all of his training as a Phantom Warrior to keep him rooted in place as Caitlin drank her fill.

The last time a woman had looked at him like that she'd

ended up on her back with her legs spread wide and his face buried between her thighs. If Caitlin kept this up, she'd find herself in a similar position. The thought was beyond tempting.

He gripped the material to keep from reaching for her. "You asked me to remove my shirt. I have done so," he said, feeling the hot lick of her hungry gaze caress his overheated skin.

Caitlin cleared her throat. "S-so I did," she said, breathlessly.

"If you like, I can remove more." His gaze pinned her in place, daring her to ask for what she so obviously desired.

Her eyes widened and her hands shot out in a halting motion. "No! I mean, no, that's quite enough. I should be able to take care of everything this way." She indicated to his side, but her traitorous gaze kept returning to his chest.

* * * * *

CHAPTER FOUR

Caitlin couldn't tear her eyes away from Arctos. He was a work of art in flesh form. Other than the scratch marks on his side, there wasn't a blemish marring his pale skin. She'd never seen a chest so plated with muscle. The heavy folds of his eight-pack rippled at his waist, forming a deep 'V' that disappeared into the bottom of his snowsuit. He was flawless. Impossibly so. And by far the most beautiful man that she'd ever laid eyes on.

Until this moment, Caitlin had never understood how Allie could fall for a guy at first sight. Her friend had called it 'lust at first sight'. According to Allie, love quickly followed. Caitlin had always considered the notion fanciful and beyond shallow. Something that would never—could never happen to her. And for twenty-six years it hadn't…until now.

"Caitlin?" he asked.

Moisture drained from her mouth, leaving it drier than a daisy in the Sahara. She blinked when he repeated her name. A fresh wave of embarrassment hit as she realized what she'd been doing. Oh my god! She, Caitlin Kelly had been *gawking* like an unschooled teen.

"Sorry." She forced herself to look away. "Almost ready," she croaked.

She turned back to the first aid kit and rifled through it, even though she'd already gathered everything she needed. Caitlin used the moment to get her pounding heart and scattered wits under control. Somehow she'd wandered into foreign territory and was now clearly out of her depth. Where was Allie when she needed her?

Caitlin seriously considered running to the bathroom, so she could call her friend for advice. The idea was quickly dismissed when she realized there was no way she could get to the phone without Arctos seeing her. Besides, she had pretty good idea what Allie would say already. Caitlin took a deep breath. *You can do this*, she thought. *Just think about cleaning toilets, scrubbing dirty pots, or waiting tables.*

"Ready." She turned back to him.

Arctos' lips twitched in amusement. "Where do you want me?"

She groaned inwardly as a small voice inside her head screamed 'the bed'. "The chair is fine." She pointed to the one closest to the fire. "Have a seat over there in the light. I want to see how bad it is."

"It's fine," he said. "Soon it will be completely healed."

"So you keep saying."

The light from the flames danced over his skin as Caitlin bent over to take a closer look at his injury. She tried to hold her breath, but all that accomplished was to make her dizzy. She inhaled, focusing on the nearly healed wound. Arctos smelled of woods and man. Caitlin closed her eyes and counted to five. As she did, his scent seemed to change, growing richer, muskier, almost sensual in nature. Caitlin stood abruptly and swayed.

Arctos reached out to steady her. "Are you okay?" He peered up at her, his lids resting at half-mast, effectively veiling his eyes.

"Fine." She stepped away abruptly, shaken by the

sensations buzzing through her body. "Just had a bit of a head rush. Probably didn't eat enough. I'm going to get the salve." Caitlin hiked her thumb over her shoulder.

* * * * *

Arctos watched her reach for the small jar and unscrew the top. He could smell the changes happening in his body. There was only one reason his aphrodisiac-like pheromones would flood his system—to ensnare his mate. Could that mean Caitlin really was his true-mate or was it a sign that the first bond had taken hold? Hope balanced on a fine blade of fear. Arctos wanted—no needed more than a forced connection between them.

Caitlin returned with her fingers covered in goo. "This might sting," she said, then rubbed the thick substance onto the scratches.

Arctos flinched as she ran her hand over his bare flesh.

"Sorry." She gently blew on his side.

Goosebumps rose on his arms, hardening his flat nipples. Blood rushed from his head straight to his shaft, filling it in record time. He gripped the arms of the chair until his knuckles turned white.

"It should stop hurting in a minute." Her gaze skittered away from his blatant erection.

Arctos clenched his jaw until his teeth ached. "The pain I feel isn't due to the treatment."

Caitlin swallowed audibly, then picked up the bandage. She placed it over the wound and taped it to his uninjured skin. "All done." She started to walk away, but Arctos stopped her.

"Thank you." Their eyes met and held. Need, fear, hunger, and uncertainty flashed between them in an instant. It was the latter that was his downfall. He slowly pulled her onto his lap. Arctos gave Caitlin plenty of time to get away. She didn't try. When their lips met, it was only long enough to exchange a breath, then he released her.

Caitlin's small breasts rose and fell like she'd just run a marathon. Her pupils were dilated and she practically trembled with need. Arctos couldn't look away. He was afraid he'd miss something vital if he did. She licked her bottom lip, seeking out his taste, but otherwise didn't move.

"You are temptation in Goddess form," Arctos ground out, holding onto the chair for dear life. "I want to touch you so bad that I ache for it."

Caitlin started to speak.

"Wait! Please hear me out," he said. "I know that your heart belongs to another and that given a choice you would not have picked me."

Caitlin's mouth dropped open a second before she laughed. She stared at him, then laughed again. "I can't believe that you're serious. You actually think…" She shook her head, then pinned him to the chair with a look. "Let's clear up a few things. I think you're gorgeous. I've never seen a man so beautiful, so perfect in my life. You could tempt the Devil himself with that body, but I'm not the type of girl to fall for a handsome face or dive into bed with a stranger."

"You find me attractive?" he asked.

"Oh please." She rolled her eyes.

"But your heart belongs to another," he said, as some of his newfound hope diminished.

Caitlin hesitated, then said, "My heart belongs to me and only me."

Their gazes locked. "So there is a chance…"

"A chance for what?" she asked.

Arctos hesitated, then said, "A chance that someday you'll put your heart in my hands for safe-keeping."

* * * * *

Something melted in Caitlin's chest. Guys like Arctos

just didn't exist in the real world. She had loads of firsthand experience to prove it. Yet something inside of her wanted desperately to believe that he was different. That he'd somehow prove her wrong. His hand slid down her arm until he grasped her fingers. The tug was so slight that she almost didn't feel it. Caitlin found herself being drawn into his arms.

Their faces were mere inches apart. The warmth of his breath caressed her cheeks, while the musky aroma that seemed to emanate from his skin grew sweeter. He ran his free hand up her arm and over her shoulder, massaging along the way. His palm came to rest at the back of her neck. Arctos cupped it gently and closed the distance between them.

Caitlin knew she should tell him to stop. This wasn't like her. She didn't do things like this. Maybe staying with Allie had somehow rubbed off on her. Or maybe, just maybe, she wanted this as much as he did. Whatever the reason, she allowed him to continue.

Arctos stopped, as their lips were about to touch. Caitlin's heart was hammering so hard in her chest that she couldn't hear anything but its steady thud. His breath mingled with hers, tempting her to finish what he'd started.

What was he was waiting for? The tension rose between them, coiling tight. Caitlin could practically taste it on her tongue, feel it crackling over her skin. He wanted her. Of that there was no doubt. His entire body felt like iron beneath her.

She had told him that she didn't fall into bed with men. Was that why he'd stopped? Did he want her to make the final decision on whether this went any further? Caitlin stared into his fathomless eyes. They were so dark now that they appeared ringed in red. Arctos didn't say a word. Did nothing to influence her decision in any way. In the end, that's what tipped her over the edge.

Caitlin's mouth found his. Arctos groaned and his grip on

her neck tightened as he joined her in the embrace. She'd been kissed before. Lots of times. The kisses had varied between chaste to slobbery. Caitlin considered herself a pretty good kisser, but she didn't have anything on Arctos.

He ran his tongue along her bottom lip, then dipped inside as she gasped for air. Their tongues touched, then tangled, a controlled dance that ratcheted up her need. Arctos deepened the kiss, his strokes, flicks, and nibbles seemed aimed at building desire. Fueled by lust, Caitlin slipped her arms around his neck and allowed her body to free-fall. His taste filled her mouth, spicy and bitter from the coffee and chili-mac, yet utterly addictive. She clung to him, trying to get closer, wanting more.

Arctos growled, the sound rumbling out of his chest. He pulled back, his lungs heaving. "I need you," he said, taking a shaky breath. The confession came from the depths of his soul. His forehead dropped forward until it rested against hers. "I know you do not give yourself to men easily. For that I am truly grateful. But if you could do so this one time, I swear that I would consider it a gift beyond measure."

Caitlin brushed a stray hair away from his face. "You are too good to be true," she murmured more to herself than to him.

"I'm not," he said, emphatically. "I am selfish." Red slashed his cheeks and pain flashed in his eyes.

Arctos may be many things, but selfish wasn't one of them. Caitlin kissed him again in order to banish the thought from his mind. His taste and his smell continued to overwhelm her. Even now, she found herself craving more.

She thought about her friend, Allie. She knew what she'd do in this situation. Allie wore her heart on her sleeve for everyone to see…and crush, but it never stopped her from trying to find love. If Caitlin were being perfectly honest, she'd admit that she envied Allie's ability to pick herself up, dust herself off, and start over. Unfortunately, she'd lost her rose-colored glasses long ago.

She looked at Arctos. His lips were slightly swollen from their kisses and his brown eyes were glazed with passion. Caitlin had no doubt that she looked the same. Could she let go of her rigid self-control for *one* night of passion? Their gazes met once more. His heated to inferno as she watched.

Allie would be proud, she thought as she hopped off his lap and grabbed him by the hand.

Caitlin led Arctos back to the bedroom. His eyes widened when he saw the bed, then dropped to slumberous once more. She backed into the room until her shoulders hit the half wall that separated the bedroom from the bathroom. Caitlin watched as Arctos slipped off his boots, then slowly grasped the edges of his snowsuit and pulled it down.

Holy mother of Adonis.

Her breath caught in her throat, as he stood naked before her. For a moment, all she could do was stare. He was *impressive* in every way imaginable. She was almost afraid to remove her own clothes, since there was no way she could live up to that body.

Arctos took the decision out of her hands by pulling her into his arms and kissing her senseless. He'd obviously been holding back earlier. Caitlin's toes curled and skin grew taut. His chest brushed her nipples and she gasped as they went rigid. Arctos didn't stop kissing her. His hands slipped down to her sides and under her long underwear. The second his fingers touched her bare flesh, heat flooded her.

He bunched the material in his fists and yanked it over her head, dropping it down beside them. His dark eyes drank in the lacy cups of her padded bra. "Remove it," he said, his voice a rough rasp.

"I really hope you're not a boob man," she said.

"I'm not." His gaze dropped to her butt.

Caitlin's fingers trembled as she unhooked the front latch and her bra fell open. Her hands automatically rose to cover herself.

"No," he said, stopping her. Arctos stared at her small

breasts like he'd never seen nipples before. His hands slowly released hers, then glided over her skin until he reached her small mounds. He cupped them, squeezing them gently at first, then rolled the hard peaks between his thumbs and forefingers. "Must taste," he ground out a second before lowering his head and latching onto one nipple.

Caitlin's knees wobbled and she gasped. Her back arched with each pull of his mouth. His tongue swirled around her rigid flesh, teasing it with experienced strokes. She slid her fingers into his white hair, the strands like silk beneath her palms. Caitlin yanked him closer, urging him to take more.

Arctos obliged. His teeth scraped her, then he bit down hard enough to send a zing of pain to her brain. He followed the move with a gentle swipe of his rough tongue, soothing the sting, then began sucking her again.

Her legs quaked, threatening to give out. "Arctos, please," Caitlin begged, not sure what she was asking him to do.

He laughed around her nipple, then slowly released her a second before he popped the other one into his greedy mouth and began to devour it. Caitlin's knees gave out, but Arctos caught her before she fell. He lifted her without breaking contact with her aching nipple, then carefully placed her on the bed.

Caitlin felt an odd pressure building in her womb. It wasn't possible. He hadn't touched her anywhere, but her breasts. Yet, there was no mistaking the familiar sensation. Arctos teased her nipple, sucking hard, then releasing her. Only to return once more. The pressure continued to grow until Caitlin could no longer lie still.

As if sensing her impending release, Arctos began to worry her sensitive flesh with his teeth. He didn't let up or allow her to catch her breath. It can't be, she thought. A flick of his clever tongue sent her sailing over the edge. Caitlin cried out. Blood roared in her ears and her body trembled as her release swept through her.

For a second, the world around her faded, then came back into sharp relief. Arctos continued to lazily lap at her flesh, his big hands holding her firmly against the mattress.

"That was incredible," she gasped. "I didn't even think that was possible. I mean I've read that some women have super sensitive breasts, but I'm not one of them."

Arctos stopped what he was doing and glanced at her. A second later his lips canted. "You have been with the wrong males," he said with an over-abundance of confidence.

Caitlin opened her mouth to call him on it, but realized after what had just occurred he'd earned a bit of cockiness. He smoothed his hand over her abdomen, frowning when he reached the scratch.

"It doesn't hurt," she said.

Arctos didn't respond. Instead, he ran his palm down her thigh, barely skimming her skin. Her legs quivered.

"You have no idea how long I have waited to have you beneath me," he said, his voice harsh.

She arched a brow. "It couldn't have been too long, since we only met today."

A wry smile was his only answer.

Arctos slid his hand to the bottom of her heel and rubbed. Caitlin's head dropped back onto the pillow and she groaned. He planted his thumb at the center of her foot and kneaded.

"You're not playing fair," she said, curling her toes under in delight.

"When it comes to lovemaking and war," he said, rubbing even harder, "there is no such thing as fair play."

* * * * *

Arctos switched to Caitlin's other foot, watching her writhe in pleasure. It was a challenge to keep his gaze focused on her face, when the moisture between her thighs teased his senses.

He shook at the thought of burying his nose in her sex, tasting her honey with his lips, teasing her with his tongue. Arctos had no doubt that Caitlin would taste as good as she smelled. He worked his way up to her calves, massaging them with just the right amount of applied pressure.

She wiggled on the bed, her swollen breasts bobbing with each jerk. He'd gotten a little carried away when he'd bit her the last time. Her perfect flesh now held the faint outline of teeth. Sharp teeth. Beast teeth. If she looked too closely, she'd notice that they didn't match a human bite-mark.

Arctos decided he'd just have to keep her busy, until she forgot everything including her name. He worked his hands up to her thighs. Caitlin's legs dropped open. Even in human form, his beast recognized the invitation. He swallowed hard and kept working her sore muscles.

"Turn over, Caitlin." He needed to get the temptation of her moist opening out of view until he could get himself under control.

She didn't argue. She immediately rolled onto her stomach and moved her hair out of the way so he could reach her shoulders. Arctos grinned now that she couldn't see him. Her skin was soft as silk that had been warmed upon a flame. Everywhere he touched, heated. The round globes of her bottom were now bare and more beautiful than he'd imagined. Arctos had the overwhelming urge to lean over and take a bite out of one.

Instead, he focused on working her stiff muscles. He wanted her relaxed before he mounted her. His hard shaft continued to dig into his abdomen. Arctos did his best to ignore the pain. One hand manipulated the flesh on her back, while his other smoothed over her waist. He paused there for a minute, letting Caitlin's reactions be his guide. Her honeyed scent filled the room stronger as he lightly stroked her bottom.

She twitched, but didn't brush him away.

His grip firmed and he cupped her. Caitlin whimpered a

second before her butt rose in the air like an offering to the Goddess. Arctos prayed for the strength to take things slow. "You smell like the heavens," he said, licking one globe, then the other. "Your body tempts my control."

* * * * *

Caitlin turned her head and smiled, cracking one lid open. Arctos' attention was locked onto her bottom. "That feels so good," she said, finally catching his eye.

He grinned, but it looked pained even in the low lighting. "I fear I cannot wait much longer." His hand dipped, brushing her back entrance as it made its way to her moist opening. With one finger, he circled her, teasing her, while avoiding her throbbing clit.

Caitlin bit her lip as he pulled his finger out and slipped it into his mouth to suck on her juices. His chest shuddered and his eyes closed in ecstasy.

"I knew you'd taste like the boldest wine, the richest treat."

She couldn't breathe, couldn't think. Had she ever wanted anyone like this? Had anyone ever wanted her this bad? Her gaze remained locked on him as he gently parted her thighs and slipped between them. His hard shaft rested in the crease of her ass. It pulsed once, twice, then he shifted his hips until the head of his shaft was notched at her entrance. Caitlin opened her mouth to remind him to wear a condom. Before she could utter a single word, Arctos surged forward, burying himself to the hilt.

Caitlin cried out as her body tried valiantly to adjust to the sudden invasion. Arctos was thick, really thick, and incredibly long. She felt stuffed and stretched to the breaking point. She tried to catch her breath, but then he moved, pulling slowly out before ramming back in, deeper and harder than before. Heat burst inside of her. She'd never felt anything like it, like him.

"You'd better be safe," she gulped. "Because I am."

Arctos stopped, his big body quivering with the effort. "I know not what you mean," he said, kneeing her thigh out so he could sink even deeper into her.

"Disease. You'd better not have any diseases." She tried to glare at him, but couldn't get her eyes to focus.

"I am healthy. I would never put your life in danger. You mean everything to me," he said, the stark truth etched in his handsome features.

Her heart somersaulted in her chest. Fear chased elation, nipping doggedly at its heels. Caitlin wasn't ready for that kind of sincere honesty from a man. She wasn't sure if she'd ever be. It was that kind of honesty that led to things like *commitment*. And there was no way she was going down that road with Arctos or anyone else.

Arctos rolled his hips and hit something inside her that Caitlin hadn't believed existed outside of 'how to' books. Her thoughts scattered and she moaned. "That feels so good. Do it again."

He nipped her ear. "It's about to feel a whole lot better."

* * * * *

Arctos' body trembled as he sank his length into Caitlin. She felt perfect. Better than perfect if there were such a thing. Her warm sheath gripped him tight, squeezing his shaft until he could hardly breathe. The beast in him demanded that he finish, but Arctos knew the second he bit Caitlin it would destroy the precious connection that they'd just forged.

He tamped the bear down with faint promises and focused on bringing pleasure to the woman beneath him. How could he have thought that the Goddess had gotten it wrong? Caitlin was perfect in every way.

He thrust, driving deep, the bone in his shaft keeping him hard as stone. His kissed her womb with another drive of his hips. Soon he would flood her with his release, marking her as his mate. When the bond was complete, she would be able to carry his offspring. His hearts ached at the thought of Caitlin's stomach swelling with their child.

Arctos rolled his hips and surged forward at the same time. She clutched at the blankets beneath her. He gripped her hips and held tight until his claws threatened to unsheathe. He released her before they did, snagging the side of the bed instead. The sound of ripping material reached his sensitive ears, but Caitlin didn't seem to notice.

Forcing his claws to recede on one hand, Arctos circled her swollen nub. Caitlin whimpered, so he did it again. His thumb flicked it, then he pinched. Her entire body shook. She was so close. Arctos could feel it, but he wasn't ready to let her fly just yet. He wanted her to get used to his weight upon her, the feel of him inside her velvet sheath, the smell of his heated skin. He wanted those things so ingrained that by the time they were finished Caitlin wouldn't be able to imagine her life without him.

Arctos already felt that way about her.

Her sweet scent filled the room, mingling with the richer aroma of sex. His pheromones now covered every inch of her skin. Arctos palmed her bottom, grinding his hips as he captured her mouth in a searing kiss. "I want you," he murmured.

Dazed, she said, "You have me."

"No." He shook his head. "I don't have you yet, but I will...soon." The bone in his shaft from his beast would keep him erect for hours if necessary. Arctos had a feeling it would take that long to win Caitlin's affections.

Not affections, a little voice inside said. *Her love.*

Since when did finding a mate and falling in love need to go together? Arctos paused as he pulled out until only the tip of his shaft remained inside of her. His body shook as the truth struck. It meant *everything*. He couldn't true-mate with a woman who didn't love him.

Caitlin's hands moved to his thighs, gripping them tight as if she feared he would leave her teetering on the edge. He kissed her shoulder, making his way to the small of her neck. His teeth scrapped, dangerously sharp against her tender flesh. Arctos snapped his jaw shut as he realized what he'd been about to do.

He growled low in his throat, then lifted her to her knees, spreading her until her pink puffy sex was angled just right. Instead of entering her, he dropped to his hands and licked her from bottom to top. Caitlin trembled and her arms gave out, leaving the lower half of her body thrust high into the air. Her juices ran down his chin as Arctos continued to feast.

"I will never get enough of the taste of you." He held her so his mouth and tongue could explore her thoroughly.

Caitlin's thighs quivered and she mewed into the pillow, gripping it tight. She didn't try to pull away as he devoured her swollen flesh. When she trembled, Arctos doubled his efforts. He plunged his tongue deep inside her channel and latched onto her clit at the same time. Caitlin screamed, her whole body convulsing as her release rocked her.

Arctos wasn't nearly finished, but he sensed her exhaustion. He lapped her folds tenderly while the tremors shook her, catching the last of her moisture on his tongue. When her breathing returned to normal, Arctos positioned himself at her entrance. This time he didn't hold back. He wanted to mark her, needed to mark her. He thrust hard, his entrance eased by a flood of wetness. Each stroke glided easily in and out of her as her body opened to accept his relentless invasion.

He held her waist, pulling her back to meet his demanding thrusts. Arctos felt his balls draw up. His breathing grew ragged as his release neared. Caitlin bucked and her body clamped down on him. The frantic pace Arctos was setting faltered. He wouldn't last much longer. Light flashed behind his eyelids. He shuddered and lost all rhythm.

Her channel fluttered again, milking his shaft.

Arctos bellowed, his grip near crushing as he jerked her tight, holding her snug as his essence spilled inside of her.

* * * * *

A wall of heat incinerated Caitlin the second Arctos cried out. She felt herself shatter as his grip tightened and he lodged himself against her core, fusing them together. His scalding chest rested against her back as his big body jerked repeatedly, sending wave after wave of fresh warmth pulsing inside of her. She'd never felt anything like it. Arctos' climax seemed to go on forever.

It was several minutes before he eventually pulled out of her. He was still hard. He kissed her back, then licked the base of her neck. "Thank you," he said, his voice full of awe.

Caitlin rolled onto her back until they were staring eye to eye. "That was wow." She brushed his hair away from his face. "I'm sure you hear that a lot, but it's true."

His lips quirked. "I was inspired," he said, winking at her.

Caitlin laughed. She couldn't help it. "I don't know about you, but I could really use a shower." She thought about the bathroom situation and frowned.

"What's wrong?" he asked, searching her face.

"There isn't a shower in this cabin, only a bathtub. If I want a bath, I'll have to heat up snow."

Arctos grinned. "Is that all?"

"What do you mean is that all?" she asked, getting perturbed. He made it sound like it was no big deal, when she knew hauling snow would be a pain in the butt. Okay, so maybe it wasn't the snow that was really bothering her. Maybe it was the feelings that Arctos was stirring up inside of her.

"I'll fix you the bath that you desire." He rolled off the bed.

The instant lack of warmth from his body left her feeling

oddly ill at ease. Caitlin crossed her arms over her chest and looked around the room for her clothes. "It's going to take forever to heat that much snow," she said.

"Leave everything to me."

"You're crazy," she tossed back, gathering her things.

He winked again and something inside her chest fluttered wildly. "Trust me."

This couldn't be happening, she thought. Sex was sex. That's all. Even as the words flitted through her mind, Caitlin was loath to admit that they didn't ring true. She didn't trust men or relationships. Never had. So why did she want so desperately to trust Arctos?

Arctos came inside carrying the first of many pots of snow. He went back and forth so many times that it actually made her dizzy to watch. When he came in with the last pot, she pushed her way into the bathroom. Sure enough, the tub was overflowing with… snow.

"I don't mean to sound ungrateful, but shouldn't you heat that first?" She shivered at the thought of bathing in cold water.

He arched a brow. "I'm not finished yet. Could you please give me some room to work?" Arctos raised his hands. "On second thought, could you go into the other room and pour me another one of those cups of…what was the name of that dark brew you gave me at dinner?"

"Coffee?"

His face brightened. "Yes, that's it."

Caitlin snorted. "Fine, I'll be right back."

* * * * *

Arctos waited to make sure Caitlin was gone. When he was sure that she'd wandered into the other room, he walked into the bedroom and grabbed his weapon. He strolled back into the bathroom, then adjusted the laser so it wouldn't sear a hole in the tub. He aimed the beam at the snow and fired.

Within seconds the snow melted and the water began to steam. He leaned down to check the temperature. Satisfied, he put the pistol away and waited.

Caitlin came back into the bathroom a couple of minutes later, carrying two mugs of coffee. She nearly dropped them both when her gaze landed on the tub of steaming water. "How did you? What did you?" She put the cups down on the small table that held the basin and rushed forward, shoving Arctos out of the way. She hesitated, then dipped her fingers into the tub and sighed.

"I—" was all he managed to get out before she kissed him, cutting off his words.

"Right now, I don't care how you did it." Caitlin shrugged out of her clothes once more.

The sight of her naked had Arctos' shaft stiffening again. His whole body tensed when she bent over to swoosh the water around. He swallowed hard and took a step back to give her room. He had no doubt given her tightness that she was sore from their earlier encounter. The warm water would go a long way toward soothing her inner muscles. Goddess how he wanted her. If she'd let him, he'd take her right here, right now.

Arctos forced himself to move. It was either that or join her. The thought was tempting, beyond tempting. He focused instead on the coffee cup. He picked it up and took a sip. The hot liquid rushed down his throat, searing his chest, but did nothing to ease the need building inside of him.

"I'm going to go check on the fire," he said, clearing his suddenly dry throat.

Caitlin sighed as she sank into the tub. She closed her eyes and dropped down until the water reached her chin. Arctos stood mesmerized, unable to look away. She cracked one eye open.

"I thought you were going to check on the fire?" she asked.

He straightened. "Yes, the fire. I'll be back in a little

while. Enjoy your bath."
"Oh, I will," she said, closing her eyes once more.

* * * * *

CHAPTER FIVE

Caitlin had been soaking for several minutes when the panic over what she'd done set in. How could she have slept with a stranger in this day and age? She'd obviously lost her mind, along with her panties. The fact that Arctos acted like a perfect gentleman only made matters worse. She was used to jerks or at least guys who were only interested in a good time.

Despite his amazing looks that didn't seem to be Arctos' style. He'd said he wanted her. He'd fought a bear to protect her. And no matter how much Caitlin hated to admit it, she was monogamous by nature. That didn't mean she believed in forever or happily-ever-after. Far from it. But it did mean she wasn't used to falling into bed with men that she'd just met. It was one of the reasons she'd never considered sleeping with Michael.

She dipped down deeper into the water until it covered her mouth. The warmth soaked into her bones, relieving some of the soreness that came from a fabulous bout of lovemaking. Caitlin paused as the thought popped into her mind. She wanted to discount it outright, turn it into lust-filled sex, but that would be a lie.

Sure, there'd been lust involved. That was how they'd ended up naked in the first place, but sometime during the act something had changed. Warmth pulsed through her, spreading to her limbs.

Caitlin quickly squashed it like a bug. That way led to unhappiness. She wasn't about to ruin the moment with regrets. She took a deep breath and sank below the surface, letting the water swallow her whole. She was down there staring at the surface, when a familiar face came into view.

Arctos reached into the water and pulled her up. A frown furrowed his pale brow. "What are you doing? You cannot breathe in that environment."

She swished a hand over her face to get the water out of her eyes. "I was thinking," she said.

"Under the liquid?" he asked, confusion clearly visible upon his face.

"Yes, I do my best thinking while I'm underwater. It allows me to tune out the rest of the world."

"The fire has been fed." He proceeded to strip off his clothes.

"What are you doing?" she asked, her eyes growing rounder by the second.

He halted mid-motion. "Joining you," he said as if that should be blatantly obvious.

"I don't think that's such a good idea," Caitlin said.

Arctos slipped in behind her and pulled her against his chest. His large hands stroked her stomach, making lazy circles. It didn't take long for the flames inside her to flare once more. Caitlin dropped her head back, resting it upon his shoulder. Arctos' fingers glided over her wet skin until they rested beneath her small breasts. He cupped the mounds a second later and began to knead, carefully avoiding her nipples.

Caitlin moaned. "Okay, you can stay."

"Thank you," he said, muffling what could've been laughter with a kiss to her shoulder. His mouth skated across her skin, coming to rest at the base of her neck. Arctos nibbled until she arched her back, shoving her breasts more firmly into his hands.

He squeezed, tugging at her nipples until they grew tender and rigid.

"Yes," she hissed.

He lapped at the base of her neck, while continuing to torture her breasts. He let go of one side and slipped his arm around her waist. Amazingly, he lifted her one-handed, until her opening rested above his hard shaft, then slowly released her, allowing her weight to carry her down.

Caitlin sank down onto him, feeling him fill her inch-by-inch. She bit her lip as her body opened to accept him. Arctos waited until she was fully seated, then grasped her by the waist and lifted her again. She slipped over his turgid flesh, her tender channel stretching to accommodate his wide girth.

"You are perfect in every way," he said, kissing her and laving her neck like someone had dumped melted chocolate onto her skin.

His rough tongue made gooseflesh rise on her arms, but it was quickly dispersed as he allowed her to sink into the warm water. Arctos' chest rumbled as he guided her up and down, each time making her body take him deeper and deeper.

"Arctos," she gasped.

"What do you want, my Cat?" he asked, nipping her ear.

She ground her hips against him as water splashed over the sides of the tub. "You," she said, repeating the movement.

"That you can have whenever you desire," he said. Arctos' hands clamped onto her sides and he picked up the rhythm, shafting her until Caitlin couldn't remember why this was such a bad idea.

One hand found her clit. She fought for breath as her body tightened, reaching the breaking point. Arctos continued his sensual assault, until she couldn't take another second.

"I'm…I'm." Caitlin shattered, her strangled cry filling the small space.

Arctos continued to pet the crisp curls that covered her mound as she rode out her climax. When the shudders quieted, he leaned her over the rim of the tub and rose up behind her.

"You okay?" he asked.

"Yes," she murmured.

"Good." He grasped her hands. His fingers twined with hers a second before he entered her.

Primal grunts filled her ears as he drove into her body. Each joining seemed more demanding, more feral than the last. Everywhere he touched, everywhere he tasted, a sting of pleasure-pain lingered. Like a man possessed, he took her, branding her flesh with his insatiable passion.

At this rate, Caitlin would never get enough of him.

Water splashed onto the wooden floor with each hard thrust. The delicious fragrance of his skin surrounded her, enveloped her, until she was drowning in his male essence. Caitlin couldn't smell anything but him. Her channel clamped down hard as another orgasm took her by surprise. He groaned once, twice, then stiffened behind her as he found his own release.

Arctos placed kisses along her spine. When he reached her waist, he pulled out of her. Once again Caitlin was left feeling empty. This time the ache from his sudden absence was far worse. He made no attempt to leave the tub. Instead, he dropped down onto his hands and knees, parted her cheeks, and lapped at her swollen folds.

His chest rumbled in what sounded like a gruff purr. "Your taste, your sweet musky scent is maddening. I can't seem to get enough. Every time I look at you, you make me hard."

Caitlin gripped the side of the tub, her body torn between

pleasure and exhaustion. Tired won out. "Let's wait a while. I need to get my second wind."

"Of course." Arctos licked her one more time, swirling his tongue around her entrance, then climbed out of the now cooling water. A rough towel appeared in his hands and he held it out for her to step into. Caitlin did and nearly collapsed as he began to dry her.

"You need rest," he said. "Forgive me for being so demanding. Where you are concerned, I cannot help myself."

She laughed and stepped out of the circle of his arms. "You're not alone." Caitlin found her long underwear and put it on. It may not be sexy, but it was warm. The second Arctos slipped into bed beside her, she realized that she shouldn't have bothered with the clothes. His body radiated enough heat to shame an electric blanket.

"Get some sleep," he said, kissing her tenderly. "We'll talk in the morning."

* * * * *

Caitlin woke to falling snow. She was snuggled under the blankets, but Arctos was nowhere to be found. She frowned and looked around the room. Everything was as she remembered. Was it all a dream?

She shifted, feeling the aches that could only come from mind-blowing, body-melting sex. No, not sex. *Love.* Every tender kiss, every fevered touch came rushing back. Caitlin sighed, resting her forearm over her eyes. What had she done?

The cold light of day highlighted some harsh realities. She needed to set Arctos straight before he got any crazy ideas that this was anything serious. Pain radiated from her chest. This couldn't be happening.

"You of all people should know better," she chastised, then swung her feet over the edge of the bed and got dressed.

Caitlin searched the cabin, but Arctos was nowhere to be found. For a second, fear overwhelmed her. Had he left her here all alone? Even as the thought filled her mind, she knew in her heart that he'd never do anything like that. *He's probably out gathering more wood*. Yes, that made more sense.

She picked up the rabbits he'd caught the night before and did her best to prepare and cook them. Not exactly her ideal breakfast, but it beat the heck out of starving. The rabbits were stewing away over the fire, when Caitlin heard the first rumble outside. "Arctos?"

There was no answer.

It would've been so easy to ignore the noise, except the sound came again. This time it was answered by another and another. Caitlin tiptoed across the room and glanced out the window. She counted five polar bears before fear took over and she moved away. Their little haven was surrounded. Her gaze shot to the rabbits cooking over the fire. They'd smelled the food. Even as the thought entered her mind, she was already searching for a weapon.

They hadn't tried to break in yet, but Caitlin knew it was only a matter of time. She shoved one of the chairs in front of the door, then snatched the poker out of the fire and stood back. Where was Arctos?

She glanced at the bubbling pot. Should she toss the rabbits outside? Would that make the polar bears go away? Unfortunately, that would require opening the door.

Caitlin didn't think that was such a good idea given the circumstances. She glanced around the sparse cabin. Other than the small window in the bathroom, which a greased squirrel couldn't fit through, and the one facing the front, there was no other way of escape.

It made perfect sense given the cabin's purpose, but was of little help now. If she could just hold them off until Arctos returned… The crazy thought entered her mind, then was quickly dismissed. What could he do? It was one thing to scare away a single polar bear. Quite another to chase away five. She scanned the rafters. The ceiling was a crude pitched design that didn't hold any beams. So there was no way she could climb up and hide.

There was a loud snuffle at the door. Caitlin took a step back. Acting on autopilot, she grabbed her backpack and fumbled for her phone. She punched in a number that she knew by heart. It rang and rang, then eventually Allie picked up.

"Allie," she whispered, even though there was no doubt that the bears could hear every word.

"Caitlin? Why are you whispering?" She sounded sleepy and somewhat out of it.

"I'm whispering because I am surrounded by polar bears and I think I'm going to die." In that moment, all Caitlin wanted to do was see Arctos one more time.

"What?" Allie shouted.

"They smelled the food. I didn't think…Oh God, there's nowhere to hide." Caitlin whimpered as sharp claws raked the outside of the door.

"I'm coming," Allie said. "Just stay on the line, so they can trace your phone."

"It's too late for that," Caitlin said as the clawing grew in volume.

"Don't say that." Allie sniffled. "Where's Arctos?"

Tears welled in Caitlin's eyes. "I don't know. When I woke up, he was gone."

"I love you, Cat" Allie said, no longer trying to hide her crying.

"I love you, too," she replied.

"Just hang in there. Help is on the way."

Caitlin hung up. The last thing she wanted was for her friend to hear her die. Where was Arctos? Something hit the door—hard. She screamed. There was another loud thud and the wood cracked. Caitlin grabbed a kitchen knife to go along with the poker and backed into a corner. She wasn't going down without a fight.

* * * * *

Arctos heard Caitlin scream. He'd been out hunting so they'd have enough food to ride out the snowstorm. His blood chilled in his veins, when he scented the air and caught the musk of several bears. Before he had time to think, Arctos took off running. His mate was in danger. He'd left her unprotected. If anything happened to her…

He reached the cabin in time to see the first polar bear break down the door. Arctos' bellow of anger filled the air a second before his bones and muscles twisted, giving way to his beast. He charged the cabin, knocking the other polar bears aside as he hit the male who'd gained entry.

Arctos tackled the bear, clamping onto his sides, pulling him back until he tumbled out the door. They fought, clashing as only beasts can battle over territory. He bit, scratched, and clawed at the male all while sensing Caitlin's unbridled fear. If he could sense that, then it meant she was still alive. His relief was short-lived.

The other bears fought to get past him, each lured by the promise of food. Arctos fought valiantly, disappearing and attacking, as only a Phantom Warrior could. He eventually chased the bears off, but at great personal cost.

Exhausted and bleeding heavily, Arctos collapsed onto the snow, his limbs twitching from the battle. His body shifted back into human form in an attempt to seal the wounds. It didn't work. Warmth trickled down his side and wetness covered his chest. His lungs burned as he gasped for air. At least he would die with honor, having successfully defended his mate.

What felt like an eternity later, Caitlin appeared. The color leached from her face and moisture filled her stormy eyes as she stared at him. "You're hurt. Bad," she said, glancing at his mangled body. "They even tore off your clothes."

Hot, fat, salty drops hit his face as she bent over him. "I'll live," Arctos said, unsure if he spoke the truth.

Her gaze darted around the clearing. "We need to get you inside in case they come back. Help is on the way, so hang on."

Arctos heard her, but her words made no sense. The Phantom ship wouldn't be here for another day. So how could assistance be coming?

Caitlin put her hands beneath his shoulders. "You have to help me. I can't lift you."

He did what he could, but the intense pain hampered his movements. "Just leave me," he said.

"If I leave you, they'll come back and eat you. Even if they don't, it's below zero. You'll freeze to death," she said, sniffing loudly. "I'm not going to let that happen."

Arctos wouldn't freeze to death, but he couldn't tell Caitlin that, she was already distraught. It was more likely that he'd bleed to death. He didn't think she'd take that news any better, so he tried to rise, only to stumble back into the snow.

"Come on," she goaded. "You're not going to let a little scratch keep you down, are you?"

He glanced at his shredded chest. Scratch? Had the woman lost her mind? Arctos gritted his teeth and tried again, wobbling from side to side. His legs didn't want to work. He forced one foot in front of the other. Caitlin shouldered much of his substantial weight and guided him toward the broken door, up the stairs, and into the cabin. She shut the door the best she could, then dropped him into the nearest chair.

"Don't move. I'll be right back," she said.

* * * * *

Arctos awoke on the bed with covers tossed over his

waist. He blinked and looked around, trying to recall how he'd gotten there. It was then that he noticed Caitlin quietly sitting in the corner. She had pulled one of the kitchen chairs into the room. Her legs were tucked against her chin and she held the same weapon he'd seen her point at the bears. She hit a button and several clicks filled the air. Arctos glanced down, expecting pain, but saw only fresh bandages.

"What are you doing?" he asked in confusion. His memory was coming back quickly. He recalled the fear that had clutched him the second he'd heard her scream. The frantic race back to the cabin only to find it surrounded by bears. Then the brutal fight to protect his mate.

Caitlin didn't immediately answer, her gaze drawn instead to something on the weapon. Arctos winced when he tried to sit up.

The sound caught her attention. "You should lie still. Don't want to reopen those wounds." She raised the weapon again and fired. A flurry of clicks later, she stared once more at the back of the weapon.

He'd left her rifle. Now he was thinking he should've left this weapon behind, too, since she seemed determined to shoot him with it. Arctos ran a hand through his hair and inhaled. Her scent, though sweet, held a tinge of sourness. She was scared and angry. The fear he could understand, but not the anger. He scanned her from head to feet. She didn't appear to have any injuries.

"What are you looking for on that screen?" he asked, watching her closely.

"Did you know that I found you lying in the snow naked and bleeding?" she asked instead.

Arctos' mind raced for an explanation, but came up blank, so he said nothing.

She pointed the weapon at his face and shot. "You know," she said. "When we first met, I asked you how you were able to get away from the polar bear. You said something like 'I challenged it'. Even though I knew the odds of that happening was unlikely, I gave you the benefit of the doubt."

"I spoke the truth," he said, as tension caused his muscles to go rigid.

"Yes, you did…you just didn't tell the whole truth," she said softly, her face going pale. "Did you?"

Arctos swallowed hard. "What are you looking for?" he asked again.

"The bear," she said without inflection. "It has to be here somewhere."

Silence filled the space until it became hard to breathe due to the building pressure. They stared, gazes locked, each one measuring the other. Eventually Caitlin took a deep breath and let it out slowly, then asked, "What are you?"

And there it was the question that Arctos had hoped to avoid for a little while longer. At least until he'd completed the bond. He'd hoped to give Caitlin more time. Hoped that if they spent enough hours together that she too would see that they were meant to be together. But his time had run out and Arctos knew it. He stared at Caitlin. Was she ready to hear the truth?

His hearts clenched. He somehow doubted it. "Please put the weapon down," he said, carefully. "It is not necessary."

Caitlin frowned. "What are you talking about?"

He pointed to the thing in her hands.

She laughed, but the hollow sound held no humor. She lifted the object. "This isn't a weapon. It's a camera."

His brow furrowed.

"I use it to capture images," she said. "Tell me the truth, Arctos."

He sighed. "As you have already surmised, I am not from here," he said.

Caitlin shrugged. "I'm not from Alaska either."

He shook his head. "I'm not talking about Alaska, my Cat."

"Don't call me that," she said, putting the camera aside so

she could wrap her arms around her knees in an attempt to distance herself.

Arctos searched for the right words, but there didn't seem to be a good way of telling her that he was a species from another planet, so he blurted out the news. "I'm not from Earth."

Color rose in her cheeks and she straightened in her chair. "What do you mean you're not from *Earth*? You have to be. Where else could you come from?"

"You know, my Cat, or you wouldn't have asked me what I am. Something in you senses my Otherness, even if you're not ready to face the truth."

Caitlin dropped her feet to the ground and climbed out of the chair. "That's crazy. You're crazy. Allie was right." She hugged herself and began to pace.

"I am not insane. You would not have given me the gift of your body had you truly believed that to be the case," he said.

* * * * *

Oh my god, I slept with an alien!
Caitlin thought her head was about to explode. The pressure in her temples throbbed out a steady beat, promising to blossom into a migraine. No matter how she analyzed his words, they just didn't make sense. There was no such thing as aliens, so how could Arctos be from another planet? Scientist couldn't even agree if alien bacteria from Mars existed and he was telling her that he was a little green man.

She glanced at him. He didn't look green or gray for that matter. His pale skin was flushed with blood and his dark eyes were rimmed with red. Why would he make something like this up? Logic told her that he wouldn't…unless he was crazy. He hadn't seemed crazy. A little odd, maybe, but not insane.

Caitlin stopped and pinned him to the bed with her gaze, when he threatened to get up. "You cannot just say that you're an alien and expect me to believe it. You have to know how that is going to sound."

"I do," he said quietly, almost as if he were trying to stay calm so that she wouldn't go into hysterics. Well, it was too late for that. She was freaked out. Big time.

Caitlin thought about the bears that had attacked the cabin. She'd been too afraid to glance out the window until silence reigned. One minute she saw a polar bear, panting and bleeding, the next she saw Arctos lying in the snow naked. It had to be snow blindness or maybe it was some kind of brain freeze. Yeah, that made more sense than the fantastical. She began to pace again.

"What about the bear?" she asked. "How do you explain that?"

"You are referring to my beast," he said, as if to make sure he understood her correctly.

She stopped. "Your what?"

"The creature you mistook for another polar bear is actually my beast. My other half. It rests inside of me and is as much who am as the man you've lain with," he said.

"Are you telling me that I slept with an animal?" Before he could answer she blurted, "I think I'm going to be sick." Caitlin rushed into the bathroom and pulled up the lid on the port o' potty. Her stomach lurched and she proceeded to throw up until nothing came out. Trembling and in shock, she turned to the washbasin and splashed some freezing water from the melted snow over her face, rinsing out her mouth at the same time. It took a few minutes before she was composed enough to return to the room.

Arctos' face flushed with fury. Gone was the warmth and understanding that had been simmering in his brown eyes. Blood red irises now stared at her. His jaw clenched and unclenched. He opened and closed his mouth several times as if to speak, but anger halted his tongue.

Caitlin took a step back.

He exhaled, which sounded more like a snort than a breath, then rose. Blood seeped through the bandages, but Arctos didn't seem to notice. His gaze was riveted on her. "I am a Phantom Warrior from the planet Zaron. Like all Phantom people, I carry a beast inside of me. The beast is part of me, not a separate entity. We are one and the same," he said through teeth that appeared sharper than they had only moments ago.

Caitlin took a breath. He growled, his red eyes flashed in warning, when she thought about interrupting.

"You did not sleep with an animal, when you laid beneath me. You surrendered to me and only me. And whether you like it or not, you are my mate," he ground out, not looking at all happy with the idea.

The film snapped inside Caitlin's head. "I can't be your mate. I'm not anyone's mate nor will I ever be. If that's what you were looking for, you should've pursued Allie."

Arctos shook his head. "You do not understand," he said, taking a step closer.

She took a step back and held up her hands.

He stopped. Pain flashed across his face before his expression became unreadable. "I had no choice in the matter. You were dying. I couldn't allow that to happen." Arctos fell back onto the bed and his chin dropped to his chest.

"What do you mean I was dying?" Caitlin touched her side.

He looked at her, guilt shadowing his eyes. "I wasn't fast enough. I didn't reach you in time."

She shook her head in denial. "It's just a scratch." Panic welled inside of her.

Arctos glanced at her. "You were bleeding to death. I had no choice."

Caitlin's heart hit her ribs, sending pain crashing through her chest. "What did you do?"

This time when he met her gaze, his didn't waver. "I bonded my essence to yours." His voice cracked. "It was the only way to save you. Not that it matters. The Goddess decided our fate long before we met."

"I don't believe in bonds or fate. And I certainly don't believe in destined love," Caitlin said, even though it hurt her to do so. She wasn't ready to admit how much Arctos had gotten under her skin. Now she wasn't sure that she'd ever be. What had started out as a wild night had turned into something altogether different and it scared her to death.

Arctos looked at her, pity shimmering in his eyes. "Where I am from, there is no other kind of love. When you have so few women, you learn to cherish each and every one of them."

It hurt to look at him. Arctos was laying himself bare and asking her to do the same. Caitlin couldn't do it, even if she wanted to. She'd spent her whole childhood being shuffled from house to house. Change was the only thing *permanent* that she could count on. Love was fleeting, not ever-lasting.

"I don't believe you," she said, hoping to push him away.

Arctos rose, not at all concerned with his nudity. One second he was standing by the bed, the next his image shimmered and a bear appeared. Caitlin screamed and wedged herself in the corner. The bear didn't move, but still managed to take up a big part of the room.

No, not a bear. Arctos.

Caitlin had been so spooked by his appearance earlier that she hadn't really *looked* at him. Now that she did, she realized the creature had the same red eyes of her lover. She paused. Since when did she think of Arctos as her lover? She tucked the thought away.

"It's really you, isn't it?" She took a small step forward.

The creature bobbed its head, then shimmered into nothingness.

Caitlin gasped, then searched the room. Arctos and the bear were gone. Where? Warm hands slipped around her waist and pulled her against a hard chest. She squealed. "How did you?" was all Caitlin got out before she noticed it wasn't just his chest that was hard.

Arctos rocked his hips, his shaft gliding over her bottom. He kissed her neck, then nibbled on her earlobe.

"You're hurt. Remember?"

"Not anymore," he said, nuzzling her.

"I don't know if I can handle this," she said.

"You are stronger than you think," he countered.

Caitlin bit her lip and closed her eyes as sensation shot through her. "What do you want from me?"

"Everything," he murmured, holding her tight.

Before she could wiggle around to look at him, he latched onto her neck, his sharp teeth breaking the skin. Moisture trickled down her back and the sweet copper aroma of blood filled the air. Caitlin struggled to get away. Arctos growled deep in his chest and she instantly stopped moving. A second later, she heard him swallow.

He's drinking my blood. Why am I not freaking out?

The shaft at her back seemed to grow impossibly larger. He slid his hands up her body and cupped her small breasts. This time there was no gentle touches. Gone was the man. All that remained was the beast.

The pain from the bite quickly melted into pleasure as Arctos lapped at the spot. One hand left her nipple and slid between her thighs. Caitlin whimpered as he pressed two fingers against her sex.

"You are mine," he said in a guttural voice that she hardly recognized.

"You're making a mistake," she murmured.

"No mistake," he said.

The metallic glide of a zipper reached her ears. A moment later, he shoved his hand down her pants and gripped her sex, her very moist, very swollen, totally turned on sex. His thumb quickly found her clit and savaged it, while his fingers filled her.

Caitlin's hips bucked and she moaned. "We should talk about this some more," she said. "You can't just drop something like this on me and expect everything to be okay."

"No more talk," he grumbled.

There were all kinds of reasons that this was a bad idea, but for the life of her, Caitlin couldn't think of a single one. Her mind remained focused on what Arctos was doing to her body. Like a woman possessed, she rode his thick fingers. He didn't let up. Never let her catch her breath. Arctos continued to push her until she didn't think she could take another minute.

He pressed down on her clit and she writhed in his arms, throwing her chest out. Her bottom slammed against his rigid shaft. Arctos grunted, but continued ravishing her. Out of control and half out of her mind, Caitlin tumbled over the edge.

* * * * *

Arctos kept his fingers buried inside her and his thumb pressed against the core of her pleasure. He wanted her to admit the truth. The truth he could smell upon her skin. She wanted him. More than wanted him. Caitlin cared about him. He saw the pain in her eyes, when she'd leaned over his still form in the snow. There'd been real fear there and more than a little concern. It had flooded his nostrils until he could smell nothing else.

If he had to, he would fuck Caitlin into submission.

Now that he'd completed the bond, Arctos wasn't about to let her go without a fight. She would learn that soon enough. He kept his hand inside her pants and guided Caitlin over to the bed. There he quickly stripped her out of her clothes and slipped between her parted thighs. He was hard enough to drive a hole through an airlock.

"Caitlin," he said.

She didn't respond, only continued to pant as shudders

wracked her body.

"Open your eyes, my Cat," he said, palming her wet sex once more.

Caitlin squirmed. "I can't," she said, swallowing hard.

"You can and you will." Arctos slipped an inch inside of her.

Her lids shot open and her hips rose encouragingly. He pushed in another inch and felt her velvet sheath embrace him.

Arctos hid his smile. "You are mine, Caitlin Kelly," he said, using her given name for the first time.

She shook her head in denial.

"It would be easier on us both, if you simply admitted the truth," he said, sliding a little further, but not nearly far enough.

Caitlin met his gaze and rolled her hips.

Arctos kept himself still, even though it hurt to do so. "Not so fast," he said. "Not until you admit it."

"There's nothing to admit," she said.

He did grin then. "You are a very stubborn woman. I look forward to breaking you of this bad habit." He teased her with his hard length, then quickly pulled back out.

"Hey, not fair," she said.

He kissed her. "I am a Phantom Warrior at war for a mate. I am fighting to win. Fair is not part of the strategy."

Caitlin reached between their bodies and clasped his shaft. The breath left Arctos' lungs. "Okay," she said. "I'm good with fighting dirty." She stroked his length to prove her point.

Arctos trembled. "It's never smart to tease the beast," he rasped, feeling his Other self rise behind his eyes.

"I'll take my chances."

* * * * *

The spot on Caitlin's neck itched where Arctos had bit

her. Her skin felt too tight for her bones and far too sensitive. The aroma that she'd always been drawn to seemed to intensify, filling the room until she smelled it with every breath. Even though she'd just had one of the most amazing orgasm, her channel felt empty and she actually ached to have it filled. That had never happened before. Ever.

His shaft slipped free of her grasp. She clutched his back to keep him in place, her short nails digging into his skin. "What did you do to me? I want...I need..." Her back bowed.

Instead of answering, he pounced on the nearest nipple and sucked. Heat started at Caitlin's breast and spread like a wildfire through her body. She'd never been this turned on in her life. Was it the brush with death or something else?

Arctos made little growling noises in the back of his throat as he pleasured her. He used his lips, teeth, and tongue to torture the swollen flesh. Every pull of his mouth was answered by growing throb between her legs. It was like his lips had a direct line to her clit.

Caitlin's grip tightened. The sound he was making increased in volume. It was then that she realized he wasn't actually growling. He was chanting the same word over and over. Ignoring the riot taking place inside her, she listened closely.

"Mine. Mine. Mine," he repeated like it was his own personal mantra.

Her heart leapt, then began to race. No one had ever wanted her like this. Sure, Michael had been interested in dating her and he'd certainly hinted at wanting more, but he'd never aggressively pursued her. Caitlin was pretty sure that if she'd told him that she wasn't interested, he'd have been upset for an hour or two, then would've quickly moved on. No looking back. No second thoughts. Not so with this man...beast...alien...whatever.

Arctos released her nipple after giving it one last lick, then latched onto the other. He held the lower half of his body just out of reach of her seeking hands. It was beyond frustrating. "Why are you doing this?" she asked.

He looked up at her from beneath heavy lids and slowly blinked. The sheer determination on his brutally handsome face should've scared her to death, but somehow it didn't. Instead, it fueled the fire burning inside of her. Caitlin dug her heels into his bottom and jerked him forward.

Arctos' weight came down upon her. Caitlin gasped, relishing the feel of his hard shaft brushing against her, but it wasn't enough. She wiggled until he was notched against her clit. A fresh gush of moisture flooded her channel. His nostrils flared. This time Arctos did growl, sending vibrations through her nipple, before the sound spread through the rest of her body.

The grip she had on his back tightened. There was a tearing sensation followed by a warm trickle of moisture. Caitlin yanked her hands away, only to find them slippery with blood. "Oh my god!" She tried to push Arctos off her, but he refused to budge. "You need to move. I think I've re-opened your wounds." She stared at her hands in horror.

Arctos smiled at her.

"What's the matter with you? Why are you smiling? This is serious. They could become infected," she said as her lust-soaked brain tried desperately to switch gears.

"I am smiling because you've marked me," he said.

"I did no such thing." Caitlin stared at her short—okay not so short—nails as if she'd never seen them before. There were crescents of red beneath each one and they were longer than before. When had they grown? "You need to get up so I can put more salve on."

His grin grew and he slowly shook his head. "I am not finished with you yet. I'm not going anywhere until you admit that you're mine," he said.

"Then we're going to be here a long time," she said tartly.

This time when Arctos smiled, he didn't bother to hide

his very sharp, very white teeth. "I sincerely hope so."

Caitlin balked. This was crazy. This whole situation was crazy. Maybe she was lying in the snow dying. That would explain the bear hallucinations and the whole invisibility trick.

"I'd be more than happy to thaw you out." His eyes sparkled in amusement.

"How did you? Wait, what? Did you read my mind?" she asked, completely flabbergasted and utterly horrified at the thought. The last thing she wanted was for him traipsing around in her brain. There were things in there she didn't want him to see. Things that she wasn't ready to face yet.

"Yes," he said unrepentantly. "Though I must say that it would've been easy enough to do by your expression alone."

"How?" she asked, not really sure she wanted the answer.

"You are my mate. I have marked you as such. Just as you have marked me," he said. "Soon you will be able to do the same."

"That was an accident. I didn't mean to scratch you," she said.

He arched a pale brow. "Didn't you?"

Caitlin opened her mouth, then closed it quickly. Had she meant to somehow mark him? It didn't seem likely, yet she couldn't deny the urge had been there.

"Enough! You're thinking too much, when you should be feeling." Arctos surged inside of her.

Caitlin's thoughts exploded, leaving only sensation behind. This was what her body wanted, needed. A man filling her. No, not *a* man—Arctos. Only he could take her to such heights, wring every last drop of pleasure out of her, and still leave her panting for more. Of course, she'd never tell him so.

His lips quirked.

Too late, he already heard. She stuck out her tongue, only to have him capture it with his lips. He sucked it into his mouth, daring her to play. And play she did. Caitlin wrapped her arms around him, pulling his big body against hers, so she could deepen the embrace.

Lips and teeth collided in a battle for supremacy. She chased Arctos' tongue with her own, swirling and dipping, laving and flicking. It wasn't enough. She wanted more. Her hips rose to meet his next thrust, fusing them so tight she thought they might never be separated. Each stroke plunged deeper and harder until she felt him touch the wall around her heart.

Arctos' expression turned to one of sheer determination.

* * * * *

He was so close he could feel it. Arctos continued to ride her body, demanding without words her acceptance. She was cracking. He could hear it in her thoughts, see it in her face. His hips bucked wildly. He'd never been so hard in his life. Already Caitlin's scent was changing. It was still sweet, but becoming more like his own.

She closed her eyes and threw her head back, gasping for air.

Arctos saw his chance. He closed his eyes and morphed his form, passing straight through her. The first time he'd done it to save her life. This time was to solidify their bond. He flipped Caitlin over before her brain could process what had happened and impaled her on his throbbing shaft. Her eyes flew open in surprise as she straddled his waist.

"I'm yours," he said. "Take me."

She hesitated, but for a moment, then rose to her knees and dropped back down. Arctos reached up to play with her pert nipples. The heavily engorged nubs called to him. He leaned forward to pop one into his mouth. He loved the feel of the rigid flesh against his palate. He couldn't seem to get enough of the taste of her. Arctos doubted he ever would.

Caitlin pushed him onto his back, forcing him to release her. Arctos scowled playfully, then switched his attention to her sex where it remained locked. From this angle, he could see his shaft sinking inch by inch into her wet channel. Every time she rose, it came out covered in her sweet dew. Caitlin ground her hips against him, eliciting a groan.

"Like that, do you?" she asked.

"You know I do," he said, licking his suddenly dry lips. He should've let her take him like this sooner. From this angle, Arctos could see everything—her sex, his shaft, her swollen breasts, and best of all her eyes. The light gray now held a ring of red. He'd never seen anything more beautiful in his life.

He tried to keep his hands to his sides, but with every bounce she was becoming more feral. His beast had scented her. To him, she smelled like a female in heat. And in a way she was. Caitlin was changing rapidly and she didn't even know it yet.

Her face flushed and her body lost rhythm as she neared her release. Arctos found the hidden bundle of nerves, now fully engorged with blood, and began to slowly stroke it. The pace was maddening, he knew. Caitlin jerked, nearly slipping off him. One hand found her waist, while the other continued the pleasurable torture.

"You are mine," he snarled.

"No," she snapped back, her voice lower and far more guttural than it had been earlier.

"Yes, you are and I'll prove it," he said, keeping her on a razor's edge.

She bit her lip, drawing blood, and tried to find release with his fingers, but Arctos denied her. She whimpered.

"What was that, mate? I didn't hear you."

"Don't make me beg. I need…"

He pressed down on her clit. "I know what you need, but I need something first." Arctos knew he wasn't playing fair. He'd warned her that he wouldn't. Not when so much was riding on his success. She had to face the truth. She had to accept him for who and what he was.

"What? Just tell me what you want me to say," she said, grinding her hips on him. Already her nails were lengthening, along with her teeth. Soon she'd have trouble speaking.

He wanted her to tell him that she loved him. That they were meant to be together. Arctos knew he'd have to settle for the latter, since Caitlin wasn't ready to face her emotions yet. "Admit that you're my mate and I'll help you find release."

Caitlin cupped her hands over her breasts and began to play with her nipples. Arctos yanked them away.

"No, you will not find release by your own hand. Not today," he said. His beast rose to the surface.

She snarled back at him, her eyes going ruby red.

The leash that held Arctos' beast snapped. He grabbed Caitlin by the waist and lifted her off his body, then quickly pinned her beneath him. Her soft back brushed his chest as she tried in vain to escape. His sharp teeth latched onto the base of her neck as he kneed her legs apart. With one thrust, he buried himself in her. Caitlin lashed out, trying to get free, but it was too late. He had her right where he wanted her.

She hadn't shifted yet, but it wouldn't be long now. He wanted her admission before she did so.

Arctos dominated her as only a Phantom Warrior from the Tooth Clan could do. He held her in place with his strong jaw and clamped his claws into her sides, then fucked her.

Two hours later, he was still drawing whimpers from her raw throat, while one release blurred into the next. Painfully hard, but more determined than ever, Arctos continued to work her body. "You're not done, are you?"

"Not again," she mewed. "I can't."

"You will," he said, building her toward another orgasm. It was then that Arctos felt her finally *submit*.

Caitlin's body went limp beneath him and she carefully tilted her head, baring even more of her throat. Arctos instantly released his grip on her neck and licked the spot where he'd bit down. Her grumbles turned to a strange sort of murmur. He sniffed the air to determine the cause. Pure unadulterated satiation filled his lungs.

"Mine," he said, kissing her shoulder.

"Yours," she repeated, softly.

Arctos brought her to climax, this time with a slow rolling boil, then finally sought his own release. He filled Caitlin's body with his essence, flooding her with what he hoped would become new life.

He had just slipped from her warm sheath, when a loud crash rocked the small cabin.

* * * * *

CHAPTER SIX

Caitlin fell out of bed at the sound of the door crashing in. The bears were back. Her brain went from replete to alert in seconds. She waited for the familiar slivers of fear to grip her, but they never materialized. Instead, a wall of anger slammed into her, demanding that she fight.

What was that all about?

Arctos was already moving. One minute he was behind her, the next he was gone. As far as she could tell, he was still naked.

More bangs followed. Caitlin jumped up and scrambled into her clothes. She wasn't about to let Arctos take on the polar bears by himself. Her fingertips burned as she rushed into the room ready to attack.

Caitlin didn't realize she was snarling until she saw Allie's startled face. What was she doing here? Where were the bears? It took her a second to remember that she'd phoned her friend, when she thought she was going to die. Allie must have had the police trace her phone. Well duh? How else could they have found her?

Her gaze moved to the rest of her rescuers. She didn't recognize any of the faces, except one. Mike stood in the doorway with a shotgun aimed at Arctos' bare chest.

"She doesn't look like she needs rescuing to me," he said. Mike's finger twitched above the trigger.

In her mind, Caitlin saw the gun go off and Arctos fall. She watched the life drain from his beautiful brown eyes. Pain ripped through her. She couldn't let it happen. He was hers.

"No!" she shouted. Caitlin didn't think. She reacted. With one leap, she crossed half the room and landed lightly in front of Arctos, her small body doing its best to block his larger one. She growled again, this time the rumble sounded like a pissed off wolf who'd just discovered her vocal cords.

Allie's face drained of color and she took a step back.

Caitlin's eyes locked on Mike. He hadn't moved an inch, but his expression had certainly shifted. Gone was the concern she'd spotted at first. It had slowly been replaced with…fear.

"Put the gun down," she snapped, taking a step closer. Her voice came out garbled.

Arctos grabbed her by the waist and gently shoved her behind him. Caitlin tried to push him out of the way, but it was like trying to move a tank. Her body seemed to have a mind of its own. One moment her teeth were short, the next they were long. The hair on her arms appeared to thicken, then thin. What in the world was happening to her?

"Arctos?" she said, hearing the distress in her voice.

He turned, gathering her close. "It's okay. Everything will be okay," he said.

Soothed by his touch, she melted into his body. "I don't understand," she said as tears filled her eyes.

* * * * *

Arctos would've taken a thousand gunshots over seeing Caitlin cry. Each tear ripped a hole in his hearts. If she kept this up, there'd be nothing left to beat inside of his chest. He glared at the people around them.

"Is she going to be okay?" Allie asked. "She doesn't look right."

He sighed. "She'll be fine. She just needs a moment to calm down and compose herself. We thought the bears had returned." Arctos had known it wasn't bears at the door. He'd smelled the stink of anxious sweat and the oil that had been used on the guns. His gaze shifted to the man, who'd very nearly shot him. So this was Mike. He'd snatched the name from Caitlin's jumbled thoughts, before panic overwhelmed her.

The man continued to glare at him. It probably didn't help that he hadn't bothered to clothe himself. Not that Arctos cared about nudity, but it was more than clear that this group did. Everyone, but Allie kept their gazes focused above his waist.

"Give us a minute." He guided Caitlin into the bedroom and shut the door behind them. The space smelled of sex, heat, and animal musk. Arctos sat her down on the bed, then kneeled in front of her. "Breathing helps control the shift," he said quietly, knowing that the others would try to listen in.

Her brow furrowed in confusion. "The what?"

He dropped his chin, resting his forehead against hers. "I'd hoped to be able to explain everything, but I fear I'm too late."

Caitlin's wary gaze met his. "Explain what?" *What else besides being an alien bear could there possibly be?*

Her thought slammed into his head. Arctos would've laughed if she hadn't looked so lost. "There's much more to being my mate than admitting it."

She sniffled. "Yeah, I kind of got that, when I leapt across the room. I've never been athletic and now I'm some kind of super hero."

He frowned. "I know not what that is," he said. "But you were amazing. Very brave...don't ever do that again. My hearts could not take the strain."

Caitlin grudgingly agreed. "You got it. Now tell me what's happening, so I can go out and explain it to the group."

Arctos paused. As much as he wanted to tell her everything, he couldn't allow Caitlin to reveal the truth. For one, he had no doubt that they wouldn't believe her. Two, it would jeopardize the entire Phantom mission to Earth.

"What's wrong?" she asked, watching him.

"Nothing," he said.

She smirked. "Yes, there is. Every time something's wrong, your lips thin and a small line appears between your eyebrows."

His eyes widened in surprise. This time Arctos did laugh. "I should've known that I'd never be able to deceive my Cat."

Caitlin's expression grew serious. "You shouldn't even try," she said, softly.

"You are right." He grabbed her hand and kissed her knuckles tenderly. "You have my vow that I'll never attempt to deceive you again. It was dishonorable of me to even try. Can you forgive me?"

* * * * *

Caitlin would've laughed, if he hadn't looked so utterly miserable…and adorable. His children would probably end up with that same expression if they were caught being naughty. She tried to imagine Arctos with kids. It was surprisingly easy to do.

She waited for panic to hit. It always did before when she thought about kids, family, and her future. This time peace settled in her bones, leaving no room for those antiquated thoughts.

"You're forgiven," she said.

His face instantly brightened. "Thank you," he said in all

sincerity. "Now, I'll make this quick. I've told you where I'm from and what I am."

She nodded slowly.

"I have spoken the truth," he said.

Her shoulders relaxed.

"But I have not told you everything."

Caitlin felt the muscles in her shoulders tense. "You're not married, are you?"

He grinned. "No, I would never have taken you as a mate, if I already had one."

"Good to know." She was amazed at how calm she sounded, when inside her emotions were rioting. Caitlin did her best to put out all the little fires, but eventually had to let them burn in order to keep her sanity.

"You asked me how you were able to leap across the room," he said.

She swallowed hard and nodded again.

"When a Phantom Warrior mates, we don't simply share our bodies and essence with a female," he said.

"You sleep with men, too?" she asked as panic reared its ugly head. Caitlin didn't think she could share Arctos with anyone.

"No," he said, his lips firming. "I have only lain with women. Men..." He paused as if searching for the right words. "Our males are very dominant. Most would be unable to submit to that kind of bond. It would be a constant battle for supremacy. Though it is quite common and accepted on Zaron within the Atlantean community."

"Atlantean? Like in Atlantis?" She shook her head. "Forget I asked."

"You are taking this situation remarkably well," he said.

Caitlin snorted. "Not really," she said. "If you want to know the truth, I'm screaming on the inside."

Concern clouded his eyes.

"Don't stop now," she said.

Arctos nodded. "When we shared our bodies this last

time, I bit you," he said.

She rubbed her neck. "Yeah, I remember."

"The bite transferred some of my beast essence into your body," he said, ducking his head. "It made passing through you again far easier."

"Again?" she asked.

"It's how I healed you the first time," he said.

"Okay, that explains how I got better, but it doesn't explain the whole beast thingie." Caitlin had a feeling she knew, but her brain steadfastly refused to process the thought.

"I needed to share more of my essence in order to complete the bond," Arctos said.

"So you bit me?"

He hesitated, then said, "Yes."

She thought about her burning fingers and the snarls coming from her when she'd burst into the other room. "What exactly does your essence do?"

He sucked in a deep breath and slowly let it out. He was stalling. Caitlin could see it in how he held his shoulders. Arctos' whole body tensed.

"Tell me. Please," she said. "Before I freak out even more."

Arctos lifted his head and met her gaze. "It changes your scent, making it more like mine. That way other Phantom Warriors will know you're my mate."

"And?" she said, drawing the word out. Caitlin knew there had to be more to it.

"It gives you part of my beast." His answer was so quiet that Caitlin wasn't sure that she'd heard him correctly.

"Are you telling me that you somehow put that bear inside of me?" she asked, her voice rising with every syllable.

Arctos tilted his head and listened. "They grow restless waiting. Soon, they will come in."

Caitlin lowered her voice. "I'd appreciate an answer."

She still felt like herself—sort of. Sure, she seemed a little more aggressive than she'd been before. And maybe she was faster and a tad stronger, but was that really because of Arctos' beast?

No, a radioactive spider bit you during the night, the voice inside her head snarked.

"We share my beast now," he said. "It is part of us both. We can call upon it at any time."

"Do I get any say in this at all?" she asked, fearing his answer. Had what he done to her caused irreparable damage?

He saved your life, that same little voice whispered. Caitlin was beginning to hate that voice.

Arctos looked grim. "You are not damaged, but you have been altered. You are now stronger than a normal human. Faster. And once you learn how, you will eventually be able to take on beast form. When that happens, you'll shift. You'll heal quicker and live far longer," he said. There was sadness in his eyes now.

"What about you?" she asked, touching his cheek. Caitlin knew she should be furious with him, but she just couldn't muster the energy. It was all too much.

"I am as I was before," he said. "The only difference is that you are now my mate."

"So, you're here to stay?" she asked, hope blooming in spite of her natural pessimism.

He shook his head slowly. "You know I cannot. Already the ship I came on is approaching our location. Once it gets here, I have to go."

"So that's it? You're just going to wham, bam, thank you ma'am me?" Caitlin felt a lick of temper rise beneath her skin. How dare he make her care about him and then fly away.

Arctos opened his mouth, then closed it again. "I do not recognize this Earth saying," he said.

Caitlin jumped off the bed. "So you come down here, pass on your essence, then leave? That's pretty crappy, if you ask me."

Arctos mirrored her movements, his own temper rising to take the bait. "I had no intention of leaving this planet without you," he hissed under his breath.

Her hands moved to her hips. "Really? When exactly were you planning to ask me to go with you? As you were getting on the flight?"

The temperature in the room heated, matching the rise in pheromones. Caitlin saw Arctos' nostrils flair a second before he tackled her onto the bed. "It's not a flight," he ground out, rolling her beneath him. "It's a ship. And I would've asked you had your friends not shown up."

His hard shafted brushed her sex through her clothes. Caitlin felt her face heat. It was followed by an altogether different kind of flush. "We can't do this right now," she said sounding far more breathless than she'd like.

"Then get rid of them, so we can finish this," he said, rocking his hips.

Caitlin body softened beneath him. "You'd better let me up."

"You cannot tell them about me," he said, meeting her gaze.

"Don't worry, I won't," she said. "They'll think I'm crazy."

He rolled off her. Reluctantly, Caitlin stumbled to her feet. When she reached the door, she turned. "You still haven't asked me to go with you."

He propped his elbow up, resting his head in his hand. "Will you?" he all but purred.

"I'll think about," she said tartly, before adding, "though it may take a while to convince me that it's a good idea."

Arctos smiled, his feral grin filled with dark sinful promise. "I believe I'm more than up for the challenge," he said, glancing down, before meeting her gaze once more.

She watched him expand and lengthen right before her eyes. Caitlin giggled. "Hold that thought."

EPILOGUE

"Are you sure you have to leave?" Allie asked.

Caitlin folded the last of her clothes. "Yeah," she said quietly.

Allie came around to her side of the bed. "I'm going to miss you."

Caitlin choked. "I'll miss you, too."

"Will you at least visit?" Allie asked.

Their gazes met. "I will if I can," Caitlin said, then picked up her suitcase and camera equipment.

"I don't mind giving you a ride to the airport. I know you said that you don't need one, but it would give us a little more time together," Allie said, snagging a tissue from the nightstand.

Caitlin smiled. "I appreciate the offer, but Arctos has taken care of the transportation arrangements." The ship was cloaked right outside of town. If she hadn't seen it with her own eyes, Caitlin wouldn't have believed it.

Allie rushed into her arms and hugged her tight. Caitlin hugged her back, taking care not to hurt her friend with her newfound strength.

"I'd better go," she said. They were going to swing by

her apartment in Virginia before they headed to Zaron. Caitlin pulled away, brushing at her tears.

This trip to Alaska had turned out to be more of an adventure than she ever imagined possible. Caitlin knew that she had her friend to thank for her newfound happiness. Had it not been for Allie's stunt, she'd have never met Arctos.

"Thank you for everything," she said.

"You're welcome." Allie gave her a watery smile as Caitlin stepped through the door.

"You take care of yourself," she said.

"I will." One hand rested on the doorknob, while her other dabbed at tears. "Cat?"

Caitlin stopped to look back. "Yes?"

"Would it bother you if I dated Michael?" Allie blurted. "He kind of asked me out after we found you with the naked guy."

Caitlin blinked, then threw her head back and laughed. "Of course not. Go for it."

"Good! Because I think he's the one," Allie said.

Caitlin shook her head and smiled. Arctos appeared as if by magic at the bottom of the stairs of the apartment building. He stared at her, his warm brown eyes sparkling in the sunlight. Allie could keep Michael. There was only one man for her and he wasn't even from this planet.

"Ready?" he asked.

"Ready," she said. Caitlin took a deep breath and opened her heart for the first time. She thought it would hurt, but it didn't. Love flowed through her, raining down upon his golden head.

Arctos smiled, letting her know without words that he was there to catch her. He'd always be there. For she was his true-mate. His life. His love. And he was hers.

# # #

PHANTOM
WARRIORS
Linx
JORDAN
SUMMERS

Chapter One

The music throbbed out a steady beat, rattling his chest. Linx watched as the woman on the brightly lit stage leapt onto a gold pole, hooking one flawlessly long leg around it. She slowly circled the pole, coming to rest on the floor with her thighs spread wide. Only a thin scrap of material kept him from seeing what the human males called heaven. The woman onstage was almost as perfect as the one currently giving him a lap dance.

Linx was pretty sure that's what she'd called it. Whatever kind of dance the striking brunette was doing felt good, really good. His body approved.

The brunette swiveled her hips above his lap, brushing her mouthwatering ass over his growing erection. The blonde onstage frowned and slowly slithered toward him on her hands and knees, her pert breasts defying gravity.

Linx smiled, imagining what they'd taste like when he rolled his tongue across her peach-colored nipples.

The topless brunette on his lap scowled at the interloper.

"Don't worry, pet. I'll make sure that neither of you leave unsatisfied." He stroked the side of her face with his fingertips. "I'm famished for feminine company and I always have a ravenous appetite."

Which was the truth, but not the whole truth. Linx had done very well for himself since he'd arrived on the planet yesterday. He still had a few days left and he intended to enjoy every last minute before he got down to the business of seeking a mate. He didn't think it would take long once he set his sights on a woman.

The real question was how had Bacchus, Kegar, Talon, and Arctos managed to choose just one?

Linx glanced at the clock on the wall. It was early, not even sundown. Still plenty of time to sample a dozen more.

A man, whose face had encountered a fist or two, sat in the corner with his back against the wall, pretending to watch the show. From that tactical position the man could see the whole club, including all the comings and goings, though he seemed more interested in what Linx was doing than anything else.

Under different circumstances, Linx would've chosen the same spot, but he wasn't here to fight, he was here to fuck. And he wasn't at all concerned with human males being any kind of threat to him or his current mission.

Linx had noticed the man when he stepped into the club. It had been hard to miss the lithe auburn-haired woman draped on his arm or the sharp smell of gun oil clinging to his pale skin. Like every other human male Linx had encountered in this place, the man was armed.

A waitress rushed over with a drink on her tray. She hadn't bothered to ask the man what he wanted. She'd simply handed the beverage to him and scurried off.

On this world, Linx had no doubt that the man keeping a careful eye on him and the rest of the club might be dangerous, but in the galaxy he would be considered nothing more than a nuisance. So that's how Linx chose to view him.

The blonde, who'd been onstage, plopped down beside Linx, taking his attention away from the man in the booth. She began to massage his arms, using over-exaggerated movements that somehow emphasized her bountiful breasts. "Why don't you come with me, lover. I'll show you what it's like to get a lap dance from a pro." Her accent rolled off her tongue, making each letter vibrate in her mouth, before a word formed.

The sound was in no way displeasing. It reminded Linx of a soft continuous purr. He felt a sense of smugness as the two women continued to argue over him.

"Shove off, Nadia. I saw him first." The brunette ground her sex onto Linx's erection.

"Yeah, well, if you hadn't noticed, Eva, he's only had eyes for me for the last twenty minutes," Nadia said.

"If you mean that in between watching my act, he's glanced at you, then you're right." The blonde winked. "Shouldn't you be going home now that your shift has ended?"

"I could say the same to you," Eva said.

Linx's lips twitched. He still couldn't get over the abundance of women on this planet. Even in this *small* settlement of Philadelphia, Pennsylvania there seemed to be thousands of them. Earth was like a virtual buffet and he intended to gorge himself before he was forced to return to the ship.

He glanced at each woman. Both were beautiful. Stunning in fact. Their breasts were high, firm, and *identical*. Odd that, but he wasn't about to complain. Linx inhaled, catching the musk of their arousal. Why should he choose, when they were both so willing to fall into his bed? He leaned forward and whispered into the brunette's ear.

Eva grinned wickedly. "You are naughty."

"That's why you like me." He skimmed her hips with his nails, taking care not to break her fragile skin.

She glanced down at his burgeoning erection, then raised a brow. "That's not the only reason, sugar."

Nadia opened her mouth to protest, but before she could say a word, Linx pulled her into his arms and kissed her. She practically purred as he ran his rough hand down her bare spine.

"You're coming, too." He gently moved Eva aside and stood, offering his hands to both women.

They clasped them and rose to their feet like they were royalty.

"Shall we?" Linx started toward the front door.

"Not that way," Nadia said. "There are rooms out the back."

Linx shrugged. The closer the better.

* * * * *

Tabby pulled her hat down low on her face and adjusted her sunglasses. She took a deep breath and rubbed her sweaty palms on her pants. The moustache she'd applied tickled. She scratched her nose, then double-checked to make sure the lip hair stayed in place.

"You can do this," she murmured under her breath.

She pulled her suit jacket down and loosened the knot on her tie. It was now or never. She straightened her padded shoulders and stepped inside the dingy strip club. Smoke assaulted her nose and threatened to trigger her allergies. She choked, but managed to ward off a sneeze.

Like always, Boris Chernov stood at the door, guarding the entrance like a pit-bull promised of a nice, juicy bone. Two other enforcers, Viktor Galdin and Alexei Vazov sat at the bar, sipping vodka, looking for all intents and purposes like regular customers, their bored expressions broken only by their sharp-eyed gazes.

One snap of a finger and they'd jump to do Sergei's bidding. To Tabby's horror, she'd found out a month ago that Viktor and Alexei were known in law enforcement circles for their love of wet work. Given their cold, shark-like intensity, it wasn't hard to imagine them covered in blood.

Boris held his hand out to stop her from proceeding any farther. Tabby's heart jumped into her throat, making it hard to swallow, impossible to breathe.

He looked her up and down slowly. "That will be twenty dollars," he said in a thick Russian accent that seemed oddly out of place in this part of Philadelphia.

Tabby pulled out a wallet she'd gotten from a secondhand store and grabbed two tens. Her hands trembled as she waited for him to take the money.

"Have fun, son." He slapped her on the back. The force sent her forward a few steps.

A bark of laughter came out of the darkness. Tabby's head shot up. She'd recognize that 'snort' anywhere. Taylor was here. She took a hurried step in the direction of the laugh, but was stopped short by a heavy hand on her shoulder.

"One moment." Boris tipped her chin up and his eyes narrowed. He reached out and snatched the moustache off.

"Ouch!"

"You should not be here," he said.

* * * * *

Linx and the two dancers were halfway across the room, when a commotion started at the front entrance. He ignored it and kept walking, tugging the women along with him. In his mind, Linx was already undressing them and laying them on a bed. He couldn't wait to bury himself in their welcoming sheaths.

The man seated against the wall slowly rose to his feet. His gaze hardened as he stared across the room.

"Sergei, please don't." The woman at his side grabbed his arm.

Sergei didn't look at her. He simply shrugged her off as he faced down the new threat.

Something made Linx want to see what had captured the

human male's attention. It must be a formidable threat if he was willing to discard his lovely companion so easily. Linx turned to see what was happening.

"You're not allowed." The beefy bouncer working the door crossed his arms over his wall of a chest. His frame blocked out the person he was talking to. "We warned you that there would be trouble if you came around again." A heated argument ensued, drowning out the thumping beat.

The bouncer moved, revealing a small man wearing sensible shoes and an oversized suit. Linx frowned. This was the threat?

The man had sunglasses on and a hat pulled down so low over his face that Linx could barely make out his features. His hair had been tucked beneath the brim. If it weren't for the lone dark red wisp that had fallen out, Linx would have thought the man was hairless.

"Let me see my sister and I'll leave," he shrieked, high and shrill.

Linx cringed as the horrific sound grated his sensitive ears. What kind of man sounded like that?

The bouncer stood over him, his broken nose nearly touching the man's upturned one. "You know that's not going to happen. Taylor doesn't want to talk to you." He pointed to the door. "Now get out of here while you still can."

"Sergei can go to hell." The man grabbed onto the bar. "I'm not leaving until I see my twin."

The bouncer sighed. "Have it your way." He pried the man's fingers off the bar and lifted him into the air as if he weighed nothing.

Linx frowned. The man yelped as his hat fell off, revealing strikingly beautiful burgundy hair. Not a man…a *woman*. The long tresses easily hung past her waist. As a cat-shifter, Linx had always had a thing for nice hair.

The woman struck the bouncer in the back. "Boris, put me down!"

"Stop hitting me, Tabitha, and I'll think about it," the bouncer said.

She struggled in his arms. The man's grip tightened and his massive biceps flexed.

"You're hurting me." She gasped. "I can't breathe."

"Maybe I teach you lesson," he said in a thick guttural accent. "That way next time you listen."

Linx released the women he'd been escorting and moved across the room. He was standing at the front door before he realized what he'd done. "Put her down," he said, his voice low and exceedingly calm.

Boris squinted at him. "You should stay out of this, friend." He glanced over Linx's head at the strippers waiting by the exit. "Get back to your *dates*. This doesn't concern you."

"I said, put her down," Linx repeated. This time he allowed the threat to hang in the air.

Boris unceremoniously dropped the woman he'd called Tabitha. She landed on her hands and knees with a thud. "You should've left it alone. Now I'm going to have to ask you to leave, too." The bouncer reached out to grab Linx, but he was no longer standing where he'd been only seconds before. "What the?" The bouncer jerked his head around to find him.

Linx leaned against the bar, waiting for the big man to locate him. He felt more than saw the two men at the bar rise from their stools. The gun oil clinging to their skin tickled his nose. He glanced over his shoulder and gave them a warning glare. The men tensed, then looked over at the man who'd been sitting against the wall. Fighting with humans was almost too easy to bother with. Linx knew he could have all of them disarmed in seconds.

From the corner of his eye, he saw Tabitha slowly stand and brush off her hands. She truly did have glorious hair. His fingers itched to touch it, to see if it was as soft as it looked, though he didn't know why.

Other than her long locks, the woman was utterly unremarkable. He glanced at her, then at Nadia and Eva, whom he'd left standing by the back door. The dancers were definitely more his type, but for some reason he couldn't abandon her. She *needed* him.

Boris's eyes narrowed, when his gaze landed on Linx. "How did you get over there?"

Linx's lips quirked. "Given your lack of speed, it wasn't hard."

The bouncer's face flushed with blood and he glanced toward Sergei. He must've gotten some kind of cue because the bouncer nodded, then took a swing at Linx's head.

Linx caught his arm, stopping the motion with one hand. "You really don't want to fight me." He could feel the shift burning through him and fought hard to tamp it down. Linx had no doubt his eyes were glowing as his beast peered out at his would be opponent.

"What are you?" Boris strained to break his hold.

"A man," Linx said.

"You are no man. Release me, *Tchort*." Boris spat. Sweat broke out across his brow and he trembled. The rank odor of fear reached Linx's nostrils. The beast inside of him perked up even more. Instead of giving in to the fear, the bouncer blustered on. "Do you have any idea who owns this bar? You're bringing a whole lot of trouble down on your head, and for what? Some chick that you don't even know?"

Linx stilled. He was right. Why was he fighting for a woman he cared nothing about? Perplexed, Linx released him and turned to walk away.

"Watch out!" Tabitha cried, but it was too late.

Boris's meaty fist caught him upside his temple and spun him around. Linx shook his head and a growl rumbled from his chest. He took a step toward the bouncer, intending to show him how a Phantom Warrior fights, but the woman with the glorious hair stopped him.

"Are you insane? Let's go!" Tabitha yanked him by the

arm. Her warm touch sank into Linx's muscles and sent an odd shock zinging down his spine.

She looked over his shoulder, fear widening her dark brown eyes. Linx followed her gaze. Sergei now held the weapon he'd smelled earlier and was marching toward them.

Linx wasn't concerned, but it was more than obvious that Tabitha was, since her scent soured. He wrinkled his nose and let her lead him away. Linx stopped at the door and glanced back wistfully. The two dancers he'd planned to bed didn't follow. He watched the women hurry out the back door as Sergei approached, their names already fading from his memory.

* * * * *

CHAPTER TWO

Tabitha Shelley released the stranger she'd dragged out of the bar, then kept walking. She didn't check to see if he would follow. Now that he was safe, she didn't care.

What was he thinking? He could've been killed.

She covered two more blocks, listening to the sound of her labored breathing and pounding heart. Tabby turned back to make sure that she wasn't being followed and was surprised to see the man right behind her. He was so quiet that she'd thought he'd bailed on her.

In the dark, he'd been handsome, but in the fading sunlight the man was positively stunning. His denim blue eyes practically glittered, when they narrowed on her.

"Sorry about that whole mess." Tabby wasn't sure what else to say. She'd really botched this one. And she'd been so sure that her ruse would work.

If she hadn't heard her sister laugh, then she might've made it. The sound of Taylor had caused her to raise her head, giving sharp-eyed, dimwitted Boris Chernov enough time to recognize her. All she'd been able to do was catch a glimpse of Taylor sitting next to Sergei Belovich, a *brigadier* in the Russian mob, before Boris stopped her.

It hadn't helped that she'd also been distracted by the sudden appearance of the stranger. She stared at him. He had a face worthy of distraction and a body to match. And from that swoon-inducing smile he was giving her, there was no doubt that he knew it.

Yet, he had to be more than a pretty face. Truly shallow people only looked out for themselves. They didn't jump in to rescue complete strangers. And they certainly couldn't make it seem like it was something they did every day. Which meant he was either too stupid to live or he had ties to the mob.

Was it possible that he was a *Pakhan*? He didn't look like a typical mob boss. She glanced at his forearms. He didn't appear to have any tattoos. Maybe he was a *Brigadier* like Sergei and worked as an intermediary controlling the criminal cells for the boss? But that didn't seem likely either, since Sergei preferred to take care of business himself. He wouldn't ask someone to step in for him, would he? Was he a new enforcer?

Tabby felt the blood drain from her face as she took a step back to really look at her rescuer.

His black T-shirt hugged plentiful muscles, leaving little to the imagination. The top had been paired with matching jeans and military grade combat boots. Unless he'd shoved a gun into his snug pants, he wasn't armed.

Tabby glanced at the front of his pants and suddenly wished that she hadn't. Her mind flashed to the two strippers he'd been with. That explained his current condition. Or maybe he just got off on fighting. Either way, her gut told her that he was trouble. The sooner she dumped him, the better off she'd be. But before she did that, she needed to know a few things.

"What were you thinking back there?" she asked.

His dark brow arched. "I could ask you the same thing. From what I could tell, you have had zero combat training." His voice had no discernable accent as he chided her.

Definitely not from around here or Brighton Beach, Brooklyn, where the Russian mob made their US home base. Could be that he'd come in from California, but his skin didn't have the color of someone who'd spent a lot of time in the sun.

Tabby's face flushed. "I know plenty about fighting." She'd been fighting to get her twin sister back from Sergei for over six months now. But of course, that wasn't what he'd meant.

He stepped closer. "Then why didn't you fight, when he picked you up? There were plenty of moves that could've incapacitated him."

Her hands settled on her hips. "Not sure if you noticed, but Boris is huge. Hulk huge." Besides whatever maneuver he was referring to hadn't been covered in the hand-to-hand combat books that she'd read. Of course, Tabby couldn't exactly tell him that. He could be working for Sergei or one of the other bosses in the area. So she said the first thing that popped into her head. "He caught me off guard."

The man snorted in disbelief.

"It's true. I'll prove it," she said. "Try to choke me." Tabby braced herself, then motioned to her throat.

He blinked slowly. "What?"

"I said try to choke me." She made the universal sign for choking.

His brow furrowed. "I will do no such thing. You are a woman."

Tabby rolled her eyes. "I'm surprised you noticed given the acute case of silicone boob blindness you seemed to be suffering from when I came into the club."

* * * * *

Linx didn't know exactly what she meant, but he could tell from her tone that she'd just insulted him. So this was the thanks he got for saving her. It wasn't his fault that he hadn't known she was a woman until her hat fell off. He glared at her. She dressed like a man and screeched like a Harpy.

Until now, he hadn't encountered any women on Earth like her. And for that he was eternally grateful. Since one of her on the planet was enough.

He allowed his gaze to wander. From what he could tell, she didn't have large, perfect breasts like the others. Hers were smaller. More compact. A mouthful at most. Her thick waist led to hips that were definitely fuller than the dancers.

Yet, standing here before him with her burgundy hair glistening in the sunset and fire burning in her dark brown eyes, he'd never seen a woman look quite so *feminine*. How had he missed the fact that she was a woman? Maybe she was right about his temporary blindness.

"Why were you fighting a man three times your size?" he asked.

"I wasn't fighting. I was trying to sneak into the club." She looked at him, her gaze far too assessing for his comfort.

"Why?"

"That's none of your business."

Linx tilted his head. "You made it my business, when you cried out and I had to step in to save you."

Her jaw clenched. "I could've handled Boris. I just needed more time," she said. "I never asked for your help. You took it upon yourself to intervene."

He shook his head in amazement. "I suppose that's true. But the fact that you didn't ask for my help either makes you insane or stupid."

Her nostrils flared. "I am *not* stupid."

"So you're insane." That made the most sense given what he'd witnessed of her behavior thus far.

"Guess that makes two of us, since you just pissed off an under boss in the Russian mob," she said, as if that should mean something to him.

Linx couldn't quite figure her out. Tabitha was full of

bluff and bluster, yet he could smell the fear clinging to her pale skin. Like a good soldier, she didn't allow it to stop her from her mission. He just couldn't figure out what kind of mission a woman like her could be on.

"What were you doing in there?" he asked, this time using a gentler tone.

She crossed her arms over her chest and glared at him. For several seconds, she didn't speak.

"The sooner you tell me, the sooner I'll leave you alone," Linx said.

That seemed to brighten her mood, which in turn soured his. "I was looking for my sister."

He stiffened. "Was she one of the women I was with?" The idea left him feeling oddly uncomfortable.

"No." Tabitha shook her head, sending her hair into her face. She quickly scooped it out of the way. "Taylor is Sergei's girlfriend. At least that's what he calls her. She's more like his sex slave."

"And you know this how?" His discomfort grew.

"Because she won't return my phone calls. Won't answer her email," she said in frustration.

Linx frowned at her. "That doesn't mean that he's holding her against her will. It just means that she doesn't want to speak to you."

"Do you have any siblings?"

"No."

Tabitha sighed. "Then you wouldn't understand. Taylor and I are close. We're twins. We aren't identical, but I can sense when something is wrong. And something is definitely wrong."

Her distress bothered Linx. "What is your name?" he asked, though he'd already knew the answer.

"Sorry." She blushed. "My name is Tabitha. Tabitha Shelley. My friends call me Tabby."

"Tabitha." He let her name slide across his tongue. "Tabby…like the cat?"

She rolled her eyes again. "Yes."

He grinned to himself. "I am called Linx."

"Like the cat?" she asked teasingly.

His smile widened. "Very much so."

She held out her hand. "Nice to meet you."

Linx took it, but instead of shaking her outstretched hand, he brought it to his lips and placed a chaste kiss on the back of her knuckles.

"What are you doing?" Tabby snatched her hand back.

His brows rose in surprise. Linx had never had that kind of reaction from a woman before.

Tabby rubbed the back of her hand on her pants' leg, then scowled at him. "Don't do that again," she hissed like an angry kitten. "I'm not one of those bimbos you hooked up with in the club."

"I—" was all he managed to get out before she backed away.

"If you know what's good for you, you'll stay away from the Molotov Club. Sergei won't forget what you've done," she said. "He's a vindictive bastard who gets off on hurting people. Kind of comes with the job description." Tabitha turned to leave, but stopped short. "Why did Boris call you *Tchort*?"

Linx frowned in confusion. "I know not what that means."

Her eyes narrowed. "It means 'Dark God' or devil. Though I think in this context, Boris was calling you a demon."

"Perhaps he was referring to my devilish appearance." He waggled his eyebrows.

Tabby scowled. "Yeah, I don't think so."

Linx shrugged. "I do not know him, but Boris struck me as a superstitious man, who'd be afraid of his own shadow if it tapped him on the shoulder."

She rubbed the back of her neck. "That's probably it," she said, but it didn't sound like she believed him. "See ya."

Tabby walked away.

"Where are you going?" Linx called after her.

"Home," she said. "You should do the same."

Tabby left him standing on the sidewalk. Not only had she brushed away his kiss, she'd also dismissed him. Linx had never been dismissed by a woman in his life. Not even when he was young and inexperienced. He watched her fade into the distance. And decided he didn't like it or her one bit.

* * * * *

CHAPTER THREE

Sergei Belovich watched Tabitha Shelley pull the man out the door. He'd had a bad feeling about the guy ever since he'd laid eyes on him. His suspicions rose, when the man intervened on Tabitha's behalf. Were they working together?

He wouldn't put anything past her. She was determined to get her beloved sister away from him. She still didn't understand that once someone was his, they stayed his until he *let* them go. The woman was becoming a pain in his ass. Sergei should've killed her long ago. It would've made controlling Taylor much easier.

The spot between his shoulder blades itched. A sure sign that trouble was on the way. Was it the stranger who'd only moments ago tried to walk out the back door with two of his strippers? Or was something else coming?

Sergei's mother had always told him that Romanian gypsy blood ran through his veins. He hadn't believed her until that same itch saved him from a bullet. Now he paid attention.

He didn't like the man. Sergei could've easily chalked the whole thing up to jealousy, given the man's striking good looks, but that wasn't it. Something about him seemed *off*.

A cold breeze brushed past him and Sergei turned, expecting to see someone standing behind him, but no one was there. His eyes narrowed as he carefully scanned the smoky bar to locate the cause of his sudden unease. Other than the regulars, who'd been coming in for years, nobody stood out.

Sergei tried to shake off the feeling of being watched, but it clung to him like a maggot on rotting flesh. He surveyed the room once more, then turned back to the woman he'd been bedding for the last few months. He still enjoyed Taylor's body, but he didn't appreciate the baggage she brought with her or her clinginess.

She was getting too attached and that wouldn't do. He demanded compliance and monogamy from his women, but emotions complicated things. Sergei didn't do emotions. He'd learned that lesson from his mother early on. And monogamy, well, that was one-sided, too.

Sergei rolled his shoulders as the hair on his neck prickled. His flame-haired pet looked at him expectantly as he returned to his seat. "Your sister is bad for business," he said softly, but he saw her flinch all the same. "I can't have her coming in here causing a scene."

"I'll talk to her. That's all she wants." Taylor petted his arm in a soothing fashion, though the touch did little to douse his temper. "I'm sure once I do, she'll leave you— leave us—alone." She scooted closer, allowing her ample bosom to brush against his chest.

Sergei rubbed a knuckle along her soft cheek and felt his cock tighten. She really was beautiful. Fortunately, there were many more like her in the world. "I've already given you enough time. You said you'd handle her and you haven't. Now it's my turn."

Tears filled her hazel green eyes. "Please Sergei, give me another chance. I know I can get through to her." She choked back a sob.

He grabbed a handful of her hair and pulled it tight.

Taylor whimpered, but did not cry out. He'd taught her not to, no matter how bad the pain got. "For you, pet, I'll do this one thing, but it will cost you because *nothink* in this world is for free."

"Whatever you want, baby." She gulped and nodded quickly. "I understand."

"Do you?" He yanked harder on her hair.

"Yes," she hissed.

"Good." Sergei said, but he had no intention of keeping his word. He looked over Taylor's head at Boris and nodded. Boris's jaw tightened, but he nodded back, then walked over to the two men seated at the bar.

* * * * *

Linx remained invisible as he listened to the man's conversation with Tabby's sister. He had snuck back into the club to see if the furor had died down. He thought it had…until he approached Sergei's table.

It was uncanny how much Taylor looked like her sister, Tabitha. They weren't identical, but their mannerisms were similar. But that's where the resemblance ended. Tabitha was a fighter. Linx couldn't imagine her putting up with being manhandled like Taylor was doing. She barely whimpered, which meant Sergei had been abusing her for a while. Or maybe, she was the type of woman who liked it rough. He certainly did on occasion.

Linx watched her plead with Sergei to leave Tabitha alone. He'd agreed, but something in that look raised his hackles. Sergei didn't seem like a man used to keeping his word. Linx left the spot he'd been standing in and walked over to Boris. He didn't understand the language Boris was speaking, but he caught the words *ten minutes*. His whole body tensed. Something was very wrong. He could feel it on the air, even without the use of his whiskers.

The two men rose from their bar stools ten minutes later.

Tall, heavy and oddly lacking any discernable necks, the men ambled out the door. Linx may not have understood what they were saying, but some things—like danger, were universal. He was determined to follow them.

Linx slipped into the car with the men. The man in the passenger seat kept looking over his shoulder as if he sensed his presence in the back seat.

"What's wrong, Alexei?" the driver asked.

Alexei rolled his shoulders. "*Nothink.*" His accent thick with nerves.

"Then why do you keep looking behind us? Are we being tailed?" The man shot a glance into the review mirror. "I don't see anyone."

Alexei shook his head. "I told you it was *nothink*, Viktor. I just want to get this over with."

"Do you have the address?" Viktor asked.

"*Da.*" Alexei punched it into the car's navigation system.

Linx sat quietly, staring out the window as the city rushed by him. The men hadn't spoken since they put in the address and he preferred it that way. He'd only studied English and had no idea what language they were speaking. He could bring out his translation device, but they didn't seem the type to spill anything important.

The men drove for thirty minutes. The skyscrapers faded into a quiet neighborhood dotted with small colorful homes. They turned right on Tulip Street, then slowed to a stop.

Linx wasn't sure what they were waiting for, but like all hunters, he was patient. The men stared at a peach colored house on the left-hand side of the street. When the light in the front of the house switched off, they made their move.

* * * * *

Tabby had been studying her lock picking 'how to' books for the past hour and half. The instructions were clear. She was pretty sure she could now pick a basic lock. If today had proven one thing to her, it was that she wasn't going to get to her sister through a frontal assault. There was no doubt Taylor had seen her. Tabby had noted her twin's wide panicked eyes a second before Boris blocked her view and lifted her off the ground.

In her heart, she'd begged Taylor to come to her rescue. Instead, her twin had grabbed Sergei's arm and all but climbed onto his lap, ignoring the chaos happening at the front door of the club.

It had been a slap in the face to Tabby. Made worse when Sergei had shoved her sister aside and started across the room. She shuddered to think what would've happened if Linx hadn't intervened.

Suddenly an image of her dark-haired, blue-eyed savior flashed in her mind. Boris was right to call him *Tchort*. He was a dark god. A demon in black jeans. Once she'd gotten a good look at Linx, Tabby had been determined to ignore her attraction to him. And it had worked for all of a minute.

She knew she'd done the right thing by sending him away, but for some reason it still bothered her. Not that she would've ultimately said or done anything to act upon her attraction. She wasn't like her sister.

Instead, Tabby used Taylor's rotten taste in men as a 'What Not To Do' guide for her own life. If she found herself really attracted to a man, Tabby considered it an ominous sign and ran the other way.

She didn't date bad boys. She wasn't drawn to dangerous men. The fact that Linx tempted her to break her steadfast rules was an *anomaly*. One she'd just as soon forget. Give her a boring, unattractive man any day of the week and she'd jump at the chance to date him. Unlike Taylor, Tabby prided herself for being in control of her hormones and her personal life.

"What personal life?" Tabby snorted. Ever since her twin had hooked up with the Russian mobster, her life had been in a tailspin. She'd spent the last six months trying to sort through the mess that was Taylor. Six months? More like twenty-six years.

Had it really been that long? Tabby's shoulders sagged. She was tired. Tired of this dance that she and Taylor had been doing. Tired of always being the responsible twin. Tired of always coming to the rescue, when her sister messed up. When would it be enough? When would she get a chance to have a life?

Like so many relationships before, Taylor had convinced herself that she loved Sergei and that he loved her back. She was the only one who couldn't see that she was being used. Bad enough that her sister had begun stripping for the mobster.

The Taylor that Tabby knew would never do that, not without being heavily influenced.

Tabby hated that she was beginning to question whether she really knew her twin at all.

Stripping was bad enough, but it was only a matter of time before Sergei talked Taylor into running drugs for him. That's what he'd done with his last girlfriend and look what had happened to her. Tabby's mind flashed to the photo of the young woman, who'd been found bludgeoned and tossed into a dumpster. He'd discarded her like garbage because to him, she was trash.

She couldn't let Sergei do that to her twin. If she couldn't reach Taylor directly, then Tabby would just have to find proof of Sergei's illegal activities. Maybe if she had enough proof to take to the police, they'd finally be able to arrest Sergei. She looked at the lock-picking kit next to her instruction book. What was that old adage? It takes a thief to catch a mobster or something like that. There was more than one way to save her sister.

Tabby turned the light off. She had made it halfway down the hall, when something crashed through her front door into her living room. She turned her head to see the unmistakable silhouette of Viktor and Alexei, standing in the darkness.

Tabby's heart hit her knees, then ricocheted into her throat. She raced back down the hall toward the kitchen, her sock-covered feet silent on the carpet. Her only hope was to reach the back door before the men spotted her.

"I take bedrooms. You search rest of house. She's here somewhere," Alexei said in a thick muddled accent.

Viktor grunted.

Tabby felt along the countertop, until she found her kettle. It was still hot from the tea that she'd had earlier. She waited, trying to hear over the blood pounding in her ears. The door to the kitchen slowly opened. Tabby didn't hesitate. She slammed the kettle against Viktor's head, sending hot water careening over his face.

He screamed, then let out a flood of Russian curses as he fell to the floor.

She didn't wait for him to recover. Instead, Tabby ran for the back door and pulled. The door didn't budge. She'd locked it...and her keys were in the living room. Her gaze darted around the room. Viktor was already beginning to recover. No way would she make it past him before he grabbed her.

She could hear the pounding of heavy boots coming down the hall. Soon there would be two of them and she'd be dead. Tabby scanned the room once more and spotted the window above the kitchen sink. It was small, but she was sure she could fit.

She ran over to it and flipped the latch, unlocking the window, then pushed with all her might. The window frame creaked, then began to rise. Tabby climbed onto the sink and stuck her legs out the window. Viktor struggled to his feet and rushed her.

Tabby screamed, then screamed again, when she felt strong hands clamp down on her hips and pull her outside. Oh my god, Alexei had her! She was as good as dead. Tabby struggled, punching and kicking like a wildcat. His grasp loosened and she nearly fell, but never hit the ground.

Instead, Tabby found herself cradled against a hard chest. She looked up and saw Linx, his expression grim as he ran. A multitude of questions flooded her mind, but they could all wait until they were safe.

"We need to get to my car," she said.

"Where is it?" he asked.

"On the street." She pointed to the green Honda.

"Keys," he gritted out.

Tabby's heart sank. Like the keys to the backdoor, her car keys were also in the living room, hanging from a set of neat hooks. Then she thought about the other books she'd read. Could she do it? Did she dare try? What if Viktor and Alexei caught them before she could hotwire the car?

What choice did they have? Linx couldn't run all night, especially carrying her.

"We don't need the keys," she said, praying that it was true.

* * * * *

Linx took Tabby to her car. His heart had nearly exploded in his chest, when he'd heard her cry out. If she hadn't managed to squeeze out the window, he was pretty sure she'd be dead. He didn't want to think about. If he did, he'd only anger the beast. And he didn't think Tabby would appreciate that side of him after what she'd just been through.

Every instinct told him to stand and fight. But he wouldn't. Not if there was a chance that she'd be injured in the process.

She grabbed a rock and busted out the back driver's side window of her car. Linx frowned as she opened the front door and slid to the floor under the steering mechanism. Tabby reached into a hidden compartment on the passenger side and pulled out a metal instrument, then popped a piece of plastic off the column.

A minute or so later, she'd combined wires and slammed the metal instrument into the slot where the key normally went. She turned it a few times. On the third try, the engine roared to life and her radio blared. Tabby shut the radio off, then turned to look at Linx, her eyes wide with fear.

"Get in. They're coming."

Linx jumped in and Tabby sped off, barely giving him time to close the door. He glanced over his shoulder and saw Viktor and Alexei run to their car. Their headlights flashed and a low growling hum filled the air as they started their vehicle. They spun the car around in a perfect three hundred and sixty degree turn, then quickly gained on them.

"Hang on," Tabby said. "This might get rough." She cranked the wheel to the right and the car's back tires spun to get traction.

"Where are you going?" Linx asked. If she just stopped the car, he could take care of the men behind them. He didn't mind given what they'd intended to do to her.

"The police station. No way will they follow us inside," she said.

Linx wasn't convinced. "They seem pretty determined. What have you done to anger them so?" he asked.

"I haven't done anything other than try to get my sister away from that scumbag, Sergei. What were you doing here?" Her face paled. "Did you come with them?"

Linx wasn't sure how to answer. Yes, he'd ridden in the vehicle with the men, but no, he wasn't *with* them. At least not in the way that she was implying. He couldn't exactly tell her the truth. He knew Tabby wouldn't believe him. Linx needed to find out what was going on. There had to be more to the story than she was telling him.

He pulled out his weapon and pointed it at the car behind them.

"What are you doing?" Her head jerked to the side so she could see him. "You can't just shoot them. Someone will see you."

A car honked.

She barely avoided a collision.

"Keep your eyes on the road," he said.

Tabby did as he asked, though given the covert glances she shot his way she didn't want to. "We're almost to the police station. If that's a gun, you'd better put it away."

"It's not a gun. It's a camera." Linx aimed his magnetic pulse weapon. Viktor and Alexei's engine died instantly. The car slowly rolled to a stop. "You can slow down now," he said. "They are no longer behind us."

"What did you do?" Her knuckles were white as she slowly eased her grip on the steering wheel and relaxed her foot on the pedal.

"Recorded their license plate," he said. It was a lie, but a believable one.

"Can I see it?" she asked.

"See what?" He looked at her.

"The camera."

"I'd rather you didn't. It's a very sensitive piece of equipment," he said. "Now let's go somewhere that we can talk."

Tabby knew he was lying, but right now she didn't care because whatever he'd done had gotten Alexei and Viktor off their backs. She tried to slow her breathing. That had been close. Sergei was obviously done messing around. "You really should've stayed out of this mess."

"If I had, you'd be dead."

She flinched as the truth struck, then slowly met his eyes. "Sergei Belovich is a very bad man. He doesn't forget, when someone wrongs him. And he never forgives. If Alexei and Viktor saw you…"

"They did. I made sure of it."

"I'm sorry."

"I'm not." Linx looked at her, his gaze piercing her soul, then he slowly grinned. Two amazing dimples appeared on his cheeks, making Tabby's heart flutter and her breath catch, but the warmth of the smile didn't thaw the chill of his stormy blue eyes. "Sergei and I have one thing in common. I don't forget either."

* * * * *

CHAPTER FOUR

Tabby and Linx drove around for another hour. It took that long for Tabby's hands to stop shaking. Linx kept a wary eye out, but Alexei and Viktor's vehicle hadn't returned.

"Pull over there." Linx pointed to a brightly lit coffee shop.

Tabby parked the car, but couldn't bring herself to turn it off. Linx reached over and twisted the screwdriver sticking out of her steering column.

"You are safe for now." He pulled the tool out of the ignition and placed it in the center console, then opened his door.

No she wasn't. Sergei had made that abundantly clear.

Linx stood outside her window. She noticed he was scanning the streets. Finally, he reached out and knocked on the glass. "Unlock your door."

It took Tabby a minute to do so. Linx opened the door and held out his hand. With trembling fingers, she reached out. He pulled her up and held her until her wobbly legs steadied.

"Let's go inside and get something to drink."

Tabby stared at the passing cars, then allowed her gaze to

trail up and down the sidewalk. "Are you sure it's safe?"

Linx's blue eyes glistened under the streetlights. "You are safe with me."

She so wanted to believe him, but after tonight she didn't think she'd ever feel safe again. He walked her over to the door and held it open until she stepped inside.

The walls of the coffee house looked as if the Sixties had exploded and dripped down them. Funky light fixtures hung from the ceilings above the six booths inside. A smattering of stools and low tables covered the rest of the floor. A narrow path led from the door to the bar where orders were placed. The air smelled of rich coffee beans and exotic spices.

Linx rested his hand on the small of her back and guided her to the counter. Tabby knew she should pull away. He was a stranger. But for some reason, she couldn't bring herself to. The warmth of his touch chased the chill in her bones away, relaxing her tense muscles in the process. She found herself leaning into his touch.

"Two café lattes, please." She started to reach for her purse, then remembered that it wasn't there. Tabby sighed.

Linx dug into his back pocket and pulled out a wad of cash. "Allow me." He dropped a few bills on the counter. "Why don't you grab us a booth?"

Tabby nodded. She found a booth that gave them a good view of the front door and the street beyond. If Alexei or Viktor showed up, they'd see them coming. Part of her wanted to go to the police. It was the logical thing to do. But Tabby knew if she did that, Sergei might hurt Taylor.

Linx came over to the booth carrying two cups of steaming hot coffee. He placed one in front of her and the other on the table. Instead of sitting across from her, he sat down next to her, forcing Tabby to move over. He might say he wasn't worried, but that didn't stop him from wanting to watch the door.

He waited until Tabby took a sip of her coffee, then

spoke, "Tell me what's going on." His voice was low, unthreatening, but there was a thread of tension running through it.

Tabby sighed. "Honestly, I don't want to get you involved."

"You might not have noticed, but I'm already involved," he said, his frustration obvious this time.

"There's still a chance Alexei and Viktor didn't see you." It was remote, she knew. But she'd take any chance she could get.

Linx laughed, but there was no humor in the sound. "I told you that I made sure that they saw me."

"Why would you do something like that?" Tabby took another sip. "This is my fight. Not yours. If you're smart, you'll leave this city and never come back."

Linx's lips canted. "Fortunately for you, I've never been accused of being bright."

She shook her head. "Why would you want to get yourself killed over a stranger?"

His eyebrow quirked. "I have no intention of dying."

"Nobody does, until the moment comes." Her voice faded under the weight of sorrow. Her parents had been so vibrant, full of life. One day they were there, the next the police were knocking on the twins' door with news of the accident. From that moment on, life turned into an endless blur of foster homes and distant relatives, who wanted nothing to do with them.

The second Tabby and Taylor graduated, they moved out and had been living on their own ever since. It had been rough going those first few years, but eventually Tabby graduated from college and landed a job at the library. Taylor had drifted from job to job, boyfriend to boyfriend, trying to fill the emptiness left behind from their parents' death.

* * * * *

Linx watched the pain flash across her face. Her throat worked up and down a few times as she choked on it. He hated to see her like this. She'd gone from being a fighter to being fearful and he didn't like it one bit.

She was right about one thing. They were strangers.

He wasn't foolish enough to believe that he knew the woman. Linx wasn't even sure that he wanted to know her better, but he was a Phantom Warrior. And a warrior *never* turned their back on a woman in need.

"Start from the beginning. How did your sister meet Sergei?" he asked.

Tabby's knuckles turned white as she gripped the coffee cup. "We had a rough childhood growing up. My parents died when we were in our early teens. Our home life after they passed was unstable to say the least. I did my best to adapt. Taylor rebelled."

"You never wanted to do the same?"

"No," she said.

Linx let the lie pass. He lifted his cup to his lips and took a drink. It tasted bitter, but like all cats, he liked the cream. "How did she rebel?" Linx was pretty sure he knew how, but he wanted to hear it from Tabby.

She sunk lower into the booth. "Taylor always liked the boys with bad reputations. It started out innocent enough, but soon she was sneaking out of our bedroom at night to meet up with them. By the time I enrolled in college, she'd been through a string of hot losers." Tabby put her cup down. "It was like she couldn't get close enough to the danger. You know?"

He did, but Linx didn't say so. Much of his childhood had been spent courting danger and bedding women. Each was dangerous in their own way. It seemed that he and Taylor had much in common. The only difference being he was as deadly as the danger he courted. "So how'd she meet Sergei?"

Tabby ran her fingers around the edge of her coffee cup.

"She applied to be a cocktail waitress at one of his clubs. He told her that she was 'star' material and would be wasted waiting tables. He convinced Taylor that all her problems could be solved by dancing." She snorted. "What a crock!"

"So your sister started dancing for him?"

Tabby nodded. "Yes, but it wasn't long before they were dating. She introduced me to him at a charity event. Until that moment, I didn't know who she had been seeing."

"What about you?" Linx asked.

Tabby frowned. "What about me?"

"You've mentioned your sister's colorful social life, but you haven't mentioned anything about yourself."

* * * * *

She fidgeted. "There's not much to tell. I went to school and worked full time to keep a roof over our heads. There was no time for socializing. Not really." Tabby cringed as the words left her mouth. She sounded pathetic. Like she didn't have a life.

An ache started in her chest and blossomed as the truth spread.

"I dated. Some." God, that sounded even worse. "Listen, this isn't about me. We're here to help Taylor."

Linx sat back. "I didn't mean to upset you."

"You didn't upset me," she snapped.

His lips twitched. "I can see that."

Tabby crossed her arms over her chest. "Do you have family?"

Linx hesitated, then said, "Not in the manner in which you speak."

"Then you have no idea what it's like. When you have family, you'll do anything to keep them safe—even if it's from themselves."

"I am trying to understand." *You're not making it easy* was left unsaid.

"Sergei is a dangerous man. People who are around him for long end up getting hurt or worse. It's only a matter of time before Taylor draws the short straw," she said.

Linx's brow furrowed in confusion. "Short straw?"

"Before he hurts her, too."

"Ah." Linx looked at her, his blue eyes unreadable. "Is that why he sent men to your house?"

Tabby nodded. "Sergei knows that if I get access to my sister, I can talk her into leaving him. He doesn't want that to happen. His ego couldn't handle it."

"From what I witnessed, your sister wasn't being held against her will," he said, watching her closely.

She met his gaze. "I love my sister, but sometimes, she's an idiot and doesn't know what's good for her. This is one of those times."

"Sometimes we have to let the ones we love learn from their mistakes," he said.

"True," she said. "As long as it doesn't cost them their lives."

Linx looked at her. Really looked. For the first time in her life, Tabby felt like she was being seen. It was both exhilarating and disconcerting. She tried not to squirm in her seat, but Tabby failed. She'd never had a good-looking man focus his attention on her. She had no idea what Linx saw when he looked at her, but he seemed to reach some kind of conclusion because he said," I take it that you have a plan."

Could she trust him with her secrets? God, she wanted to trust him. Something about the man drew her like a lodestone. Tabby found herself wanting to tell him everything, when she'd never really been a sharer.

Sure, he'd helped her escape Alexei and Viktor, but how well did she really know Linx? The answer worried her. It was one thing to drive through town in order to escape two assassins, it was quite another to let him in on her slightly illegal—okay, *very* illegal—plan to stop Sergei.

"I appreciate all the help you have given me, but you've

done enough," she said. Tabby couldn't risk telling Linx the truth. Too much was riding on her success. What if he went to the police? What if he *was* the police? What if he wasn't and he went to Sergei with her plans? She shuddered and picked up her now cold coffee. She couldn't take the chance.

His dark brows lowered dangerously over his eyes. "Are you dismissing me again?"

It was Tabby's turn to frown. "I wouldn't call it dismissing."

He turned to face her. "Then what would you call it?"

"Saving your life." She blew out a heavy breath. "I won't be responsible for your safety." It was hard enough being responsible for her and Taylor.

His jaw clenched. "I never asked you to be."

"No, you didn't." She shook her head. "But I'd still *feel* responsible if I brought you in on my plan," she said.

"So you do have a plan? I knew it," he said triumphantly.

Tabby scowled at him. She hadn't meant to admit that much.

"I think tonight proves that you're in over your head. Even the best warriors sometimes rely on others," he said.

"All tonight proves is that I'm getting close and Sergei is worried," she said.

Linx's humorous expression vanished in an instant. "Sergei is not worried about you. You annoy him. He wants to rid himself of the annoyance."

Tabby trembled and rubbed her hands over her arms. "How do you know that?" Only someone close to Sergei would have those kinds of details. The thought sent ice slicing through her veins. Dread filled her, making her feet feel like lead. Why had she opened up to him? It was as if she couldn't keep silent. And now, it might cost Tabby her life.

"I overheard him talking," Linx said, but didn't elaborate.

Was he reading her mind or had he spoken the truth? Tabby had never been good at poker. She couldn't bluff. She also couldn't tell when someone else was bluffing. That was the most difficult thing about being around professional liars. She stared at him, attempting to divine the answers. She'd have had better luck trying to read a Sphinx.

She needed more time, but that was the one thing she was out of. Tabby had to get proof of Sergei's criminal activities before he made another attempt on her life. Everything was riding on her success.

It pained her to admit it, but Linx was right. She couldn't do it on her own. She'd tried going to the police. She'd tried sneaking in. Nothing had worked and it had only made things worse.

Alexei and Viktor had come close—really close to stopping her for good. Tabby wasn't sure if they'd been sent to her home to kill her or just make her wish that she were dead. Either way, she had no intention of giving them another chance to get their hands on her.

She met his unflinching gaze. "Tomorrow night I plan to break into Sergei's club and search his office for proof that he's a criminal."

* * * * *

The woman was insane. Linx had pegged her right the first time he laid eyes on her. She was determined to get herself killed.

"And exactly how do you plan to do that?" he asked.

She looked away. "I've been practicing my lock-picking skills. I have a book and the right equipment. I know I can get into the club through the back door."

"You've done this before?" Maybe he'd misread her completely. Was he dealing with a thief who only played the part of a righteous innocent?

Tabby glared at him defiantly. "No, but I know I can."

Linx inhaled deeply, allowing his beast to discern the truth. She was serious. There was no doubt. Even if her expression betrayed her, she couldn't hide her scent. Her *delicious* scent. He inhaled again and smelled...*cookies.* Linx's stomach growled.

Since when did she smell like cookies? He glanced around the coffee shop, thinking he must've caught a whiff of something behind the counter, but other than scones and a few pastries, there were none.

"Were you eating cookies earlier?" he asked.

Tabby looked at him like he'd sprouted a third nostril. "No. Why? Are you hungry?"

Not for food. Linx shook his head and snorted to get the aroma out of his lungs, but like the crazy woman beside him, it refused to leave. The aroma wrapped around him, until his head began to spin. He looked into his coffee cup. Had she somehow drugged him? The creamy pale elixir held no answers.

How had he gotten himself into this mess? He'd come to the planet determined to experience all of its delights and he'd succeeded until this afternoon. Now he was on the run from something called the Mob with a woman who had no concern for her own safety. It was insane. Ridiculous.

And the most fun he'd had in years.

"I can't ask you to do this with me," Tabby said. "It's illegal."

"You don't have to ask," he said. She couldn't keep him away if she tried.

"What I'm going to do is dangerous," she said, her voice pleading.

"All the more reason for me to come with you." He gave her no wiggle room.

She glared at him. "I don't want you to come."

Linx glared back. "Too late for second thoughts now."

Tabby growled like an angry kitten. "Has anyone ever told you that you're a pain in the butt?"

"Yes. Quite often as a matter of fact." Linx grinned and winked at her. She flushed like a ripe apple. "But I grow on you."

"Yeah, that's what I'm afraid of," she muttered and looked out the window.

* * * * *

It was one thing to risk her own life, quite another to risk... She glanced at the smoking hot stranger beside her. *His* life. It would be a waste for all that loveliness to end up bloodied and lifeless.

"What if you can't find proof?" He looked far too casual given the seriousness of their conversation.

Tabby couldn't even consider the possibility. Sergei had to be hiding something in his office at the club. "I will." She sounded petulant to her own ears.

"I'm sure," he said. "But what if you don't?"

"Then I'll have to think of something else." She hated the idea that Linx might be right. What if Sergei was smart enough not to keep incriminating evidence lying around? What then?

He sat back in the booth and crossed his hands behind his head. "Let's say that you do find what you're looking for. What then?"

"I'll grab Taylor and run," she said. There had to be somewhere on this planet that Sergei wouldn't look. But even as the thought filtered through her head, Tabby knew it wasn't true. If she managed to get something on Sergei, he'd move heaven and earth to find them and kill them. Nowhere would be safe. They'd have to spend the rest of their lives moving from place to place.

Linx tilted his head back and closed his eyes. "And if your sister doesn't want to come with you…what will you do then?"

Tabby bit her lip. She really hadn't considered that Taylor might refuse to come with her. It was inconceivable. "I'll kidnap her if I have to," she said, knowing it was the truth.

"You'd risk your freedom, your life, death, everything for your sister?"

She glanced at him. "Yes, wouldn't you?"

Linx pinned her to the booth with his sharp blue eyes. "I'd risk everything to gain what I most desire."

The intensity glowing in those dark depths scared her silly. Tabby could barely breathe as she nodded in agreement, though at that moment she didn't think they were talking about the same thing.

"I'm curious," he said. "Would your sister do the same for you?"

She opened her mouth to respond, then slowly closed it without saying a word. The answer in her heart hurt too much to utter aloud.

* * * * *

CHAPTER FIVE

Tabby's hand shook, causing the glow of the flashlight to skitter over the pavement. Linx's leg shot out, his foot tapping at the schizophrenic beam of light. She stopped to look at him. "What are you doing?"

Red slashed his cheeks. He straightened and slowly lowered his leg. "Nothing," he said, but his eyes remained locked on the faint glow.

Tabby jerked the flashlight to the right and watched his sharp gaze track the beam's movement. Just to be sure that she wasn't imagining things, she reversed direction. Linx didn't move, but his body tensed. Sheer will kept him in place. Tabby had seen videos online where dogs and cats chased the red beams of laser pointers, but she'd never seen a human do so.

She bit her lip to keep from laughing and whirled the flashlight around a few more times.

"Knock it off!" Linx said, as his foot came down on the beam of light.

He might be good-looking, but he definitely had his quirks. Tabby supposed that was a good thing, since any sane person would've refused to help. Like it or not, she needed Linx's assistance. With him here, she at least had a chance of getting Taylor back.

How many men would knowingly break the law for a virtual stranger? Not many. Beggars like her couldn't afford to let a little thing like insanity get in the way of her mission. Tabby knew she'd work with the devil himself if it meant getting her sister away from Sergei. Given Linx's dark good looks, she wasn't altogether sure that she wasn't.

Linx had gone from chasing the flashlight beam to suddenly sniffing the air. Tabby inhaled, but other than the eye-watering stench coming from the dumpster nearby, she couldn't smell a thing.

"If you're having second thoughts about helping me, tell me now." She prayed hard that he wouldn't take her up on her offer.

The statement startled Linx out of...whatever he was doing.

"What brought that up? Are you having second thoughts about your plan?" He didn't have to sound so damn hopeful.

"No," she said. "Are you?"

"I told you that I would assist you and I will."

Tabby ran her hands over her arms. "Sorry, I'm just nervous. I've never broken the law before," she said. "It doesn't help that you seem distracted."

"Don't mistake my actions for distraction." His stormy eyes seemed to glow in the dark. "I am trying to get a feel for our surroundings. I don't think you want anyone sneaking up on us."

She glanced around warily. "No. That wouldn't be good." Tabby didn't want to go to jail, but she was desperate. The fact that Sergei had sent his men to do...she shuddered at how close she'd come to being hurt or worse. It was only a matter of time before he turned his anger on Taylor. Her sister was just too blinded by her attraction to the knuckle dragger to realize it. She stared into the darkness. "There it is."

* * * * *

Linx followed her outstretched finger. A lone gray door appeared like a smudge next to the off-white paint. Every hair on his body stood on end. He didn't sense any humans nearby, but Linx couldn't seem to shake his growing unease. "Perhaps we should do this some other night?"

Tabby shook her head. "He's already sent his assassins after me once. Sergei knows by now that I got away. What if they don't miss next time? Or heaven forbid, what if he takes his anger out on Taylor?" She clutched the tools in her hand and shined the flashlight in his eyes. "I can't take that chance."

Linx reached out and lowered the light. "Are you sure that you can get the door open?"

She nodded, but was unable to meet his gaze.

His brave little thief was in way over her head. She was too proud to admit it. He couldn't fault her for that, since he suffered from the same frailty. All Linx could do now was make sure that she came to no harm.

Tabby's blunt white teeth kept gnawing on her bottom lip, drawing his attention again and again to her lush mouth. She'd made it more than clear that she didn't want anything to do with him, but that didn't stop Linx from wondering what was hiding under that gruff, sensibly clothed exterior.

"Are you in or are you out? I need to know now before I get to work on the locks."

Linx listened to her heart rate accelerate. Sweat dotted her brow, even though the air was cool. Her sour scent took on the sharp tang of fear. "I'm in." The little fool would do this with or without his help. He had no doubt.

Tabby approached the door and carefully opened her toolkit. She rolled out the instruments and ran her fingers over each one. She picked out two and stared at the lock. "Keep an eye out. This may take a while." She slipped the flashlight into her mouth.

Twenty minutes later, Tabby was still struggling with the lock. She'd changed tools twice to no avail.

"Do you need help?" he asked.

She pulled the flashlight out of her mouth. "No! I got it."

Linx stepped back, allowing himself to blend into the shadows. He watched for a minute more to make sure Tabby's attention remained on the lock, then closed his eyes and let his body fall away into nothingness. Linx stepped through the wall and walked over to the door. Red lights flooded the space, illuminating the room and the various exits. He could hear the scratches the instruments made as Tabby continued to pick the lock.

At this rate, they'd be here when the afternoon shift arrived. He sent out his senses to ensure they were alone. Other than a few rats scrounging for food in the walls, the place was empty. Satisfied, Linx unlocked the door, then hurried back over to where he'd slipped through the wall. He felt himself solidify a second before Tabby squealed in triumph.

"I did it!" Her face split into a wide grin as she turned the knob and opened the door. "Told you that I could."

Linx's hearts kicked a beat at her obvious pleasure, but he kept his expression placid, so she wouldn't suspect his intervention. "Congratulations."

"Thanks!" She stepped into the hazy darkness, holding the door open for him to follow. He'd already noted the lack of a system alert, but he didn't understand its absence.

"Why are there no alerts on this building?" he asked.

Tabby frowned. "Alerts?"

"Protection devices."

"Oh, you mean alarms." Tabby shrugged. "Because most people know who owns this place. This neighborhood. They wouldn't dare steal from him unless they want to end up dead."

Linx held out an arm to stop her from going deeper into the club. "You are here to take something." He thought it pertinent to remind her of the fact, since she placed her welfare far below all others.

Tabby slithered out of his grip. "That's different." She rubbed the back of her neck. "I'm here to save my sister. I am not going to rob Sergei."

"Will he note the difference?" Linx watched her pale before his eyes.

Tabby swallowed hard. "You don't understand. You don't have family." She flicked off her flashlight.

Her words cut him. Perhaps that had been her intention. Linx knew it was the fear talking, so he let her escape...for now. They wound their way through the back area, getting turned around a couple of times before ending up on the stage. The soft red glow of the exits bathed the room. Linx recognized the gold poles, but what surprised him was Tabby's reaction to them.

She froze and looked around wide eyed as it dawned on her where they were. She approached the nearest pole and carefully ran her finger around its circumference. The second she realized what she was doing, Tabby jerked her hand back.

But Linx hadn't missed the curiosity in her eyes or the *longing*. "Have you ever danced?"

"What?" She gasped. "Me? No! I'd never..." Her voice trailed off. "Why would you even ask that?"

He kept his stance casual. He didn't want to spook her anymore than she already was. "I find it odd that you've never been curious about what your sister does for a living?"

She scowled at him. "Haven't you ever heard that curiosity killed the cat?"

Linx licked his lips. "It takes far more than curiosity to kill a feline. Trust me, kitten. I know."

"Don't call me that. And don't look at me like that."

Linx lowered his voice. "How am I looking at you?"

"Like you want...like you...just stop. Okay?" Tabby huffed. "I know what you're thinking, but I'm not a prude."

"I never said that you were." He cocked his head and watched, as she got even more flustered. It was obvious that she'd given dancing some serious consideration.

Linx's body tightened as he envisioned Tabby naked, slowly twirling around the pole, her long hair flowing down her bare back, nipping at her waist. The thought of seeing this buttoned-down woman let loose brought an unexpected wave of desire coursing through him. *How curious...*

She stared at the floor. "I've seen my sister...dance, if that's what you want to call it."

Linx arched a brow. "And?"

Tabby scowled and glanced at him. "And what?"

* * * * *

Taylor had looked beautiful, sensual, and oddly happy as she twirled around the gold pole, displaying herself like the goddess that she was. Is that what Linx wanted to hear? And why did that bother her so much?

She knew she shouldn't be surprised. He had been leaving with two gaudy strippers when she met him. It was more than obvious that Linx had a type and that type didn't include the average woman.

Her shoulders slumped as she glanced down at her less than stellar figure. Tabby did her best to work with what she had, but she had to admit it wasn't much.

She wasn't like Taylor, who was magnificent, commanding, powerful. Her sister didn't need a ton of makeup or padding to look beautiful.

After Tabby had gotten over the initial shock of seeing her half-naked twin in front of a room full of strange men, she'd had to admit that part of her was...*envious*.

What would it be like to enthrall a room full of men with just a sway of your hips? The thought was titillating and terrifying, since part of her was convinced she couldn't enthrall a twig. She licked her suddenly dry lips.

"There's no one around but us. You could always dance for me." Linx's warm breath brushed the sensitive skin of her ear. He was sin and temptation all rolled into one perfect male package.

His tongue darted out and touched her other lobe. When had he moved? And why hadn't she heard him or seen him? He gave her a quick nibble and delicious shivers trickled down her spine, leaving every nerve in her body thrumming.

"Dance for me."

The breathy request left her dizzy...and tempted. Could she? Should she dare? *When would she get another chance to live out her private fantasy?* A little voice inside her whispered. Tabby shook her head. "We don't have time," she said. "We need to find proof that Sergei is a crook and get out of here."

The heat from his body poured over her in waves. "Doesn't have to be a long dance."

His words dripped with raw desire, making her shudder. "Why are you here?" she whispered.

"I told you that I want to help." Linx ran his finger down her arm, scorching her skin.

Tabby bit her lip. "I can't." But oh, how she wanted to. Just this one time be irresponsible. What would it feel like? What would it be like to dance for a man like Linx?

"Sure you can," he murmured. "We have time. Dance for me. And only me."

She closed her eyes as need warred with commonsense. "One song." She cracked a lid and looked at him. If he tried to bargain for more, Tabby knew she'd back out of dancing. Part of her hoped that he would, so she had an excuse. While the primal side, she rarely acknowledged, prayed that he wouldn't.

"One song." He gave her a Cheshire grin that did funny things to her stomach and made her knees wobble.

"You can't be onstage with me, if I do this," she said. No way would she make it through a whole song with him standing next to her. Was she really going to do this? Tabby pulled out her phone and selected some music, while Linx swaggered across the stage and dropped down onto the floor. He sat in a seat next to the stage and waited, his attention riveted on her.

Oh my god! She was really going to do this. What if she looked stupid? Tabby had never been super coordinated, but from the expression of longing on Linx's face, she didn't think he'd care.

She pressed play and the music started with a blare of horns and a straining bass beat. A man with a soulful voice started singing, telling her to take off her coat, then her shoes. Tabby did as he asked and swayed her hips from side to side to the ballsy beat. She wasn't wearing a dress, but she did have a hat on, which she promptly pulled off, even though the singer told her that she could leave it on.

Tabby ran her fingers through her hair and let the long locks fall to her waist. She couldn't believe that she was doing this, but somehow was unable to stop. It was as if something inside of her had been unleashed. A wild side she refused to admit even existed within her. Now that it was loose, there was no stopping it. No stopping her.

She slowly began to unbutton her shirt, turning her back to Linx, so she could look at him over her shoulder. His eyes practically glowed red under the emergency lighting. He sat poker straight on the chair, his attention locked on her ass as she swayed from side to side, twirling her hat on her finger.

She pulled her shirt off one shoulder, then winked at him. Tabby wasn't sure if it was the sexy music or the real her finally coming out to play. Whatever the case, she now knew how Taylor felt, when she had a gorgeous man's undivided attention. It was embarrassing to admit, but Tabby loved it.

She dropped the shirt on the ground, unconcerned about her less than perfect figure for the first time in her life. Instead of removing her bra, her fingers slithered down her waist to the clasp on her pants. She flicked the button and wished that she'd actually put on sexier underwear.

Like every other day, she'd dressed for comfort, not appearance. Tabby faltered until she looked at Linx. His breathing had deepened and he looked as if he were ready to jump across the stage to get to her. She took a steadying breath and shimmied out of her pants.

She twirled around the pole in her white cotton briefs, allowing the music to take her away. She'd never been more turned on in her life. Tabby allowed her body to slide down the pole until she was on her knees, then she swayed, running her hands over her bare skin. Her eyes flew open and locked with Linx's glittering gaze. She bit her lip and slowly unhooked her bra, catching it before it fell.

He swallowed hard. His eyes shimmered in the darkness.

The music spoke of love. She glanced around the club one last time to ensure they were alone. Satisfied, Tabby let go of her bra and prowled across the stage on her hands and knees.

Linx couldn't tear his gaze away from her. It was more than obvious she'd never danced for anyone before. The thought thrilled him more than it should. After tonight, Tabby would no longer be able to deny the sensual nature she kept hidden from the world. It was now on full display...for him. And him only. The idea pleased Linx beyond measure.

Despite her blatant inexperience, he'd never been more turned on in his life. He wanted this woman. Wanted Tabby. And Linx was determined to have her.

She rolled her hips and his shaft leapt to attention. Linx wasn't sure how much longer he could stay in his seat. The music thumped a sensual beat and she followed the rhythm. Linx knew his eyes were glowing. He couldn't help it. Tabby reached behind her and unhooked her bra, teasing him.

She had no idea what she was playing with, but he did. She dropped the material, revealing her small breasts. Despite the fact they were nowhere near the size of the other women he'd seen dance, his mouth went dry. His palms itched to touch her, cup her, mold her. Linx longed to pull Tabby onto his lap and take her nipples into his mouth, sucking first one, then the other. He'd feast upon her until he'd driven her as mad as she was driving him.

Linx crooked a finger and beckoned her over. Tabby crawled toward him, exaggerating each step. His cock felt like it was ready to explode in his pants. Linx had to touch her, taste her—take her.

Tabby hesitated at the edge of the stage as the music wound down. Linx reached for her before she could change her mind and pulled her into his arms. His mouth crashed down upon hers in a punishing kiss.

He'd never tasted anything so sweet. She didn't immediately respond until his thumb brushed her nipple, then Tabby moaned and plunged her fingers into his hair, yanking his head closer.

Linx deepened the kiss, his tongue exploring the seam of her lips. When she finally opened for him, he dove inside. Heat swept through his body, making his already stiff shaft even harder. He growled and tightened his grip on her hip.

Tabby wiggled around until she straddled his thighs. She swayed her hips one last time before the music died. Linx's growl turned to one of desperation. He pulled back from the kiss so he could run his hands over her small breasts and cup them. Her nipples perked to tight pointed peaks. He pinched and squeezed them until they flushed rose, then urged her forward so he could take her into his mouth.

The second he sucked her eager flesh between his lips, Linx knew he was in trouble. She tasted like *home*. The kind of home a cat like him would want to return to every night. This could not be happening. Even as the thought crossed his mind, Linx knew he couldn't stop. He sighed and flicked his tongue over her nipple, feeling it quiver. He nibbled on Tabby's flesh until she threw her head back.

"I want you." He rubbed his face back and forth between

her breasts, leaving his scent all over her.

* * * * *

Tabby gasped and clutched his head. She was lost in a sea of sensation. She'd felt his hard shaft, when he'd pulled her onto his lap. But the second he kissed her, she'd lost all reason. The man could kiss. She'd give him that. She had never been kissed with so much passion. He'd poured every ounce of his hunger and need into that kiss and she'd felt it all the way to her toes. Even now her core moistened and throbbed, demanding release.

She'd never wanted anyone like she wanted Linx and it terrified her.

What in the world had possessed her to dance for him?

It had seemed so natural at the time. But there was nothing natural about the heat building between them right now. He flicked his tongue. Her nipple beaded painfully. She dug her fingers into his hair and pulled, but he didn't let go.

His hand slid down her waist to her underwear. Linx knotted his fingers into the fabric and pulled. Tabby's underwear ripped, then dropped onto his lap.

"Touch me," he growled.

It was a request and a demand. One she could not ignore.

Were they really going to do this? Even as she asked the question, Tabby's hands had already started to move. They fluttered down the front of his shirt until they reached his pants. He was so hard, she couldn't get the clasp to open, so she ran her hand over the outline of his shaft.

Linx hissed and his gaze locked on hers. "Do it again."

She did and felt him grow beneath her fingertips. Tabby bit her lip. "You're going to bust a seam if I don't get these off you."

He swallowed hard and seemed to force himself to release her so that he could help. With a quick flick of his wrist, his pants sprang open and his shaft surged forth.

Moisture pooled between Tabby's thighs. He was so big, so thick. She had to look again just to be sure she hadn't imagined his size. *She hadn't.*

One thick finger reached between her legs and ran down the length of her moist seam. Tabby's hips jerked as Linx skimmed her clit.

"Like that, do you?" he asked.

All Tabby could do was nod.

He pulled her close and kissed her deep. At the same time, Linx plunged his finger into her drenched channel. Tabby gasped against his lips as he added a second, then a third.

"You're so tight. I don't want to hurt you," he whispered, before raining kisses over her face and sucking on her earlobe.

Coming from any other man, she'd have laughed, but Linx had something monstrous to brag about. He sucked harder. Tabby's thighs trembled and she nearly collapsed onto his lap. She was so close. If he kept working his fingers in and out of her like that, she'd explode. "Linx, please."

She felt more than saw his smile. "I love it when you beg me."

"Jerk," she muttered, then yelped as he nipped her ear.

"You love it." Linx choked as she grasped him and began working her hands up and down his length. "Don't do that," he said.

"It's only fair." She groaned as he plunged his fingers deep and rotated his hand until his knuckle dug into her clit.

* * * * *

"I can't wait much longer." Linx continued to play with her flooded channel. From this position, he couldn't taste her and he desperately wanted to.

He thumbed the hidden bundle of nerves guaranteed to send Earth women into ecstasy. Tabby's thighs gave out, trapping his hand inside of her. He took advantage of the position, feasting on her breasts while he continued to tease her clit. Her body trembled and she released a keening cry that was pure music to his sensitive ears. She shuddered in his arms and her skin flushed as her release swept through her body.

Linx carefully pulled his fingers out, then brought them to his mouth and licked each one. Her eyes flared as she watched him and she flushed even deeper.

He'd never seen anything so beautiful in his life. And she was all his. Tabby just didn't know it yet. Linx continued to brush her clit until her trembling eased, then he lifted her and grasped his cock.

She opened her mouth to say something, but he covered her lips with a searing kiss and dropped her onto his shaft. Tabby was so wet that she slid down the length of him. He could feel her body stretch to accommodate his size. So hot. So perfect. *Mine.* Linx arched his hips, sending his shaft even deeper.

Tabby gasped.

He rocked again.

She moaned. "Oh god, you feel incredible. I—I..."

Linx thrust, finally seating himself completely inside of her tight channel. If he'd had doubts before that they'd be perfect together, they were gone now.

"Ride me." His breath rushed from his chest as she rose up and dropped down on him.

Tabby rolled her hips.

Linx's jaw clenched as her body clamped down around him. "I want you."

"You have me." She ground her sex into his.

Linx shook his head. "You don't understand."

"Too much talk." Tabby bit his bottom lip. "More action."

His eyes shot open and he growled. Biting was an important part of Phantom mating, but there was no way that

Tabby could know that. "Why did you bite me?"

"I don't know. Seemed like the right thing to do." She shrugged. "Didn't you like it?"

"Oh, I liked it alright. Too much." Linx grabbed her hips. In less than a second, he flipped her over the arm of the chair and was powering into her from behind. He draped his hard body over hers and bit down on her shoulder.

Tabby cried out. In shock? In pain? Linx didn't know. Didn't care. He was too far gone. Whatever the reason, it must've been fleeting, because she raised her butt higher to give him better access to her entrance.

He was so big, his body practically surrounded her. Tabby had no idea how she'd ended up beneath him, bent over the arm of the chair, but somehow he'd managed it. His huge shaft continued to tunnel into her, digging deeper, driving her to new heights.

Taylor had always said there was sex, and there was ruin. As long as you stayed on the sex side of the fence, you'd be okay. Tabby knew beyond a doubt that she'd slipped from sex to ruin five minutes ago. No way would any guy be able to match Linx. She was officially ruined for life.

He thrust hard, rocking her forward with his powerful hips. His grunts turned animalistic as he did his best to fuck her into oblivion. Linx licked and kissed her neck where he'd bit her. It had only hurt for a minute. The burn quickly turned to pleasure and seemed to tingle under his touch.

Tabby felt her body begin to tighten. She'd already climaxed once. She recognized the building throb between her thighs, though she couldn't believe it was possible.

Linx must have sensed the tension too because he increased his speed. Tabby's world narrowed in the low lighting, then exploded in a wash of white as her second orgasm struck. She bucked beneath him.

Tabby moaned.

Linx clamped his hands onto her hips. His nails bit into her skin as he slammed forward, taking her breath away. He did it twice more, then stilled, buried to the hilt inside of her. His bellow sounded more like a roar as his hips jerked and warmth flooded her.

Tabby's body shuddered as a third release took her. This one smaller, but no less powerful. Not that she was complaining, but it was odd. She'd never been this responsive. Ever.

Linx's big body melted over hers and his warm spicy scent filled her nostrils. He took a deep breath and his chest rumbled in what could only be described as a loud purr.

"Mine." He gently kissed the side of her neck.

Tabby's heart jumped. It was one thing for someone to cry out in the heat of passion. It was quite another for them to say endearments after the fact. What had she gotten herself into? She, Tabby Shelley, had just had unprotected sex with a stranger. She'd obviously lost her mind. Or maybe it was the stress of dealing with Sergei and Taylor? Whatever the reason, she needed some serious questions answered, but they'd have to wait until they got out of here. "We'd better hurry. We've already been here too long."

Linx reluctantly slipped out of her. He didn't want to. Already he could feel his body twitching as it slowly came back to life. In another few minutes, he'd be ready to take her again.

Tabby shimmied out from beneath him. She picked up her underwear. Frowned, then dropped it back onto the ground. She climbed onto the stage to get her clothes and dressed quickly. Linx noticed she didn't look at him.

Again, not the response he was used to getting from most women after he'd made love to them. But Tabby wasn't like most women. She was stubborn, obstinate…and adorable. The kind of woman that would make a good *mate*.

The word didn't bring panic like it used to. Odd, that. He eyed Tabby closely. Was she? Could she be? There'd be plenty of time to find out the answer once they finished their mission.

He hadn't removed his clothing, so it took but a moment for him to once again be fully dressed. Tabby still wouldn't meet his gaze as she switched on the flashlight and made her way across the club.

"His office is back here somewhere." She didn't check to see if he'd followed.

Linx didn't care for the change in her demeanor. He could sense her pulling away. And that was something he could not allow. Linx had no intention of letting Tabby go. Not until he knew for sure. The sooner she understood that, the better.

* * * * *

CHAPTER SIX

Sergei's office turned out to be nothing like the gaudy club. It was neat, organized, and empty of anything incriminating. Tabby had searched the place twice, even going so far as to knock on all the walls and the floor to see if there were any hidden compartments. Other than a Glock and a shotgun, which weren't illegal, there was nothing that could be used against him.

"We have to go," Linx said.

"I know. Just let me look through the filing cabinet one more time," Tabby said.

Linx stopped her before she could open the drawer. "You've already searched it twice. There is nothing here."

Angry tears filled her eyes. "There has to be. I know he's dirty. I know it."

Linx's expression softened and he caressed her face. "You're right, but he is smart enough not to get caught so easily. We'll have to think of something else."

"Like what?" Tabby slumped down into Sergei's chair. "I thought for sure that he was hiding something here."

"We could always kidnap your sister." He grinned at her.

"Then what?" A lone tear slipped down her cheek before

Tabby could scrub it away. "There will be nowhere on Earth that we could hide."

Linx gave her a strange look that Tabby couldn't begin to decipher. "I may be able to help in that regard."

"Oh yeah, you have a Bond villain hideout that we can use?" she asked.

"No, but I have something far better. I know of a place where Sergei would never look, could never find," he said.

Tabby wished that magical location truly existed, but she was a realist. "Sergei and his network have eyes everywhere. It's the nature of their business."

Linx stared at her. "Not everywhere," he said, but didn't expand upon his answer.

They put everything back in place, until it looked as if they'd never been here. "Let's get out of here." Tabby glared at the empty office. For the first time, she was worried that there was no way to defeat him.

* * * * *

"Boss, you'd better come see this," Boris said.

Sergei Belovich rose from his booth and followed his bodyguard to the back of the club. "What is it?"

Boris pointed at the back doorknob. "Viktor brought this to my attention after his daily walk around."

Sergei leaned over and looked at the knob. There was no mistaking the scratches on the door or what they meant. "Has anything been taken?"

"Doesn't look like it," Boris said. "I'm about to check the video now."

Sergei glanced at him and back at the door. Those marks showed the signs of an amateur, but he'd been in this business too long to take anything for granted. It's why he'd recently installed the recording system. "Let me know what you find."

"*Da*, boss," Boris said.

Sergei strolled back to his booth and ordered another drink. The music in the club changed and Taylor came strutting out on stage. He sat back and sipped his whiskey as she took to the pole like she was born for it. Her lean hips swayed as she performed a bump and grind just for him. Sergei felt his shaft begin to harden. If the club wasn't busy, he'd take her right here in the booth, when she finished her dance. Taylor would let him. It was one of the things he liked about her.

Boris came tearing out of the back office, his eyes wide and sweat pouring off his face. He wheezed, then took a gasping breath.

Sergei sat up straighter. "What's the matter?"

"The tape." He heaved another breath. "You're never going to believe what's on the tape."

Sergei surged to his feet, Taylor already forgotten. He followed Boris into the back office and sat, rolling his chair over to the video screen.

"Watch this." Boris hit play. "You won't believe it. I still don't trust my eyes."

A man appeared on the screen, who seemed to blend with the shadows. He stood in the darkness next to someone else, then he dropped down off the stage and took a seat. A woman came forward a minute later and touched the pole. "Is that..?"

"Just keep watching," Boris said.

The woman started to sway seductively, doing a striptease to rival the pros. But that wasn't what surprised Sergei the most. No, it was what the woman did next that had his eyebrows disappearing beneath his hairline.

"She's screwing him," Boris said.

"I can see that!" Ms. Prim, neat, and proper was really a hellcat underneath. Sergei should've known. It was always the righteous ones who had something to hide. "Can you get the image cleaned up? I want a clear shot of her face."

"*Da*, boss."

"*Horohsho!*" *Good.* Sergei sat back and grinned as the woman rode the man. "I want the cleaned up copy of the video back here by three. Send the boys to pick up Tabitha Shelley. She has some explaining to do."

Boris left.

Sergei continued to watch the video. He was just about to turn it off, when the man looked up at the camera. His eyes glowed red like twin coals stoked in a fire. Cold washed over Sergei. It had to be a trick of the low lighting or the recording equipment. Human eyes didn't glow like that. Only predators and evil glowed like that. He thought about Boris's earlier rants about the man being inhuman. He'd dismissed it as superstition, but something had spooked his bodyguard.

As Sergei stared at the screen, he finally understood why.

* * * * *

Tabby finished up her shift at the library. Fortunately, it had been a busy day thanks to a rush of students in to study for their midterms. She'd been grateful for the chaos. It kept her mind off what had occurred last night. Between breaking into the club and becoming an exhibitionist, she'd sunk to a new low.

She still couldn't believe that she'd stripped for a total stranger and then had sex with said stranger. At the time, it had felt so natural, like Linx wasn't a stranger at all, but in the cold light of day, the situation seemed like something else entirely.

Tabby wasn't a reckless person. She didn't do reckless things. She knew she was damn lucky that Linx was disease free. He'd been affronted when she'd asked…until he saw how much the answer meant to her. Maybe digging Taylor out of so many binds had finally caused her to snap. That might explain some of her behavior last night, but not all.

The sun blinded her as she walked to her car. She'd left Linx sleeping in his hotel room this morning and went to work. He'd insisted that she stay last night and she'd obliged, not wanting to go home to her broken front door.

Tabby knew she was a coward for sneaking out, but she just couldn't bring herself to face him. She was too embarrassed. She was still trying to come to grips with how she felt about Linx and this new unexpected side of herself, when Tabby ran into Alexei Vazov and Viktor Galdin. This time there was no getting away.

* * * * *

Linx awoke to a cold bed. Tabby was gone. He'd known it before he opened his eyes. Her sweet scent was already fading, which meant she'd been gone for a while. He rolled over and groaned, throwing his arm over his eyes to ward off the sunlight.

Last night had been...*unexpected*. He hadn't really been looking for anything other than a distraction. Tabby had certainly provided that and more. Even now he wanted her—and not just for sex. Though he wanted that, too. His little Tabby cat had somehow sunk her claws into his skin and there was no getting her out.

His lips twitched at the irony of finding a woman who didn't really want anything to do with him. Linx closed his eyes. If he concentrated, he could still see Tabby prancing across the stage and swinging around the pole. When she'd crawled toward him on her knees, it had been his undoing. It had taken every fiber of his being to not lunge for her.

She'd surprised him again, when she'd straddled his thighs and demanded his cock. When a woman does that, a sane man doesn't say no. Linx was Phantom enough to give her what she wanted. He just hadn't expected to get caught in the process.

Linx was honest enough with himself to know that he hadn't really tried to get away. He smiled and reached for her pillow. He pulled it to his face and inhaled. Her scent was still there, lingering like a pleasant dream.

He wondered what she was doing. Where had she gone? Was she thinking about him, too?

His stomach growled. Linx was hungry. Once he devoured Tabby again, they could decide where to go eat.

* * * * *

Alexei and Viktor drove Tabby to the club and parked around back. Alexei pulled out a cellphone and made a quick call. A minute later the back door opened. Boris gave her an odd look, then stepped aside so they could enter.

They escorted her to the same office she and Linx had searched. Tabby's stomach dropped and it became difficult to breathe, when she saw Sergei sitting behind his desk grinning like a boa in a mouse nest.

"Tabitha, Tabitha, Tabitha, you are a woman filled with surprises," Sergei said.

Someone whimpered. Tabby turned to see her sister, Taylor sitting in the corner. Her makeup was running down her face and there were signs of a bruise starting to form on her cheek. She rushed forward, only to be stopped short by Viktor.

Tabby straightened and faced Sergei. "What did you do to her?"

He didn't answer. Instead, he kept his attention on a video screen. "You know, when I came into work today my men told me that someone had tried to break into the club. I didn't think much of it, until I saw the video."

Tabby felt the blood drain from her face. "What video?"

He hit play. Tabby saw herself walk out onto the stage and within minutes begin to dance. Linx sat in the front row of seats, watching.

Sergei glanced her way, before his gaze slid back to the screen. "I had no idea that you were so talented. I suppose it runs in the family, right?"

Taylor sniffled. "You should've left it alone, Tab."

"With moves like these, it makes me think I picked the wrong sister to work at my establishment," Sergei said. "Had I known you wanted to dance so badly, I would've given you an audition." He pointed at the screen. "Maybe I can have him watch again. He really brings it out of you."

Tabby watched the recording with growing horror. The dance had ended and now she found herself performing a different kind of dance. It was like watching a stranger bob up and down on Linx. There was no doubt what they were doing. What they had done.

At one point in the video, Linx looked right at the camera and stared for what felt like an eternity. Almost like he 'knew' it was there. Her face flushed and bile rose in her throat. Tabby swallowed repeatedly to keep from throwing up. Had the whole thing been a set up? Had Linx betrayed her? She'd thought for sure there was something developing between them. She'd felt it, or at least Tabby had thought she'd felt something special. Had she imagined everything?

You're a fool, she told herself.

When the recording stopped, Sergei began to clap. The slow methodical sound made her flinch. "That was quite a performance," he said. "Definitely an 'A' for effort. My only advice is that you might want to lose the underwear. White isn't very attractive onstage unless it has sequins."

Tabby's body flashed from hot to cold. The one time she'd chosen to shed her inhibitions and just let go had come back to destroy her. "What do you want?"

Sergei's hard gaze made Tabby tremble. "You know what I want."

"I'm not going to dance for you," Tabby said. She wouldn't do it. No matter what he threatened to do to her.

Sergei snorted. "Not that." He tsked. "Though I admit it would bring me a level of satisfaction. No, I want what I've always wanted. I want you to stop causing trouble for my business."

"What about Taylor?" Tabby asked.

"What about her?" Sergei countered. "She's happy with me. Aren't you, dumpling?"

Fresh tears filled her twin's eyes and spilled down her cheeks. "Yes." She sniffed. "I want to stay."

It was a lie and they both knew it. Did Taylor finally understand why Tabby had been trying so desperately to get her away from Sergei? If she did, then the loss of Tabby's livelihood would be worth it.

"So what happens now? Are you going to call the police?" Numbness engulfed Tabby until she couldn't feel anything at all. He had her where he'd always wanted her— at his mercy.

Sergei tilted his head and took a deep breath. "I've never cared for the police. I prefer to handle my own business."

Tabby wished he'd just get to the point. They both knew he could do whatever he wanted and there was nothing she could do about it, as long as the video existed. "What now?"

Sergei grinned again. "I'm so glad that you asked. You are going to walk out my club and never come back. If you even think about interfering with my business again, I am going to send this recording to your work and of course post it all over the Internet." He turned to Boris. "How much do you think we could make if we sold this tape?"

Boris scratched his head, giving the question serious thought. "I don't know, boss. At least ten thousand, if we shopped it to the Internet porn sites. Possibly more, if we can clean it up and bring out the details." He glanced at Tabby's small breasts.

If that recording hit the Internet, life as Tabby knew it would be over. There was no doubt the library would fire her. She'd be hard pressed to ever work in a library again. Most of her co-workers would stop speaking to her and she'd lose what few friends that she had.

"I'm sorry, Tab," Taylor said.

Sergei scowled at her. "You did nothing wrong. Your

sister is the criminal."

"Can I go now?" Tabby asked, unable to meet Taylor's gaze.

"*Da,*" Sergei said. "You may leave, but remember, one more wrong move and the world gets to see your little dance." He threw his head back and laughed, a big barking sound that sent shards of pain through her.

Tabby's body shook with barely suppressed anger as she forced herself to leave. What was she going to do now? She'd blown her one chance at getting Sergei and all because she couldn't keep her pants on.

She phoned a taxi to come pick her up. The driver dropped her off at her car and she drove home, seething. She thought of Linx. How he'd encouraged her to dance. How he'd pulled her onto his lap. How he'd stared right at the camera, all but grinning, as she lay splayed beneath him as he drove himself inside of her.

Oh god, how the betrayal hurt. Taylor was right. There was sex and there was ruin. And thanks to last night, Tabby had done a bang-up job of ruining her life.

How many times had she lectured Taylor about dating men that were bad for her? How many times had she told her that she was behaving out of character? That she deserved better? And what does she do the first chance she gets?

Tabby strips and has sex a total stranger. Some example she turned out to be. No wonder Taylor could barely look her in the eye. It wasn't just fear of Sergei. It was disappointment. But her twin's disappointment was nothing compared to the disappointment Tabby felt in herself. How could she have been so wrong about Linx?

The thought that he was somehow involved or connected with Sergei ate at her all the way home. Tabby couldn't let it go. She had to find out the truth.

She arrived home and looked around her small house. It had taken years to furnish it and fix it so it was exactly what she wanted. And now with the click of a button, it would all disappear. Tabby wasn't naive enough to believe that Sergei wouldn't send the video out.

He was only toying with her. Making her believe that she was 'safe'. Soon he'd tire of the game and put the video up on the Internet and life, as she knew it, would be over. *It was already over.* Only the mirage of her old life remained. She scanned the room, not really seeing it anymore.

Tabby wasn't surprised by the knock on the front door. She knew who it was and she was ready to face him. She walked over and looked through the peephole, though she needn't have bothered, since the door was only hanging by one hinge. Linx stood on her porch with a wide smile on his face.

For a second Tabby's heart stuttered and she forgot all about being angry. But the second passed quickly and the anger returned once more. She opened the door.

Linx brightened when he saw her, then his smile slowly faded. "What's wrong?" he asked.

She stared at him. For the life of her, Tabby couldn't see through the facade. From all outward appearances, he looked concerned. The man deserved accolades for his acting ability. "Come in," she said, not answering him yet. Tabby didn't trust herself to speak.

Linx stepped through the door and grabbed her arm.

"Don't touch me." She jerked away and shut the door behind him.

Linx's sharp blue eyes narrowed, but he didn't try to touch her again. "What happened? I thought that we had a good time last night."

Tabby snorted. Good time was an understatement. Last night had been the best night of her life. She should've known something was up for that reason alone, but she'd been too busy enjoying herself.

"Why did you do it?" Her voice remained strong, without a quaver of emotion to betray her true feelings. "Was it for money? Did you owe a lot and this was how you decided to pay up?"

Linx's brow lowered over his eyes. "I don't know what you're talking about."

Unable to contain her fury any longer, Tabby turned on him. "You knew! Last night, you knew that we were being taped and you still let me get on stage and make a fool of myself."

Linx's eyes widened.

Bitterness welled within her. Tabby was angry. Angry at him. Angry at herself. Angry that she'd allowed herself to care for this man. "How much did Sergei pay you?"

"Pay?" His jaw clamped shut and a muscle flexed as he ground his teeth.

"Pay you to sleep with me," she grit out.

His nostrils flared and white lines bracketed his mouth as his lips thinned over his teeth. "We exchanged no money. I do not charge for sex."

"So you screwed me for free. Oh that makes it all better." Tabby curled her hands into fists and glared at him. "How could you? You looked right at the camera. You all but winked at it, when you were..."

"When I was what?" His voice dropped in warning.

Tabby knew she was treading on thin ice, but she didn't care. She wanted someone else to hurt as much as she was hurting. It only seemed fitting that it be the man who'd helped ruin her life. "You know what."

* * * * *

Linx felt the beast inside of him rise. It took every fiber of his being not to shift as Tabby's accusations flayed him. She'd all but accused him of being dishonorable. "Are you implying that I somehow coerced you into laying beneath me?"

That was a charge the Phantom people and the Atlanteans took very seriously. A man found guilty of coercing or forcing a woman to have sex was executed.

He saw the temptation in her eyes to lie. Linx also saw the second she decided to go with the truth.

"No, you didn't force me." She shook her head, sending her long wine-colored hair into her face. "I was the idiot who convinced herself that last night was different. Somehow special."

Linx reached for her again, but she dodged away. "It *was* different." At first, he'd tried to convince himself that last night was just sex. Amazing sex. But still just sex. By the afternoon, Linx had almost believed it, but seeing Tabby again brought the truth crushing down. He was no longer in denial.

Tabby laughed painfully. "I'm such an idiot. I should've known. The night was too perfect to be real."

This time when Linx reached out, he didn't allow Tabby to escape. She struggled in his arms, until he guided her over to the wall and pinned her back against it. She attempted to squirm away, until he pressed his body into hers. The second hard met soft, Linx felt the tension in her fade. "Tell me what has happened."

Wetness hit his chest and Linx stilled, afraid to move, to breathe. Tabby's shoulders began to shake and the moisture increased. Oh goddess, he could handle anything, but tears. Linx wasn't sure what to do. Tabby let out a loud sob and something inside of him crumbled.

"How could you?" She sniffed. "I trusted you…with everything."

"What is it that you think that I've done?" Linx asked. He needed to know so that he could fix whatever it was.

She heaved a shuddering breath. "You let him tape me. Tape us."

"Let who?" Linx rubbed her arms, his thumbs gently caressing her bare skin.

She sobbed again. "Sergei."

"He taped us?" Linx wasn't sure what taping meant, but

he knew from the context that it wasn't anything good. "What was taped?"

"Us," Tabby cried. "Me! Everything..." She indicated to her body.

Linx rocked her as his mind raced. He needed to find out exactly what Sergei had done so that he could take away her tears. "He knows about us breaking in last night?"

She looked at him with watery eyes. "He knows about *everything*. He's seen everything. Sergei plans to release it onto the Internet."

Linx knew that the Internet was used for the spread of information. "How do you know this?" This time when Tabby pulled away, he reluctantly released her.

"He showed me the tape. You looked right at the camera. I saw you," she said. The accusation in her voice was still there, but had lost some of its ferocity.

"I knew of no camera," he said softly.

"But you looked at it," she said.

Had he seen it and not known what he was looking at? It was possible. Linx wasn't familiar with all of the inventions on Earth. Still had he suspected there was something wrong with the situation last night, beyond the obvious, he would've never allowed Tabby to be placed in such a vulnerable position.

Of course, she would never believe him. The only way he'd convince her was if he righted the situation.

When he didn't answer immediately, Tabby said, "I'd like you to leave. I have a lot to think about and I can't do that with you here."

"Tabby, let me explain." His chest tightened at the thought of leaving. It went against every fiber of his being. Warriors didn't abandon their...mates.

She shook her head. "It doesn't matter now. The damage is already done." Tabby walked over to the door and opened it. "Please, leave."

"I can fix this," he said.

"Don't! You'll only make things worse for me and for Taylor," she said. "Now go."

The emotions he'd kept carefully contained rioted inside of him as Linx stepped out onto Tabby's front porch. He turned back to look at her one last time and found himself staring at her closed door. How had things gone so right and so very wrong in such a short period of time?

Linx pulled out his translation device and looked up 'taped'. He read the definition twice, convinced that there had to be some kind of mistake. But there was no mistake.

Anger boiled in his gut, threatening to explode.

Did she really think so little of him that she'd believe he'd do something so low? The answer Linx got didn't sit well. Tabby had all but accused him of having no honor. He may not take life or this quest very seriously, but he'd given her no reason to question his honor. It was the one area of his life that Linx never joked about. That fact that Tabby did...hurt.

Somehow he'd fix this mess. He had to. His life and future were riding on his success.

* * * * *

Making Linx leave was the hardest thing Tabby had ever done in her life. She'd thought it would be easy. Just push him out the door and forget about him. Trouble was Linx wasn't the type of man that a woman forgot about. He was the type of man that a woman remembered fondly in her twilight years. The kind of man that could still bring a twinkle to her eyes no matter how much time had passed.

And she'd just kicked him to the curb.

"You did it because he betrayed you," she muttered. "He knew about the camera and never said a word."

Except...Linx had looked genuinely confused when she'd accused him. Almost like he didn't understand what she meant, which was impossible. Only a simpleton wouldn't get it. She'd been direct—thanks to a burst of courage prodded by a sharp stick of anger.

Of course now that he was gone, Tabby was still in the same bind she'd been in when she arrived home.

She thought about calling the police to report the abuse she'd noted. But Tabby knew that Taylor would never press charges. And since she hadn't actually 'witnessed' Sergei hit her sister, there wouldn't be much the police could do. Taylor could say she walked into a door and that would be the end of it.

Tabby's thoughts turned to Linx once more. How could she have been so wrong about him? She'd always prided herself on being a good judge of character. Had lust destroyed her brain cells? Probably, but last night hadn't all been about lust. And that hurt most of all.

Tomorrow she would go into work and give her notice. They would be shocked, but she had no choice. Better that than have them learn the truth. She had a little savings. Enough to live on for a few months. After that, maybe she'd change her name. Dye her hair. She glanced down at her long burgundy hair and fresh tears began to flow. The thought of having to change her hair was too much. She'd already sacrificed enough. How much more did she have to lose?

* * * * *

CHAPTER SEVEN

Linx hailed a taxi and returned to the strip club. He may be angry at Tabby's refusal to believe him, but Linx was furious with Sergei. No way would he let the man get away with threatening her.

He paid the taxi and watched it drive away. He gazed up and down the street, but no one was around. There were no cars parked outside the club yet, which was perfect for what he had in mind. Linx walked up to the front door and turned the knob. It opened. He found Boris inside, sitting on a barstool watching some kind of sporting event.

The beefy wall of a man stood and glared at him. "What do you think you're doing here?"

"I want to speak with Sergei." Linx watched as Boris raised his hand and gave some kind of a signal. Alexei and Viktor slipped out of the shadows. He eyed the men and grinned to himself. At least now it would be somewhat of a challenge.

Boris glanced over his shoulder. "We have a slow one." He nodded in Linx's direction. "He thinks because of his porn debut last night that we're going to just let him walk in here and talk to the boss."

Viktor laughed and muttered something about a big dick under his breath.

Alexei moved in closer. "We owe you for that little stunt you pulled the other night. Don't know how you did it, but we had to replace our car."

Linx arched a brow and leaned against the doorway. "And I owe you for taping me and my lady friend in a rather delicate position."

Alexei snorted. "You missed your calling, pretty boy. You could've made some serious money with that dick of yours, but now it's too late because nobody's going to hire you once we get done messing up your handsome face."

"I've heard of this. Is this what they call 'trash talk' here on Earth?" Linx asked.

"*Duratski*!" Viktor said.

"You're right, he is an idiot," Alexei added.

Bolstered by the other men's nearness, Boris made his move. The big man came in swinging, but Linx was ready. He caught Boris's massive fist in his hand and squeezed. Bones crunched beneath his fingertips.

Boris howled in pain.

"What..." Viktor reached for his gun, but before he could pull it out of the harness beneath his jacket, Linx was on him.

Alexei rushed forward and barreled into Linx, sending him flying through the air. Linx flipped end over end and landed lightly on his feet, then rushed them. The beast rose inside of him and claws sprang from his fingertips. He felt his teeth lengthening and his vision shift.

Alexei helped Viktor up. Both men faced him.

"What is he?" Viktor asked.

Boris cradled his hand and stared in horror. "He's a *Tchort*. A demon. The devil himself."

"Kill it!" Alexei shouted.

The men drew their guns and fired wildly. Linx leapt into the air and landed on Viktor, who in turn fell into Alexei.

Boris's gun wavered as he tried to get a clear shot. Linx didn't give him the chance. He faded and appeared behind the big man. He grabbed Boris around the neck and slammed his head into the bar. He went down hard and didn't get back up.

Linx disappeared again, then reappeared long enough to rain blows upon Alexei and Viktor. The men swung and missed, nearly hitting each other. Linx kicked Viktor in the solar plexus, doubling him over and slammed his fist into Alexei's throat. The big man wheezed and dropped to his knees. Linx punched him in the head. Alexei fell over. Viktor moaned and Linx backhanded him. By the time he was finished, all three men were unconscious.

Sergei came out of his office with a shotgun in his hand. "What did you do to my men?" he asked, surveying the carnage. "Do you have a death wish?" He cocked the gun.

"No, but you must," Linx said. "Did you think I'd let you get away with threatening Tabitha? A man who threatens defenseless women has no honor."

"You're a dead man," Sergei said. "You just don't know it yet." He fired. The concussion of sound from both barrels going off was deafening.

Linx faded instantly. When he reappeared again, he had Sergei by the throat, his claws sinking deep. "Do not make threats you cannot keep."

Sergei choked and blood trickled down the front of his shirt.

Taylor came running out of the back office. "What are you doing? Are you trying to get us killed?"

"He will not harm you or your sister. If he does, I will return and strip his flesh from his bones." Linx glared at Sergei, making sure the beast glowed in his eyes.

Taylor scrambled back with an alarmed cry. "What are you?"

Linx spared her a glance. "It's not important 'what' I am. All that's important is that Sergei understands what will happen to him if any harm comes to your sister." He squeezed and heard the man wheeze. "Nod if we understand each other."

Sergei's jaw clenched and he glared in defiance.

Linx tightened his grip and felt the blood flow increase. "I said, nod if we have an understanding."

Sergei looked over at Taylor, a promise of retribution in his eyes, then he nodded.

Linx squeezed until he passed out, then stared at the woman whose face was so much like the one haunting him. "You're coming with me."

Taylor backed away. "I can't go. If I leave, he'll come after me and kill me."

Linx shook his head. "No, he won't."

She rubbed her trembling hands over her arms. "You don't know him like I do," she said. "He doesn't forgive and he never forgets. By coming here and doing this--" Taylor motioned to the bodies on the ground. "You've signed mine and Tabby's death warrants."

"I have ensured your safety," Linx said. "A simple thank you would be enough. Now get your things. You're coming with me."

Taylor backed away.

"After everything he's done to your sister, you still want to stay with him?" Linx could understand her fear, but not her misplaced loyalty.

"I have no choice."

"Fine, we'll do this the hard way." Linx took out his weapon, flicked it to stun and fired. Taylor's eyes rolled back in her head. He caught her before she hit the dirty carpet.

Linx carried the unconscious woman out the back door and found a sleek, black vehicle parked in the alley. The design told him it was built for speed with its highly polished paint and shiny silver wheels. The dark windows gave the driver total anonymity, while the car all but screamed for attention. Linx knew it had to belong to Sergei. He was the only man that he'd met vain enough to need it. He gently placed Taylor on the ground and went back inside to retrieve the keys. He located them in Sergei's office shoved in a drawer.

After liberating the keys, he walked back out into the alley and opened the car door. He lifted Taylor and slipped her onto the backseat, then jumped behind the wheel.

He wasn't altogether certain how to operate the machine, but he'd watched Tabby and the taxi driver enough to have a pretty good idea. Linx figured if he could drive a spaceship, this land vehicle shouldn't be much of a problem.

It turned out he was right about operating the vehicle, but he could've done with a better understanding of what the various lights and signs meant. Linx didn't think Sergei was going to be too happy with that four-foot long 'scratch' running down the side of his '*Porch*'. At least that's what Linx thought the vehicle was called, although after the last turn, it might've been missing a few letters.

It took some backtracking, but Linx eventually found Tabby's home again.

Tabby stepped out onto the front porch when he pulled in, her eyes widening when they landed on the car. "What are you doing here? How did you get Sergei's car?" Suspicion dripped from every syllable.

"He didn't loan it to me, if that's what you're thinking." Linx's temper flared, but he bit back words guaranteed to provoke her. He put the car in park and stepped out of the vehicle. "I took care of the problem."

Tabby frowned. "The only problem I have is you."

"I'll be gone soon enough. In the meantime, I'd appreciate some help getting your sister out of the car."

Tabby rushed forward. "What is Taylor doing here?"

"I couldn't exactly leave her after my *conversation* with Sergei and his men." Linx smirked. "I thought you'd be pleased."

"I am." She stepped closer. "Now tell me about this

conversation you supposedly had." Tabby looked inside the car. Her eyes widened when she saw Taylor slumped forward in the front seat. "What have you done?"

"I got your sister back for you," Linx said. "You said that's all you wanted. All you *cared* about." He didn't try to conceal his bitterness or the pain that came from her rejection.

"What's wrong with her?" Tabby glared at him.

Linx glanced at his passenger. "She's stunned, but is otherwise unharmed."

"How did that happen?" she asked. This time there was something on her face that Linx hadn't seen before...fear. Tabby slowly backed away.

"I would never harm you or your sister. She didn't want to leave Sergei after I'd spoken to him." He gave her a pointed look. "It was not safe for her to stay."

Understanding dawned and Tabby nodded.

"If you help me get her into the house, I will leave you and you'll never have to see me again." She had no idea how much it cost Linx to say those words. He felt as if his two hearts were being ripped from his chest. But if his absence would ensure Tabby's happiness, then somehow he'd force himself to leave.

The beast within him snarled, but he steadfastly ignored it. He'd just have to find another woman, another mate.

Even as the thought crossed his mind, Linx knew he wouldn't be able to replace Tabby so easily.

* * * * *

For some reason the idea of never seeing Linx again, didn't sit well with Tabby. She may not know him fully or understand his motives, but thus far he'd come through for her when she'd needed him. Of course, that knowledge didn't stop the growing concern in the back of her mind from kicking its way to the forefront. She knew there was more going on here, than what he'd said.

Tabby examined Linx from head to toe and noticed that his knuckles were red and slightly swollen. "What exactly did you say to Sergei?"

"I asked him to leave you and your sister alone," he said.

Tabby wasn't buying the look of innocence on his face, even if there was something about it that made her heart melt. "What did Sergei say?"

Linx shrugged. "Not much at first, but eventually he agreed that it would be in his best interest to do so."

"Uh-huh, sure." There was no way Sergei would just agree to something like that. He was a man used to getting his way in all things. "That's such a nice story. What are you leaving out?"

"Nothing," he said.

She knew it was a lie, but didn't call him on it. Tabby helped Linx carry Taylor into the house. She could see the bruises on her twin's face beneath her carefully applied makeup. She wondered, not for the first time, how long Sergei had been abusing her. Linx placed Taylor onto the couch and walked to the door. Tabby's heart tripped and began to pound. He was really going to leave. And she'd never see him again.

What did you expect? It's not like you asked him to stay.

Tabby recognized panic when she felt it. "Where will you go?" she asked before she could stop herself.

"I told you that I'd leave you alone," Linx said. "I always keep my word."

Tabby glanced back at Taylor. "Thanks for bringing my sister home." She watched him walk to the door. Something inside of her cried out as he stepped outside. Tabby knew his leaving was for the best, but that didn't stop a part of her from wanting him to stay.

Linx opened his mouth like he wanted to say more, but nodded instead and left.

A lump formed in Tabby's throat as she tried to swallow.

Her eyes burned as she blinked back tears. What was wrong with her? She'd only met the guy a few days ago, so why did it feel like her heart was breaking?

* * * * *

Taylor woke with a start. Tabby had been sitting by her side for over an hour, when her sister shot up and frantically looked around.

"Where's the monster?" Taylor asked.

Tabby frowned. Maybe her sister's brain had been damaged when Linx stunned her because she wasn't making any sense. "Honey, you're at home."

Taylor stared at Tabby for what seemed like an eternity. "Where did that guy go that you were with the other day?"

"Linx?"

"I don't know what his name is. The one you had sex with on the video," she blurted.

Tabby flushed. She and her twin were close and talked about everything...or had in the past, but for some reason she didn't feel comfortable discussing Linx. And she certainly didn't want to talk about the video. She'd been reliving that night in her head ever since he walked out the door. "Why do you want to know?"

Taylor did a quick scan of the house. "Is he here?"

"No." She didn't miss him. And Tabby would continue to tell herself that until she believed it.

Her sister deflated in front of her eyes. "Thank goodness."

Tabby's brow furrowed. Why would Taylor say that, especially after everything Linx had done for them—for her? "I think maybe you need to lie back down."

Taylor stared at her, then slowly did as she'd suggested.

"Would you like a glass of water?" Tabby asked as much for herself as for her sister. It was obvious that Taylor was in shock. She just didn't understand why.

She nodded. "Yeah, that would be nice. I don't feel so well."

Tabby walked into the kitchen. More than anything else, she wanted to get her thoughts straight. She needed answers from Taylor and she wasn't precisely sure where to begin. She grabbed a glass and filled it with water, then walked back into the living room.

"What happened?" She handed Taylor the water.

Taylor's wild gaze continued to explore the room. "Are you sure he's gone?"

"Yes! I don't know why you keep asking," she said. "Did Linx hurt you?"

Taylor frowned, then her expression cleared. "No, not exactly hurt, but he shot me with something."

Tabby's breath froze in her lungs. "He shot you?" She thought about the weapon he'd aimed at Viktor and Alexei's car. Had he used the same thing? If it could do that to an engine, what would it do to a person? Tabby scanned Taylor from her toes to the top of her head and back again.

Taylor rolled her eyes. "It wasn't with a gun. At least not any kind of gun I'd ever seen before," she said.

"Was it a Taser?" Tabby asked.

Taylor shook her head. "No, I don't think so. There wasn't any electricity."

"Start from the beginning and tell me everything that happened." Tabby took a deep breath and slowly let it out. It was a good thing Linx wasn't still here or she'd strangle him.

Taylor's nose crinkled as she tried to recall. "I came out after the fight. Well, near the end anyway."

"What fight?" Tabby's heart began to pound. What had Linx done? He'd said he had made sure they were safe by speaking with Sergei. She'd known that was a lie, but hadn't questioned him further. His knuckles had been red, but other than that, he appeared unharmed. Perhaps Taylor was over-exaggerating the seriousness of the situation.

"He took out all three of Sergei's men, then he attacked Sergei himself," she said.

Or maybe not, Tabby thought.

Taylor looked at her sister. "I've never seen anything like it. One minute he was there, the next he disappeared. Like a ghost. He had fangs and claws." Her voice trailed off as she put her fingers up to her mouth to simulate teeth. "I think he might be a vampire."

Tabby blinked. "I'm sorry, did you say vampire?" She'd never heard anything so ridiculous in her life. It was more than obvious that Taylor was suffering from a concussion. "I think I need to get you to the hospital."

Her sister's chin shot up. "I know it sounds crazy, but you didn't see him. He moved so fast and fought so good. He was like a Ninja. When he got his hands around Sergei's throat, I'm telling you, he didn't look human. He looked like some kind of animal with glowing red eyes, long claws, and sharp teeth. I've never been so scared in my life." She scrubbed a hand over her face as if to erase the memory. "Boris called him a demon. I'm beginning to think that he's right."

"Linx is *not* a vampire and I'm pretty sure he's not a demon. But I'd bet my house that he is a soldier," Tabby said. That made far more sense than him being some kind of supernatural creature. She glanced at her twin. Her sister looked so sincere. Whatever Taylor had seen had definitely freaked her out. Maybe the shock of witnessing all that violence had triggered her imagination. It was compensating for the missing pieces of her memory.

Yeah, that had to be it. The other option was unthinkable.

"How do you know he's not a vampire?" Taylor asked, scanning Tabby's neck for bite marks.

She wouldn't find any. At least not where she was looking. Linx had nipped her during their lovemaking, but he'd done so on her shoulder. He hadn't left fang marks behind, but he had left a whopper of a hickey. Telling Taylor so wouldn't help bring her sister back to reality. It would only fuel her fantasies. "Listen, my name isn't Sookie. This isn't Louisiana. And I don't have any blood drinks in my refrigerator." Tabby stared at her. "And if that wasn't reason enough, then I'd like to point out that vampires aren't real."

Taylor didn't look convinced as she took another sip of water.

"I've seen Linx during the day, okay?"

Taylor scowled. "Well, he could still be a demon. They can go wherever they want anytime they want."

"Do you hear yourself?" Tabby asked. "I'm mean, really hear yourself? You're starting to worry me."

"There's nothing wrong with my head," Taylor said defensively. "I know what I saw. Sergei and the others saw it, too. It's only a matter of time before they recover enough to come looking for him. And I suspect they'll start here."

Fear slithered down her spine, settling into Tabby's gut. "Linx said that everything would be okay now. Except maybe in a church."

Taylor glared at her. "All he did was piss off an already pissed off Sergei."

Tabby looked at her. "Why, Tay? Why did you stay?" It was a question that she'd been asking herself for months. She desperately needed an answer. "You know what kind of man Sergei is."

Taylor crossed her arms over her ample chest. "He's not always an asshole, you know? When we first met, Sergei treated me like a princess."

She sighed. "Princesses don't have to strip for their boyfriends in order to stay in his good graces."

Taylor's gaze dropped, then quickly returned. "I don't strip for Sergei. I strip because I enjoy the attention. You're just jealous."

Tabby snorted. "Jealous? Jealous! Is that what you think?"

"Yes." Taylor nodded.

"Then you're delusional," Tabby said. "Did it ever occur

to you that I didn't want you to end up like Sergei's last girlfriend? She's dead, Taylor. He discarded her like week-old garbage."

"The police found no evidence that Sergei had anything to do with her disappearance and subsequent murder," Taylor said. "I asked Sergei and he was upset that I'd even think such a thing."

Tabby couldn't believe the words pouring out of her twin's mouth. "He's part of the Odessa Mafia. What did you expect him to say? Yeah, honey, I beat the crap out of her and tossed her in the dumpster."

Taylor scrambled off the couch until they were standing eye to eye. "You don't know him. You never even gave him a chance. You have always been so judgmental. Maybe if you spent time on your own social life, you wouldn't have to worry so much about mine. At least I don't date monsters," she spat.

Tabby reeled back as if she'd been slapped. All these years she'd done everything to try to help her twin out. She had no idea that all she'd been doing was building Taylor's resentment. "You don't mean that." She couldn't mean that. Didn't she understand how worried she was?

"I do!" Taylor said.

Her twin was right about one thing. Tabby had spent more time trying to fix her sister's love life than she'd spent working on her own. Well that was about to change, starting now.

"Had I known that was how you felt, I wouldn't have bothered." It was a lie and they both knew it, but Taylor didn't call her on it. Tabby thought about Linx. Maybe if she hurried, she would be able to find him at his hotel before he left town.

Taylor straightened her shirt and walked over to the front door. "I tried to tell you. You just wouldn't listen."

"Where are you going?" Tabby asked, though in her heart, she already knew.

"Back to Sergei," Taylor said. "He loves me."

And you don't was left hanging in the air between them.

"Is that why he puts so many bruises on your face?"

Taylor's hand rose subconsciously to her cheek. When she realized what she was doing, she lowered it and gave Tabby a sad look. "I'd worry about my own life, if I were you. Sergei doesn't want to hurt me. He wants Linx. And he won't think twice about going through you to get to him."

Tabby took a step forward. "You're a fool if you really believe that."

"I'm not the one dating a monster," Taylor threw back, then opened the door...and walked straight into Sergei's open arms.

Tabby tried to scream, but a large bandaged hand closed over her mouth before she could get a single sound out. She glanced up over her shoulder and saw Boris's battered face glaring at her.

"Bring her!" Sergei turned and walked back out the door, tugging Taylor along with him. "We need bait in order to catch the demon."

"How do you know he'll come, boss?" Boris picked Tabby up with one arm.

"Because for some reason, he wants her." He pointed directly at Tabby. "Personally, I don't see what he sees in her. But we'll make sure there's enough of her left for him to identify."

Tabby's eyes rounded. Her gaze sought her twin. Taylor's face had paled.

"Sergei, honey, we don't need her. We have each other." Taylor nuzzled close.

Sergei grabbed her arm and squeezed until she cried out. "No one. And I mean, no one comes into my club and humiliates me the way that bastard did. Do you understand?" He shook Taylor hard enough to rattle her teeth.

She nodded and tears filled her eyes.

Tabby felt no triumph as her twin finally realized the

truth. She wasn't dating the monster. Taylor was.

* * * * *

CHAPTER EIGHT

"Did you think you could hire a mercenary to come in and mess with me and I wouldn't retaliate?" Sergei asked. "Did you?" He growled in fury.

Before Tabby could open her mouth and respond, he backhanded her hard across the face. She cried out. Her eyes began to water as blood trickled from her nose.

"Sergei, baby. The guy's a total stranger. I swear." Taylor cuddled up next to him.

He shoved her away. "Only whores fuck strangers." The disgust he showed her was palpable. "Unlike you, your sister is no whore."

"No, she isn't," Taylor murmured, shrinking down in the seat.

Sergei glared at her. "I suggest you shut up and don't interrupt me again or maybe I'll start to *tink* that you were in on the plan, too," his accent thickened with his rising anger.

Taylor's eyes widened. "I wasn't…I'd never…I love you."

Sergei snorted. "Do you hear that, Boris? She loves me."

A chill of fear started in Tabby's stomach and slowly spread to her limbs, numbing them. By the time the cold reached her head, her teeth were chattering.

They drove in silence to the strip club. Normally open seven days a week, the closed sign on the front door only added to Tabby's sense of dread. She shouldn't have sent Linx away. Pride and fear had kept her lips sealed and it was about to cost them everything. They circled around back to the alley.

No people. No witnesses.

Boris stopped the car and stepped outside. He quickly surveyed the alleyway, then signaled to the vehicle behind him. Viktor and Alexei drove forward and cut their engine. They continued to scan the darkness, searching for unseen threats, while Boris opened the back door.

"Come on, ladies." Sergei shoved Taylor out the door, then tightened his grip on Tabby. "Let's go." He yanked her hard, pulling her off balance.

Tabby fell to her knees on the pavement, scraping her hands.

Sergei jerked her to her feet and hurried her to the back door. Tabby looked around for any means of escape. She knew if they got her inside, she wouldn't walk out again. But Sergei's grip was strong and even if she did manage to break his hold, his men would be on her before she made it twenty feet.

He shoved her through the door into the blackness. The lights flickered on a minute later. Tabby found herself at the front of the stage. The tables and stools had been cleared out. All that remained were two chairs, which had been placed on enough plastic to wrap a house in, and a long thick rope. It was also the perfect amount of plastic to wrap two bodies in without having to worry about the messy cleanup afterwards.

Her heart leapt into her throat, choking her. Tabby struggled in earnest; using every move suggested in the books she'd read. None worked.

Sergei shoved her into one of the chairs. She tried to leap up, but Viktor pulled out his Glock and pointed it at Taylor's chest.

"Sit down," he spat. "Or she's dead."

Tabby glanced at her sister. Tears streamed down Taylor's face, smearing her makeup. She said nothing, but her eyes spoke of sorrow and regret. Tabby sat.

Alexei slipped the rope around Tabby's ankles and tied her hands behind her back.

"What's this for...ahh!" Tabby managed as she was yanked out of her seat and hoisted up into the air upside down. Her hair brushed the floor as Alexei tied off the rope and quickly removed her shoes.

Sergei looked at Boris. "Turn on the music. As we know, this one is a real screamer."

Boris nodded and strolled off to the D.J. booth. A few seconds later, a familiar thumping beat poured through the speakers. Tabby's chest tightened as memories of her one perfect night with Linx flooded her mind. The pain of 'what might have been' sharpened them, leaving her raw and empty.

"Please turn off this music," she said, fighting back tears.

Sergei laughed. "I thought you liked this song. It looked like it on the video."

"Turn it off!" she screamed.

"*Nyet*! I like it," Sergei said.

Tabby thought for sure that her heart would explode in her chest. She now understood that they weren't simply going to kill her as she'd suspected earlier. They planned to torture her first. Her mind filtered through all her reference books. She'd never read anything about torture. Tabby had no idea how to combat it. Did you meditate? Brace? Did it help to scream? She couldn't think with this song playing.

"What do you want?" she growled, ignoring the blood pounding in her ears. Her nose was bleeding again. Tabby choked on the blood as it ran down the back of her throat.

Sergei stepped forward and tilted his head until he was almost upright in her vision. "I want you to tell me all about the merc you hired, so that I can hunt him down and kill him."

Tabby's heart slammed against her ribs. "I didn't hire anyone. I'm a librarian. I don't have that kind of money," she said. "I barely know him." Even if that wasn't the truth, there was no way she'd give Linx up to these men.

Sergei made a show of scratching his head, then he glanced at his men. "Did it look like she didn't know the man on the recording, Viktor?"

The big man shook his head. "*Nyet*, boss."

"What do you think, Alexei?"

Alexei rubbed his chin. "I'd say she knows him well...unless she's a whore."

Sergei looked back at Tabby. "Are you a whore?"

She grit her teeth. "No."

"Then I expect you to tell me everything that you do know," he said.

Tabby tried to twist around. The blood throbbing in her head was beginning to mess with her vision. "I don't know anything."

"Hear that, Boris? She doesn't know anything about the man who crushed the bones in your hand. Do you believe her?" Sergei asked. "Perhaps we should cut her down and let her go home."

Boris's gaze hardened. "She lies. I think she just needs her memory jogged."

"Perhaps you're right. Give me the bat." Sergei held his hand out. Alexei stepped forward with a wooden bat and placed it in Sergei's loose grip. "I am going to ask you one more time. Who is he?"

Tabby whimpered. "I don't know." She refused to betray Linx.

Sergei swung the bat onto the bottoms of her bare feet. A shock of pain sliced through Tabby, jolting her spine, making it hard to breathe. She gasped, then screamed in agony.

"I want his name," Sergei said.

Tears dripped down Tabby's forehead as her feet and legs throbbed.

Taylor surged to her feet. "It's Linx! Now let her go."

"Taylor, no!" Tabby shouted.

"Sit!" Sergei pointed to the chair, then reached down and yanked Tabby up by her hair. "A last name, please."

"He doesn't have one," she grit out between clenched teeth.

"Who does he think he is? Some kind of pop star?" Sergei released her and she fell back. He tapped the top of the bat on the ground three times like a batter preparing for a fastball, then he swung.

The bat hissed, arcing high through the air, a second before it made contact with the bottoms of her feet. This time the pain was worse. Something in her knee shifted, dislocating the joint. Tabby screamed. The breath rushed from her lungs and she nearly blacked out.

Taylor stood. "Stop it! Please, Sergei, stop hurting her!"

Sergei nodded to Viktor. The man fired a round into the wall. "The next one will be in your chest. Now sit the fuck down."

Taylor trembled and dropped onto the chair. She covered her face with her hands and her shoulders began to shake. Tabby could hear her muttering, "I'm sorry…I'm sorry…I'm sorry," under her breath, as she rocked back and forth.

Sergei shoved the bat into Tabby's abdomen, knocking the air back out of her lungs. "Pay attention. Where did you meet him?"

Tabby gasped, then gasped again. Before she could recover, Sergei hauled back and punched her in the face, sending her spinning in circles.

Something in her jaw crunched and light exploded behind Tabby's eyes. For a second she was blind, then the world came rushing back in a flurry of color and pain. "Here," she choked. "I met him in your club."

"Now why don't I believe you?" Sergei asked. "Boris, get the board."

"*Da*, boss."

A minute later, Boris ambled over and placed a small table next to Tabby.

"Untie her left hand," Sergei said.

Boris did as he was told.

"Alexei, hold her arm. Viktor, you keep Taylor covered in case Tabitha decides to attempt something foolish."

"*Da*, boss."

Alexei held onto Tabby's arm, pulling it toward the board until her hand was flat upon the surface.

"I've told you everything I know," she cried.

"I don't think so. I '*tink*' you're holding back on me. Either way, someone has to pay for what your friend did. Since he's not here…looks like it'll have to be you." Sergei's voice faded as he handed the bat to Boris. "An eye for an eye, a hand for a hand. You get the picture."

Boris took the bat and slammed it down onto Tabby's fingers, breaking them instantly. This time the cry that was ripped from her throat was more a tortured yowl. He swung the bat again, hitting her ribs, cracking them.

Tabby's eyes rolled back in her head and the world faded around her. Her last thought was of Linx. She hoped he'd gotten far, far away.

* * * * *

Linx sat in a bar surrounded by beautiful women, who were going out of their way to catch his attention. Yet, everywhere he looked, he saw Tabby's face. He'd left. Abided by her wishes, but that did nothing to ease the ache in his chest or quiet the beast within.

He'd been here for two hours. Had plenty of opportunity to lose himself in another woman's body, but every time he went to act on his instincts something pulled him back.

Damn her! What had she done to him?

They were not bound. There should be no ties of any kind preventing him from choosing another. He felt his beast's claws sink into his spine.

Linx tossed back the last of his drink and threw a few bills down on the bar. He never liked the sensation of being unsettled. And things felt very unsettled with Tabby. She may not want to speak to him or see him again, but she was going to have to. He couldn't leave things as they were. Maybe if they had it out once and for all, he'd be able to move on.

It didn't take long to reach Tabby's house. He sat outside, staring at its little windows and perfect flowerbeds. Linx had never backed down from a fight in his life, yet he found himself hesitating, afraid of a woman with long, glossy red hair. He had no idea what she might say and that alone kept him inside the car.

Everything looked the same as it had when he'd left. Everything, but the front door. Linx frowned and stepped out of the car. When he approached the house, he saw that the door was ajar.

"Tabby?" he called out, carefully scenting the air.

There was no sound from inside. Linx reached out a finger and pushed the door open. The smell of gun oil and sweat hit him first. Followed by the sour odor of fear. Tabby's fear.

Linx's hearts began to pound. He recognized that odor. Knew who it came from. He tore through the house, checking every room, but Tabby was nowhere to be found. Neither was Taylor. He inhaled again. The various scents filtered through his sensitive nose, leaving no doubt who had them. It was his fault that they were gone, his fault that they'd been taken.

If he lost Tabby now, he wasn't sure what he'd do. Blood rushed through his veins. Linx threw his head back and let out a roar that shook the windows and rattled the doors.

He ran out the door and jumped into Sergei's car. Linx threw it into gear and sped out of the driveway. He pressed a button to roll down his window and allowed part of his body to shift. He didn't care who saw him.

Their scents were faint on the wind, but they were there. Linx drove as quickly as he could, always keeping the wind in his face. When he reached a familiar part of town, he rolled up the window and slowed down.

He knew where Sergei had taken the women. He only hoped that he wasn't too late.

Linx drove into the parking lot and stopped. The club was closed, but he could hear music pounding through the speakers. He slipped out from behind the wheel and approached the front door. It was locked, so he walked around the building to the alley.

He turned the knob and the back door opened. Inside, the lights were on and the speakers pumped out a familiar song. Linx's stomach tightened as the memory of their lovemaking hit. He shoved it away, so he could focus. He inhaled, the air telling him what his eyes couldn't see. His nose crinkled, when he caught the smell of blood. Tabby!

Linx rushed forward and came out on the stage to a horrifying scene. Tabby had been hoisted up by her ankles. Her feet were bare and black from bruises. Her swollen face was covered in blood. The hand dangling toward the ground appeared mangled and inflamed. If it weren't for the faint pulse throbbing in her neck, Linx would've thought she was dead.

A red haze rolled over Linx's vision until the world bled around him. Two words pounded in his head—Protect Mate—as he stepped out of the shadows.

The men hadn't noticed him standing at the back of the stage yet, but soon they'd know he was there. And they'd realize what a huge mistake they had made before he ended their lives.

Sergei stepped forward and tossed what appeared to be

water into Tabby's battered face. She came awake, sputtering. Her confusion and pain plain to see.

"Not again. Please no more." She whimpered and tried to curl in on herself to no avail.

Linx roared and felt his body shift. His human form melted away as fur sprang from his pores. His incisors lengthened, along with the rest of his teeth. Claws sprouted from his fingertips until all that remained was his beast. The huge cat prowled across the stage.

Sergei and his men jerked their heads up at the sound.

"What the hell is that?" Sergei shouted.

Alexei and Boris drew their guns, aimed and fired, but Linx was already moving. He faded in and out, slashing here, tearing there. The men's screams filled the air, nearly drowning out the music.

"Shoot it!" Sergei shouted, his hand already moving to his own weapon.

"Where did it go?" Viktor cried.

"Behind you!" Boris shouted, but it was too late.

Sharp claws raked out, severing his Achilles tendon. Viktor stumbled forward and fell, sprawled onto the floor. Linx sank his teeth into the man's arm at his shoulder and shook his powerful head. There was a loud pop a second before he ripped Viktor's arm off. Linx spit the limb out and faded again.

Taylor and Tabby screamed in terror. Taylor pulled her legs up to her chest and buried her face in her knees. Tabby's head jerked around to try to watch what was happening, but Linx knew he was moving too fast for her to track.

Gunshots ricocheted off the walls wildly. He had to end this before the sisters were harmed. Linx leapt into the air and brought his claws across Alexei's throat. Blood sprayed into the air in a crimson arc, before raining down upon the ground.

It tasted sweet, Linx thought as he licked his whiskers. But this was no time to eat his prey.

Alexei was dead before he hit the ground.

Boris nearly shot Sergei in his rush to kill Linx.

"Watch it, you idiot!" Sergei shouted, firing in quick succession as Linx appeared and disappeared.

"Where is it?" Boris yelled. The gun barrel jerked from side to side as he searched the club.

"I don't see it," Sergei said. "What the hell is it anyway?"

Boris didn't look at him. "It's the demon. I tried to tell you."

Sergei had never experienced fear like this. He'd been tortured, shot, burned and beaten. And never in all those times, did he feel this level of terror. Was Boris right? Were they dealing with a demon? If so, who had summoned it? He glared at Tabitha. Was she a *Baba Yaga*? She didn't look like a witch, but only a powerful conjurer could call forth a demon.

He'd never believed in such things, not even when he was a child in the old country. But he had no logical explanation for what he'd seen. The large cat had disappeared and reappeared right before their eyes.

If they were dealing with a demon, then what did it want?

If it was his soul, then it would be sorely disappointed because he'd already promised that to the devil years ago.

Sergei watched the beast fade in and out, its eyes like fiery pits. There was no mercy. No compassion. Only burning fury that held the promise of retribution and death. The animal's gaze shifted to the woman hanging upside down and Sergei watched the fire fade slightly.

So that's what it wanted.

Sergei grabbed Tabby by the hair and yanked her up. "Cut her down, Boris."

Boris backed to where the rope was tethered. He tucked his gun under his arm and slowly unwound the knot. The rope went slack and Tabby dropped to the ground, but Sergei didn't release her.

"Is this what you want?" Sergei taunted, twisted Tabby's

neck until she screamed. "Come any closer and I'll snap it."

* * * * *

Tabby could see the cat out of her one good eye. Every time it looked their way, she could feel Sergei's hands tremble. He was afraid. She'd never seen him afraid of anything or anyone. He was cornered, which made him even more dangerous.

She had no doubt he would keep his word if the cat so much as moved a whisker. In all her life, she'd never seen a more beautiful animal—or one more terrifying. At first, she'd thought she was imaging things due to her injuries, but the pain and fear of Sergei's men had been all too real. She gasped, unable to take a deep breath.

The cat stared at Sergei, his red eyes unblinking. It was an unnatural stillness, the kind seen in apex predators.

The only thing she didn't get was why Sergei talked to it like it could understand him.

"It's an animal," she rasped.

He tightened his grip on her hair, pulling some out by the roots. "Shut up, bitch!"

The cat began to shimmer and slowly fade. In its place, crouched on the ground, naked and bleeding, was Linx.

Tabby couldn't believe her eyes. Had she wanted to see him so desperately that she'd conjured him in her mind? That made more sense than anything else, but it didn't explain everyone else's reaction. Her initial shock wore off quickly. It was followed closely by an overwhelming sense of relief. She didn't care how Linx got here. Tabby was just glad that he'd arrived.

"I told you," Taylor said. "I told you he was a demon."

Linx glared at her twin. "I am not a demon." His gaze moved easily back to Tabby and for the first time, she saw the pain and the fear, hiding beneath the glowing red. "I'm sorry," he said. "I couldn't tell you the truth."

Tabby didn't know what to think. If he wasn't a demon, then what was he? Did it really matter? All that was important was that he'd come for her.

He took a step forward.

Sergei twisted her neck even further. One more twist and Tabby knew he'd break it and she'd been dead.

"Go!" She gasped as pain speared her. "They're going to kill you."

He tilted his head and looked at her like she'd lost her mind. "You know I cannot do that."

"Yes, you can. Now get the hell out of here," she said with a choked cry. "I don't want you around." *To watch me die.*

* * * * *

Linx felt the air ripple around him. He kept his gaze on the two men, but sent his senses out to scan his surroundings. There, hiding in the shadows, he found what he was looking for. Bear. He made no move to expose his Phantom brother.

"I will give you one last chance to release her. If you do that, I will consider letting you live," Linx said. "If not, I will make sure you die in as much pain as you've inflicted upon her."

Sergei sneered. "You are in no position to give orders, demon."

Linx smirked. "That's where you're wrong."

A bellowing roar came thundering out of the darkness. It was the kind of roar that could only come from a member of the Tooth Clan. The shadows moved with the massive beast as it stepped out of the darkness.

Boris gave up all pretense of bravery. He took off for the door, clutching his injured hand. The baby mammoth-sized grizzly was on him before he could turn the knob. It swiped out one hairy arm. Eight-inch claws took the man's head clean off his shoulders. Boris's head rolled several feet across the ground before coming to a stop. The beast then turned to face Sergei, its glowing red eyes merciless as it lowered its head to attack.

Sergei must have realized his life was about to end because his grip on Tabby tightened and he started to twist.

Linx faded and appeared behind him before he could finish the job. He grabbed Sergei's hand and crushed the bones, then snapped the arm holding his gun in half.

Sergei bellowed in rage, pain, and disbelief as he dropped Tabby onto the ground. She fell with a grunt, then cried out as she tried to roll onto her side.

Linx clasped Sergei's head. His claws shot out, severing tendon and arteries. Blood showered his face, but he didn't stop squeezing or cutting his way through the man's neck until it hung by a mere thread of skin. Linx shoved Sergei away, then bent to check on Tabby.

She yelped and tried to scramble out of reach, but couldn't.

"I won't harm you," he said softly, his voice all but cooing to calm her. Linx knew he looked like her biggest nightmare, but it couldn't be helped. The man had hurt her badly, and it was his fault. "I shouldn't have left you." He reached out a bloody fingertip, only belatedly realizing his claws were still out.

Tabby's eyes widened as they landed on the razor-sharp weapons. Linx willed them to fade, leaving normal-sized nails behind.

Her frightened gaze met his. "What are you?" Her voice barely audible over the music.

"Turn that noise off, Riot. I cannot hear myself think." Linx sat Tabby up as his Phantom brother shifted from bear into human form.

Tabby watched wide-eyed, then fell over gasping in pain.

Linx touched her carefully. "He hurt you. Bad."

"I need a doctor," she whispered.

"There's not time for that. You're bleeding internally.

Already your heart struggles to beat. You'll bleed out before you reach a medic." He couldn't lose her. She was...everything to him. The shock of that realization winded him, but Linx knew he had to present a strong front for her sake. The decisions they made in the next few minutes would change both their lives forever.

Tabby laid her head on the ground. "I'm tired."

Linx gently shook her shoulder. "You cannot go to sleep or you will not wake up."

"I'm dying, Linx," she murmured. "You said so yourself."

"It's true, but I believe I can save you," he said with as much conviction as he could muster. Linx wasn't altogether certain he was speaking the truth. He just knew that he couldn't lose her now that he'd been given a second chance.

Tabby turned her head until she could look at his face. "How? I don't have to sell my soul do I?"

He would've laughed if the situation hadn't been so serious. "You won't have to sell a thing."

"Brother," Riot said. "The ship is nearing."

Linx gave him a sharp nod, but didn't look at him. He could feel the ship. He knew it would arrive soon. That's how Riot had been able to sense his distress. Had they been high in orbit on the other side of the planet, they wouldn't have known he was in trouble until it was too late.

"Make it quick," Riot said.

"Hold your claws, okay? I will not force her. It must be her decision."

"Then you're a fool," Riot said with a snort.

Easy for a bear to say. They had about as much finesse as a hippo on ice skates.

Tabby's eyes started to close.

"No!" Linx shouted. "Tabitha, look at me."

Her lids drooped, but she somehow forced them open. They were glazed from the pain and the shock of the injuries.

"Do you want me?" he asked.

Her brow furrowed. "What?"

"I said do you want me?" Linx asked.

She gave him an odd look, then said, "I'd love to, but I don't think I'm up for it right now."

Riot chortled. "I see why you chose her."

Linx shot him a censorious look. "I can save you, but what I have to do in order to do that will bind us together. Do you understand?"

Tabby had no idea what Linx was talking about. His words didn't make sense. Her vision faded in and out. She shivered. She was cold. So very cold. But the pain was fading. Somewhere in the back of her mind, Tabby knew that wasn't a good thing, but she couldn't bring herself to care.

"Bind, as in forever." Linx looked so serious. "We don't have much time."

She didn't doubt that he meant every word he was saying, even if it made no sense. "Forever won't matter because in a little while, I'll be dead." Tabby tried to laugh, but it hurt too much.

Linx glared at her. "I'm serious, Tabby. You need to tell me yes or no. I will not claim you without your permission."

"Claim me?" The blackness closed in. She knew whatever he meant to do, he'd have to do fast or death would take the decision away from them both. She looked at the man, who'd so easily brought out her wild side. Would spending the rest of her life waking up to that be so bad? Tabby didn't think so. "Okay," she murmured as the darkness tried to take her. She fought to keep it at bay.

"You won't regret your decision. I swear to you," he said.

She may not, but would he?

Linx let out a heavy breath and shimmered out of existence.

Tabby felt something warm tickle her insides. His hand touched her back, then in a blink it was gone. She noticed the same tickle, this time stronger.

Pain returned with a vengeance.

Tabby cried out.

"Almost done." Linx kissed her lips and disappeared.

Warmth exploded inside of Tabby, blinding in its intensity. She had no idea what was happening, but with each build up some of the pain diminished. She gasped as she felt a wrenching in her chest.

Linx appeared again, this time covered in sweat. "You should be able to heal now. I will pass through you once more after you've rested," he said.

Tabby looked down at the front of herself, expecting to see a difference, but she was still covered in blood and bruises. The warm trickle that had been oozing from her nose and mouth was gone. She tentatively licked her lips. They were dry...and scabbed over.

"How?" she asked.

Linx stared at her with so much love in his eyes that it hurt to look at him. "I'll explain everything, when you feel better."

Her eyes drooped closed again. This time she didn't fight the pull. She let it drag her under.

* * * * *

Linx untied Tabby and lifted her into his arms. He turned as Riot approached.

"Congratulations, brother," Riot said.

Linx nodded, but didn't feel relief. He wouldn't feel like celebrating until Tabby was fully recovered. Even then, it would take years to make up for failing her so.

"What are we going to do about her?" Riot pointed to Taylor.

Linx had forgotten all about Tabby's sister. "We can't leave her."

Riot scowled. "You know the rules. Only one woman per mission."

Linx's jaw clenched. "I am aware of the rules, but that one is my mate's twin."

"Her what?" Riot looked back over at the woman cowering in the chair.

Linx held Tabby's head higher. "Look at her face."

Riot did.

"Now look at her." He nodded in Taylor's direction.

"They are almost the same," Riot said.

"That's why I can't leave her," Linx said.

Riot stared at Taylor for the longest time, then slowly turned back to Linx. "We'll have to hide her on the ship. We can't let anyone know that she's there." He glared at him. "That won't change once we reach Zaron. You'll have to find a place for her to stay until you can petition for the laws to be changed. It's either that or face confinement."

Linx lifted Tabby higher against his chest. "I'll do whatever is necessary to ensure the happiness of my mate. Leaving her twin is not an option."

Riot nodded. "Where will you keep her?"

Linx looked at Taylor for a long moment, his thoughts churning. "There is only one place I can think of that will be safe and will go unnoticed."

"Where?" Riot asked.

"The Dark King's caverns."

"Hades will never allow it," Riot said.

Linx looked at him. "He will not have a choice."

* * * * *

CHAPTER NINE

Tabitha was having the most delicious dream. Her phantom lover was kissing her inner thigh, his lips teasing her flesh into alertness. A moist tongue glided along the edge of her panties, nibbling along the crease of her leg. Tabby's eyes sprang open as a warm breath cooled the liquid trail.

She jolted up.

Linx was perched between her thighs, his dark blue eyes glazed with passion. "You taste like Zaronian wine. So sweet. Tangy. Deliciously heady. You make my head spin."

"Your eyes," she whispered. "They were different." Tabby looked around, expecting to see her house. Instead, she found herself sitting in the middle of a bed inside a small cabin of some sort. "Where am I?"

"Someplace safe," he said.

She frowned. "Are we on a cruise ship?" She'd always wanted to go on a cruise, but she would've preferred doing so, when she was feeling more up to sightseeing.

Linx gave her a lazy smile. "Not exactly." He leaned down and ran his tongue along the crotch of her panties.

Tabby's eyes nearly crossed. "Stop that!" If he didn't, she wouldn't be able to carry on a coherent conversation.

He kissed her again, lingering above her clit.

"You're distracting me," she said.

Linx worried her thigh with his teeth. "Would that be such a bad thing?"

No. "Yes!"

Linx ignored her. One long finger slipped inside her underwear and pulled, tearing them away. "I thought I lost you. I don't ever want to experience that level of fear again."

Her heart raced over the sound of conviction in his voice. "We need to talk," she said.

"Later," he murmured, returning once again to the moist seam running between her legs. He nudged her with his nose and inhaled, his eyes fluttering closed, a look of sheer ecstasy on his face.

Tabby tried to push him away, but he was having none of it. Instead, Linx buried his face between her thighs and began to feast. Tabby dropped back onto the pillows and groaned.

The man had the most talented tongue. Abrasive enough to be stimulating, yet soft when he probed her depths. Linx grasped her thighs and spread them wide.

"I've missed this. I've missed you." He swirled his tongue around her entrance. "Once was not nearly enough."

Tabby curled her hands into the sheet and arched her hips. The move brought him closer, drove his tongue deeper. She gasped as he took advantage and plunged inside.

Linx made little growling noises as he at her flesh. Every flick, every nibble brought a fresh wave of moisture, until she dripped down his chin.

Tabby bucked, needing to get closer, while wanting to pull away.

Linx reached out and held her in place as he lapped at her aching entrance, then slowly glided to her throbbing clit. He didn't immediately pounce. Instead, he kissed her, gently sucking her swollen nub until stars exploded behind her eyelids.

"Linx, please."

He released her long enough to ask, "What do you want, *mate*?"

The emphasis on the last word wasn't lost on her. When Tabby didn't respond immediately, he pressed down on her clit. She cried out in ecstasy. Her orgasm so close she could taste it.

"I want you." She gasped.

"Oh, my dearest Tabby. Don't you know that you already have me? You had me the moment that silly hat fell off your head." Linx rose above her, positioning his hard shaft at her weeping entrance. He flexed his hips, then took her mouth in a searing kiss as he drove forward inside of her.

Tabby felt him surround her, take her, claim her. His thrusts took on an urgency that hadn't been there the first time they made love.

She stilled as the realization hit. They *had* made love. She'd tried to convince herself that it was just sex, but Tabby had, had sex before and it had been nothing like this. Each thrust brought him closer to her heart. Each glide of skin branded her soul.

Tabby wrapped her legs around his hips and pulled him close, locking him inside of her. Linx grunted, but didn't slow his hard and steady ride. Each downward stroke hit her clit, making it harder and hotter, until Tabby thought she'd burst.

Her hands grasped his shoulders and she sunk her blunt teeth into his neck.

Linx jerked, then bellowed. He reached between their bodies and pressed down on the bundle of nerves, throwing Tabby over the edge and into the abyss. She cried out and her body spasmed. Linx thrust hard twice, then slammed forward, locking himself deep inside of her. Warmth splashed her cervix as he found his release.

They stayed locked together, breathing hard, bodies drenched in sweat. It took a while before either had the energy or the inclination to move.

Linx cupped her cheek and pressed his lips against hers.

"What was that for?" Tabby asked, feeling exposed and strangely embarrassed.

He caressed her face. "You are an amazing woman. I am forever grateful to the goddess for opening my eyes to allow me to see you as such."

Something inside her took flight. "Thank you."

He kissed her again, then shifted, taking his warmth with him. The loss was palpable, but they needed to talk. Tabby pulled the covers close to her chest and took a good look at the room they were in.

It was a cabin of some sort. The walls were painted silver and the floors were a deeper shade of gray. There wasn't much in the space beyond the bed, a small table, and what looked to be a bathroom of some sort. If they weren't on a cruise ship, then where were they? And who thought decorating in silver was a good idea? They'd obviously never seen a DIY show on television.

"Are we in Vegas?" she asked.

Linx shook his head. "No."

The last thing Tabby remembered was being at the club. Panic hit as images flashed before her eyes. Sergei had come to her house. Taken her and Taylor. He'd beaten the bottoms of her feet, broken her ribs, and Linx... Her eyes widened. "Where is Taylor?" Her gaze skittered around the room as she searched for her sister.

"She is safe," Linx said.

Tabby glared at him. "That's not what I asked."

Linx rolled onto his back, taking most of the covers with him. He ended up with his head resting in her lap. His dark hair felt like silk as it touched her bare thigh. Tabby brushed a lock off his forehead, but resisted the urge to sink her fingers into it. Linx made a sound suspiciously like a purr.

Tabby froze. Her mind worked overtime to sort through her memories. She'd been upside down. She glanced at her ankles. The bruises were yellowed and faded. How long had she been asleep?

She concentrated, desperate to remember. There'd been a cat. No, not a cat. A wild animal. It had been big. Huge actually. And there'd been a bear. A bear? Then Linx had appeared...and disappeared.

Sergei had obviously hit her harder than she realized because nothing made sense.

But if that were the case, then why wasn't she in a hospital? Shouldn't she be monitored?

"Where is Taylor?" For some reason, it was vitally important that she see her twin. Tabby needed to know that she was alive and that she wasn't going crazy.

"She is nearby. I can take you to see her after we've talked." Linx sat up.

Tabby's heart tripped as the weight of his tone settled heavily upon her shoulders. "What happened?"

"How much do you remember?"

"More than I wish I did," she said.

Linx looked her in the eye. "You were hurt. Dying." His jaw clenched. "I saved you, but I had to take you someplace that you'd be safe. I picked the one place I knew Sergei's men could never reach."

Tabby frowned. Blood. Bodies. Claws. She shook her head. "Sergei is dead."

"I know," Linx said grimly.

Tabby sat up straighter. "You killed him."

"He hurt you." There was no inflection in his voice, only the cold calm of resolve that said he'd do it again without a second thought. "He left me little choice."

"They tortured me." Flashes of pain and waves of nausea followed as she remembered exactly what Sergei and his men had done to her. Tabby held up her hand and wiggled her fingers. It had been broken. She knew it had been broken. She'd felt the bat, heard the bones crack, and experienced the breath-stealing agony. "I don't understand."

Linx reached for her hand, but Tabby pulled away.

"Where are we?"

"On a ship like you guessed." His gaze grew wary now.

"You said it wasn't a cruise ship," she said.

"It's not," he said. "At least not the kind of vessel you mean."

"If it's not a cruise ship, what kind of ship is it?" She supposed they could be on a tanker. Just because Sergei was dead didn't mean that she and Taylor were safe. Far from it. Sergei's boss would look into his death. There was no doubt that once the remaining staff was interviewed the mob would know all about her and Taylor.

Linx stood and walked over to the far wall. "The ship we're on is a Bender series."

"A what?"

"Perhaps it would be easier to show you." Linx held out his hand.

Tabby climbed out of bed and debated whether to take his proffered hand. She knew she was being childish. After all, they'd just made love. But she couldn't ignore the warnings going off inside her head. She approached slowly. When she was within reach, he pulled her close, wrapping her in the warmth of his hard body.

With his free hand, Linx reached out and touched a spot on the wall. The metal shimmered and appeared to fade. Less than a second later, Tabby found herself staring out a window at a sky full of stars. No, not a sky. She looked down and didn't see land...but she did see planets.

Tabby took a step back, but didn't release Linx. "W-where are we?"

"On a ship." He watched her closely.

"What kind of ship? And don't you dare say Bender because you know that doesn't mean anything to me."

Linx's lips quirked. "I think you know what kind of ship we're on."

She shook her head. "No, I don't. Because that would be

impossible."

"For the human race, perhaps, but not for my people," he said softly.

Tabby staggered back. "I think I need to sit down."

Linx helped her.

"This can't be happening." She clutched the bed. It felt real beneath her fingertips. He felt real. "I saw a cat," she said, trying to make sense of things.

"Yes," Linx said.

Her brow furrowed. "And a bear?"

"You mean Riot," he said.

"What?" She looked at him.

"That's his name. The bear."

Tabby touched her head, searching for lumps. "The bear is named Riot?"

"Yes," Linx said.

"What about the cat?" she asked, grateful that she hadn't imagined it after all.

This time Linx didn't answer. He just stared at her in that unblinking way that predators had, when they focused on prey.

Tabby stared at him, her heart pounding in her chest. "Does the cat have a name?"

He nodded slowly.

"What is it?" she asked, afraid of the answer.

Linx sighed. His blue gaze dimmed and he swallowed hard. A second later, his form began to shimmer and blur, when it stopped a large cat sat where Linx had been standing.

Tabby gasped and scooted back. She closed her eyes and opened them again, but the cat was still there and it hadn't moved. It's not possible. It's not possible. It's not possible. The mantra played in her head like a broken record, but there was no denying what her eyes were telling her.

"Linx?" she asked. "Is that really you?"

The cat blinked, then let out an ear-splitting yowl. Its red eyes glowed as it stared at her. She caught a flash of fang as it lifted one leg and licked its massive paw.

Memories came rushing back. There'd been fangs. Claws. And blood. Copious amounts of blood. And now Tabby knew why.

The cat's image wavered and a few seconds later, Linx appeared. This time he was sitting in the exact spot the cat occupied.

"What are you?" she asked, even though a million other questions swirled in her mind. That seemed like the most important one. The others could wait.

* * * * *

"I am a Phantom Warrior." Linx made no move to approach Tabby. He was afraid if he did, he'd scare her to death. He knew this was a lot for any human to take in.

"What exactly is a Phantom Warrior?" She watched him closely, almost as if she expected him to leap at her.

He scratched his head. "I suppose to you and your people I'd be considered an alien."

"Are we talking Mars and little green men?" Tabby's eyes widened until they nearly took up her whole face.

Even scared she looked adorable to him.

"I have met little green men, but they did not come from Mars. That planet is inhospitable for anything other than bacteria," he said.

Tabby blinked, then blinked again. "Oh my god, you're serious."

He nodded. "Of course. Aren't you?"

She shook her head, sending her long burgundy hair flowing over her flushed nipples. Linx stared at the tempting flesh, poking through the silken strands, and remembered the taste of her upon his tongue. He wanted more. Even now his mouth watered in anticipation.

Would he ever tire of having her or experiencing this?

Linx snorted. Never. The need just continued to grow. He looked forward to their bond strengthening. He no longer felt confined, choked by the idea of having a leash around his heart. Instead, he welcomed the restriction because with it came true freedom.

What would Tabby look like after her first change? Would her hair remain red? Would she become brindle? He had no doubt she would hiss at him and swish her tail in his face. Just the thought of taking her in her other form made him hard. He ached to have her again, but mating would have to wait until Tabby understood exactly what had happened.

"This is a spaceship." Her voice held both shock and awe. "A real live spaceship. Like the ones in the sci-fi movies."

"Yes," Linx said. "This ship is one of the finest in the galaxy."

"Why take us on a spaceship?" she asked, looking around the room like she was just seeing it for the first time.

"As I said, it was the only place I knew for certain that you'd be safe. You didn't expect me to leave my mate behind did you?" He was shocked that she'd even consider such a thing.

* * * * *

Mate...

He'd used that word earlier when they'd made love. Tabby hadn't thought anything of it at the time, but given the circumstances, the word now took on a whole new meaning. Was it getting hot in here? She fanned her face with her hand.

"What exactly do you mean by the term mate?" She vaguely remembered him mentioning being *bound*, but now that she knew the truth about him, those words took on a whole new meaning. Were ropes involved? If she never saw another rope in her life, she'd be happy.

Linx's blue eyes flashed red for a second, but he didn't move. "You know exactly what I mean." His tone left no room for argument.

She was afraid that she did understand all too well, but Tabby still wanted to hear it from him. "I know what the word means on Earth, but what does it mean to a Phantom Warrior?" Given the differences in cultures on her planet, she didn't want to assume anything.

"Unlike humans, Phantoms mate for life," he said, all but daring her to disagree. "There are many sentient beings in the universe that have similar customs."

Her eyes bugged. "You mean there's more than just Phantom Warriors floating around in space?" If there were aliens everywhere, then why hadn't they found them? He made it sound like you couldn't throw a rock without hitting one.

"Of course. You didn't think you were alone, did you?" He gave her an incredulous look that made her feel silly for even suggesting such a thing. "There are many beings and creatures throughout the universe. Just because you have been unsuccessful in locating the ones in your own solar system doesn't mean that they do not exist."

Tabby glanced out the window at the blanket of stars. There were so many of them. It was overwhelming to think about. "Where are we going?" And would she like their destination when they arrived? All she knew was Earth.

"We are on our way to Zaron. That is my home planet," he said. "It is larger than your Earth, closer to the size of Jupiter."

"Oh." She was trying hard to imagine it, but her brain wasn't cooperating. The thought of never seeing Earth again made her sad and more than a little homesick. She'd taken so much for granted while she was there. Tabby wished she could go back and have a 'do over'. She'd never look at Earth the same way again. But Linx was right. They were safer here than they would've been on Earth. Thanks to her sister's lousy taste in men, the Russian mob would never stop looking for them. Speaking of which, "I want to see Taylor." She needed to see her twin with her own eyes to know that she was all right.

Linx stood, the movements silent and graceful, just like a cat. How she hadn't noticed it before she'd never know. Like most people, she hadn't been looking.

"I'll take you to her now, but there is something I must tell you before we go," he said. The seriousness of his tone brought her up short.

"Is she hurt? You said she was okay." Had he lied? Oh god, she should've demanded to be taken to her immediately.

Linx touched her shoulder. "Taylor is well, but she shouldn't be here."

"What do you mean she shouldn't be here?" Tabby crossed her arms over her chest.

Linx took a deep breath. "There are regulations for transporting humans. Stringent rules that must be followed."

"What rules? And what do they have to do with my sister?"

* * * * *

Linx didn't know how to explain to Tabby why the Phantoms were on the planet without upsetting her. He knew the second he told her that they were there looking for mates, she was going to get angry. He'd learned that much about her in the short time they'd known each other.

His mate was a fighter. She'd proven it with Sergei and she'd proven it to him. He knew he had to be careful or she'd end up getting them all held in confinement.

"Each Phantom is only allowed to bring one mate aboard," he said, waiting to see if she understood.

Tabby gave him a blank look.

"I chose you," he said, though in truth, the goddess had

chosen for him.

She didn't move an inch.

He sighed. She wasn't going to make it easy on him. "I am not allowed to bring any other females onboard."

Her brow arched.

Linx shook his head. At this rate, they'd be to Zaron before she understood. He'd have to take a more direct approach. "I had to smuggle Taylor onto the ship because I knew you'd be unhappy without your twin. What I did is against the law. But I couldn't bear to see you unhappy, when I knew that this one thing would make all the difference."

Tabby stared at him for what felt like an eon, then she slowly smiled and threw herself into his arms. Her fingers tunneled through his hair and she kissed him. "Thank you, Linx. I lov—" The word was cut short as she pressed her lips together.

Linx didn't say anything. He could barely hear over the sound of his hearts pounding. She'd said that she loved him. Or she'd nearly said so. For now, that was enough.

"Let's go see your sister."

Tabby nodded and slowly released him.

* * * * *

Linx led Tabby down a long corridor, which looked much like the interior of their cabin, except there were many doorways leading off the long spine. They ran into a few people, who he greeted formally. He'd introduced her as his mate and she hadn't contradicted him, though part of her still couldn't believe it.

They reached an elevator and went down for what seemed like a million floors. Eventually, they reached the basement or whatever it was called on a ship. The name didn't matter in Tabby's mind because it *looked* like a basement, a very big basement with a really tall ceiling.

There were cargo containers stacked from floor to what she imagined was the ceiling, since she couldn't really see it due to the low lighting.

Shadows pressed in around them as they wound their way through a maze of crates. Eventually, the aisle widened and she spotted two doorways up ahead. Linx held his hand out and stopped her. He paused, staring into the gloom, tilting his head from side to side. A moment later, he glanced at Tabby and nodded.

"It is safe to proceed."

Tabby stepped forward as the door on the right opened. A burly man walked out, his dark, disgruntled gaze landed on them, then he slowly stepped aside. Behind him, huddled on a cot, sat Taylor.

"Any problems?" Linx asked.

"None," the man said.

Tabby rushed forward. As she drew closer, she recognized the man from the club. Riot. He'd turned into something that made a grizzly look like a child's stuffed toy.

She changed course in order to give the *bear* a wide berth.

Taylor stood as she walked through the door.

"I thought you were dead." She rushed forward.

Tabby hugged her close. "I thought so, too. Are you okay?"

Taylor glared at Riot's back. "Yes, but he won't let me leave. And he hasn't told me anything. Where are we?"

Tabby glanced over her shoulder at Linx. She had no idea where to begin or how to explain. She was still trying to process what she'd seen herself. She turned back to Taylor. "We're safe," she said.

"I am so sorry," Taylor said. Gone was the reckless woman, who'd courted danger on a regular basis. This solemn creature standing before her had replaced her. "I didn't mean for any of this to happen. When Sergei tied you up and began to beat on you, I thought we were dead." Tears filled her eyes.

"We very nearly were." If it hadn't been for Linx, they'd have been an unsolved homicide or worse, their bodies would've never been found. And after a few weeks, no one would've bothered to look for them.

"Why won't he let me leave?" Taylor asked. "Am I a prisoner?"

Tabby brushed her hair back out of her face. "No, you're not a prisoner, but you weren't exactly brought aboard legally."

Taylor's face paled. "I'm a stowaway?"

"Yes." Tabby nodded. That was as good an explanation as any.

"How long do I have to stay here?" Taylor asked.

Tabby glanced back at Linx once more and frowned. He held up three fingers. She nodded in understanding. "Just a few more days."

"Okay." Taylor slowly sat back down. She looked at her twin, her eyes searching. "Do you know what they are?" she whispered.

Tabby hesitated, then nodded.

Taylor trembled. "Are we in danger?"

She shook her head. "No. That's the one thing we don't have to worry about anymore."

Taylor's narrow shoulders slumped in relief. "Okay. I'll wait until you come and get me."

Tabby grabbed her sister and hugged her tight. "Everything is going to be okay."

Taylor gave her a sad smile. "I'm sorry I got you into this mess." Her gaze drifted over to the two men, then back to her twin's face.

Tabby met her gaze. "I'm not."

Taylor stared at her for a minute, then finally nodded in understanding. She gave Tabby's hand a quick squeeze, then released her.

"I'll see you soon," Tabby said.

Taylor nodded, then laid back down on the cot.

* * * * *

Taylor had nearly gotten her sister—her twin—killed because of her dangerous taste in men. She'd been so selfish. Never caring about Tabby's feelings or concerns as she jumped from one bad boy to the next.

Well she'd learned her lesson, Taylor thought. It had come at a high price, but she'd finally learned.

She didn't know where they were going, but she trusted Tabby. If she said they weren't in any danger, then she believed her.

Her gaze strayed back to the massive man, who'd been both guard and caregiver since she'd awoke. He watched her closely like he half expected her to sprout horns and breathe fire. Heck, maybe he did.

Taylor was used to men looking at her, leering at her, but this big guy barely gave her a second look. He was here out of duty, not because he wanted to be. And for that she was grateful. It would be a long time before she was ready to jump back into any relationship.

Not that Taylor thought there'd be much chance of that, since the men she'd met thus far weren't human.

She stared at the gray, metallic wall as she reassessed her life. She'd made a lot of mistakes over the years, but she was determined to learn from them. Taylor hoped that eventually Tabby would be able to forgive her, but she knew that wouldn't happen right away. And she couldn't blame her sister one bit.

Taylor needed to prove how much she'd changed. That would take time. She wasn't the silly airhead that let men walk all over her anymore. Staring death in the face helped adjust her outlook on life.

Both she and Tabby had been given a second chance. Taylor was determined not to waste it on any man.

* * * * *

Three days later the ship landed on Zaron. The planet was lush with thick, dark purple grasses that almost looked black and fields of blue flowers. Giant butterflies the size of Frisbees glided through the perfumed air, the flap of their iridescent wings creating a gentle breeze. Two large moons glowed orange against a light green sky. In the distance, Tabby could see the beginnings of a forest buffered by a jagged mountain range.

She was surprised to find so many human women on the planet. Didn't the Phantoms have women of their own? Or had they been interbreeding with Earth for centuries and no one was the wiser?

The way Linx had spoken Tabby thought that she and Taylor would be the only ones. She was glad that wasn't the case, but it would take time to adjust to her knew surroundings. The planet's colors and buildings were alien. Though odd, they seemed to blend together giving the place a rare coherence.

"Better get used to it. This is home now," she muttered under her breath.

"It grows on you." Linx gave her an understanding smile. "I will show you the beauty of this planet. In time, you'll find it as remarkable as your own."

She already did, but that didn't stop her from missing Earth. Tabby glanced around at the kaleidoscope of colors, determined to make the best of it. She hoped her twin did the same. "What's going to happen with Taylor?" she asked.

Linx looked at her. "I will get her as soon as you're settled."

He escorted her to a complex that resembled a giant palace. There were wings that jutted off from the main hub. Each wing was filled with hundreds of apartments, but they weren't like any apartments that Tabby had ever seen.

Linx's apartment was more like a penthouse suite from

the finest hotels. It was spacious, luxurious and held a bathroom fit for a king.

"This is your home?" Tabby asked in disbelief.

"Do you like it?" His pride was evident, but insecurity shadowed his eyes.

"I love it. It's just so..." She looked around at the grandeur. "Big."

He smiled then. "Plenty of room for a family," he said softly, but she heard him all the same.

Tabby gave him a startled glance, but didn't respond.

Linx walked up behind her and wrapped her in his arms. "Do you want a family?" It was a casual question, but there was nothing casual about the grip he had on her.

"Someday." Tabby had always wanted a family. It's why she'd fought so hard to keep Taylor in her life. They only had each other. She leaned back and realized that was no longer true. "Yes," she said.

His grip on her tightened as he nuzzled her neck. "Would you like to get started now?"

Tabby laughed, but her laughter was cut short as Linx latched onto her earlobe, sucked it between his teeth, and purred. A shiver of desire sped from her ear down her spine, igniting the growing flame inside of her. "I think I can be talked into it."

"No words are necessary for what I have planned," he growled. His sharp teeth grazed the side of her throat. One second he was behind her, the next he stood in front of her. Tabby's whole body tingled. "How did you?"

Before she could finish her question, Linx slid his palms under her butt and lifted her into the air. Their gazes met and held as he carried her into the bedroom. He laid her down gently and kissed her. "Thank you."

Tabby frowned. "For what?"

"For trusting me," he said.

She pulled back and looked at him. "It wasn't that hard. I've always been a cat lover."

Linx sat back and his lips canted. Heat filled his eyes as he crooked a finger, beckoning her closer. "Well then come here, my little Tabby cat and show me what you've got."

Tabby did, and afterwards she'd lay money that the whole palace heard Linx yowl.

# # #

OTHER BOOKS BY JORDAN SUMMERS

Phantom Warriors 1: Bacchus
Phantom Warriors 2: Saber-tooth
Phantom Warriors 3: Talon
Phantom Warriors 4: Arctos
Phantom Warriors 5: Linx
Phantom Warriors 6: Riot
Hawk's Slave
Phantom Warriors Anthology Volume 1
Phantom Warriors Anthology Volume 2

Atlantean's Quest 1: The Arrival
Atlantean's Quest 2: Exodus
Atlantean's Quest 3: Redemption
Atlantean Heat 3.5
Atlantean's Quest 4: The Return
Atlantean's Quest 5: The Dark King
Atlantean's Quest Bundle Volume 1
Atlantean's Quest Bundle Volume 2

Dead World Prequel: Raphael
Dead World Prequel: Kane
Dead World 1: Red
Dead World 2: Scarlet
Dead World 3: Crimson

Moonlight Kin 1: A Wolf's Tale
Moonlight Kin 2: Aidan's Mate
Moonlight Kin 3: Nic
Moonlight Kin 4: Tristan - Coming Soon

Tears of Amun
Heat of the Night
Gothic Passions
Rose's Rapture
Paris After Dark

Ghost Hunter: Solomon's Seals

Private Investigations
Mesmerized
Hot Shot
Ride Em' Cowboy
Off Limits

ABOUT THE AUTHOR

Jordan Summers has thirty-one published books to her credit and has sold over 145,000 ebooks. She's a member of The Horror Writer's Association, International Thriller Writers, the Author's Guild, and Novelist Inc.

Connect with her online:
Twitter.com/jordanwriter
www.facebook.com/authorjordansummers
www.JordanSummers.com
Join the Endless Summers Newsletter to find out about upcoming releases and author signings.
http://www.jordansummers.com/contact/

www.ingramcontent.com/pod-product-compliance
Lightning Source LLC
Chambersburg PA
CBHW070540120726
47909CB00007B/2191